O9-AIF-076

NIGHTMARE

NIGHTMARE

BY LESLEY EGAN

Nelson Doubleday, Inc.
Garden City, New York

Originally published under the name Anne Blaisdell by Harper & Row.

Printed in the United States of America

O! sing unto my roundelay,
O! drop the briny tear with me.
Dance no more at holiday,
Like a running river be;
        My love is dead,
        Gone to his death-bed,
All under the willow tree.

THOMAS CHATTERTON

NIGHTMARE

PART
1

ONE

By itself the rain wouldn't be too bad, but the gusty winds from the west, driving the rain sidewise, produced an effect very much like fog. And quite as hampering to a driver.

Pat slowed still more at another bend in the road, and again cursed herself that she'd listened to that maundering old fool in Clun. "Oh, this is only local, miss—you'll find you'll run out of it within an hour, west." Local! It had just got steadily worse. And to think she could have been back at that delightful inn, toasting before the public-room hearth, with muffins and hot tea to come! If she'd thought there was any prospect of a sixty-mile drive in a downpour of rain on a strange road, of course she'd never have left Clun after a late lunch there. Damn it, the natives ought to know about their country—no business to go telling wanton lies to visiting foreigners so obliging as to come and look at their mingy little nation!

The thought of that casual guess, probably produced just because she was an American (to reassure her that it doesn't rain *all* the time in England), made her grind her teeth. She also thought bitter thoughts about the narrow rambling roads (good heavens, they called a three-lane road a highway!) and of course the impossibility of getting a decent cup of coffee, and peculiar hotels without private baths, and the incomprehensible money based on arbitrary units of twelve and twenty instead of a logical hundred. And the lack of ice water. And the silly notion of driving on the wrong side of the road. And in fact, for a few intensely insular moments, every single peculiar and annoying habit the English have of being so totally un-American, which every visiting American has ever darkly complained about.

"The *English!*" said Pat aloud in heartfelt tones. The windshield wipers were working manfully, but they could be only about fifty per cent effective against the deluge. Oh, *well.* She needn't have believed the yokel: it had been her own choice to come on. Anxious to get the thing over with, have it behind her. One of the civilized duties of social communication, unavoidable. Just one of those things, and the only thing that had marred her anticipation of this long-planned holiday. However, it'd soon be over, and it was little enough for her to do.

One thing she would say of the English, they knew how to build an automobile. She patted the Jaguar's wheel affectionately. Very extravagant, and there'd be the freight home too, just about equaling the import tax; but of course she needn't think about another car for years and years and years, and besides—an unarguable answer—she'd always wanted one and she'd *had* the money. Actually, she shouldn't—what was the phrase?—kick against the pricks. She'd had a lovely time so far, with only the faint shadow of this necessary visit to Stephen's mother hanging over her. The Jaguar was a dream to handle, and the weather had been wonderful all the leisurely way from London. She'd taken it very slow and easy, first because she wanted just to wander, see everything, all on her own; and second because of getting used to driving British style. She'd pretty well got the hang of it now, and felt proud of herself.

This was the first time she'd run into any inconvenience, in three weeks; it was senseless to complain. Again, just one of those things. But all the same, she'd stop at the next village which looked like having a decent inn.

The trouble was, there didn't seem to be any. Not in the last fifteen miles, since it had really turned to a deluge. She knew she'd come about sixty miles from Clun, and thus must be somewhere in Brecknockshire, but that was about all she did know. She had the uneasy feeling that she'd got off the main road somehow: even the backward English couldn't call this a major highway, could they? She had studied the map rather casually, as she was in the habit of doing. She didn't want to cover England in a series of grim set runs, today I'll get as far as Tunbridge, today I'll make it to Truro by lunchtime. When she saw something she wanted to look at, she'd stop and look at it, maybe stay the night. So she'd often wandered off the main roads.

There had been a signpost about five miles back, but though she'd stopped and craned her neck, she hadn't been able to make it out through the downpour, and she certainly wasn't going to get out in that and eventually reach civilization looking like a drowned rat. The two hats she possessed—one a serviceable rainy-day hat, one for church—were in her luggage in the trunk. No, in what the incomprehensible English called the boot.

She was bound (like Alice) to come *somewhere* eventually. Everybody knew that rural England was composed of villages about five miles apart. It was only at home that there were expanses so vast you could drive all day without seeing anything but wheat or cows.

However, she'd come a good fifteen miles from the last hamlet. She'd hesitated about stopping there, though the rain then hadn't quite reached deluge proportions, but it had been a dreary, incredibly tiny place, and its one inn had no accommodations for guests.

"Never say die," she said aloud. "Bound to be another one along soon." And there she would stop, always providing the inn would have her.

She was going dead slow, fifteen miles an hour, and had switched on the lights. In spite of three weeks' experience, she still had a tendency to shy away right when anything suddenly appeared in front of her, and she did so now, violently, as a black bulk loomed up through the haze of rain. She swerved, and tramped on the brake, and like a fool killed the engine.

Another car, motionless at the side of the road. Pat rolled down the left-hand window. Somebody stalled?

A vague dark bulk moved toward her out of the dark bulk of the car, and she heard its door slam. Thick wet mist blew in the window onto her face; it smelled of salt and lots of wet green woods and grass. "Thanks be to God," said the dark bulk. "A human face in the wilderness. At least I presume you're human? I congratulate myself—a Jaguar. I have fallen in with the elite, no mere vulgar member of *hoi polloi* in an M.G. or Hillman."

"Are you stalled?" asked Pat. "*What* a day for it. You'd better get in, I'll take you on to the next town." And at home you'd hestiate about that sort of thing, but probably in England it was quite safe. Besides, the voice sounded like that of an educated man.

He fumbled at the door and precipitated himself in beside her. "And rescued by a lady. My luck still holds. I've been sitting in that cow for an hour, praying somebody'd come along. My own fault—I'd been warned the battery was wonky, but machinery means nothing to me. It stops, I get out and walk. But not in Noah's flood. I'm eternally grateful to you."

"Not at all," said Pat. "I'll be eternally grateful if you can tell me where we are. I've got a nasty idea I'm off the main road."

"Ah, an American. Yes, that I can tell you—I *do* read maps. This is a secondary road, and we ought to be somewhere within five miles of a place called Tregarth. I beg your pardon, should have introduced myself before—I'm Alan Glentower."

Pat had started the engine again and let in the clutch, and at this she let up on the accelerator and swiveled around to look at him, groping for the gearshift. "You *are?* Well, imagine. Picking you up out of the flood like this. I'm Pat Carroll."

"How do you do," said Glentower gloomily. "If you ask me for an autograph I'll scream."

Pat laughed. "I can't very well right now. Besides, I didn't buy the book, I borrowed it."

"An honest American," said Glentower. He was very wet, even from the brief passage between the cars, and he made the Jaguar suddenly smaller, bulking beside her. "It's a sort of measure of my mental state to say let's not talk about the book. All writers are egotistical asses, generally we enjoy that kind of thing. But I'm good and fed up with hearing how Tom, Dick and Harry liked the book."

"But I did," said Pat. It was a very good book indeed, *Isle of Gramarye.* If you liked soundly-researched, well-written, exciting and action-filled historical novels; and a lot of people did.

"It's made a lot of money," said the man beside her. "I'm sorry to get the upholstery so wet. That part of it I like. But they keep coming at you for interviews on the B.B.C. or television, and those awful meet-the-author teas, and autographing parties. Like most writers, I don't like people *en masse.* Very few of us are good speakers, you know, and if we'd confess it damn shy and retiring. What's called an ambivalent situation. Watch it—there's a fence to the near side."

"How do you mean, ambivalent?"

"Oh, we're all egotists as I say. Idea of talking about ourselves very attractive, but at the same time that dreadful paralyzing shyness. I was escaping out of it. Said all solemn, going off to collect local color for another book—which is nonsense, you do *that* out of books in your own study. George told me the damn battery was down." He had a pleasant baritone voice.

"Is that a light?" said Pat. "I do believe it is."

"It is. Haven. Thank God. I have a vision of muffins," said Glentower dreamily. "And lots of tea. But first a drink."

"That sounds heavenly."

Five minutes more, dead slow, and the light resolved itself into several lights. A hamlet. Pat slowed more, peering out of the obscured window, looking for the inn. "This looks like it—yes, there's a sign. And a dogtrot, how nice, we needn't get wet."

"What in the name of heaven is a dogtrot?"

She laughed. "Oh, sorry! A porte-cochere!"

"And I already am wet. Why didn't I bring my bag, I wonder."

But it was quite satisfactory haven. She stopped under the shelter of the overhanging port, and they went in. In the light of the entrance hall Glentower was revealed as the counterpart of the photograph on the jacket of *Isle of Gramarye*—tall, dark, very thin, with a humorously craggy face all aquiline nose and black bars of eyebrows. He took off a nondescript ancient hat, revealing an untidy thatch of black hair, and looking at her said, "Rescued by a goddess, I see. How do you do again." And then a potboy or something (were there still potboys?) came up.

Glentower explained about his car. Oh, well, reckon as Tom Shipley could send Bob out to tow her in, sure. Cost extra, out of hours. If the gentleman reckoned to drive on tonight——

"I don't," said Glentower emphatically. "Not if I can stay here. Miss Carroll—it *is* Miss?—I'll offer to stand you tea and dinner."

"More like both together, isn't it?" said Pat. The clock on the mantel in the public bar said ten minutes to six.

Inquiry of the landlord resulted in cheerful welcome; indeed guests could be accommodated. Betty was sent at once to make up the beds; on Glentower's request for sherry, Martha was sent after it scurrying, while from the rear premises someone else was ordering Jenny about. "At least they seem well-stocked with maids," murmured Glentower. Pat sent the boy out for her overnight case, and repaired the day's ravages in the upstairs bath, a coffin-shaped room obviously partitioned off at a much later date than the original construction. In the one public bar, Glentower poured sherry for her. It was a very large room, and only three or four men sat about. Glentower had pre-empted a corner table by the hearth, where a companionable coal fire hissed and crackled pleasantly. The armchairs were leather-cushioned. Pat sighed and drank sherry contentedly.

"And what are you doing in England, just sight-seeing?"

"All on my own," she nodded. "I expect it's foolish of me, because I'm not likely ever to come by another legacy. And it was a very nice one—ten thousand dollars, from a great-aunt. I'm spending it all in one glorious bust. I always wanted to do this—just drive all round the British Isles on my own. I got here a month ago, and spent a week in London while I bought the car—I'll do London properly later on."

"That sounds fun. Parts of the country I've never seen myself—I may follow your example one day."

"I went up to Gloucester first, because my grandmother was born there—but no relations left now. Our family seems never to acquire them, somehow. I don't think I've even got so much as a cousin, now Aunt's dead—my parents were killed in an accident ten years ago, and I lived with Aunt after that. Well, then after Gloucester I saw a bit of Stafford and then started working my way west. I'm making for Cardigan now, on a visit to someone there, and then I think I'll go down through Wales, all the way to Cornwall, and up the coast across east. It doesn't matter how much time I take, I can just go on until the money gives out. Everybody tells me I'm crazy, to give up a good job—I'd been at the bank nearly five years—and spend all the money this way, but I don't know. It doesn't seem very sensible to go on saving up for years and then do your traveling when you're too old to enjoy it, maybe have arthritis or chronic indigestion or something."

He laughed. "I think you're being very sensible—*toujours gai!* Never know, you might invest it and lose it all, or get killed crossing the road before you got any interest on it. D'you intend staying long in Cardigan? I'm making for Newcastle, Carmarthen's my home county, and I could show you around there, give you tips on what to see. You mustn't miss the cockle women, or the Carmarthen Oak—other things."

"That's very nice of you," said Pat. "I'm—not just exactly sure how long I'll have to stay. Oh, dear, what a way to put it. And I don't mean it exactly as it sounds, but——You see, it's a sort of duty visit. A little place called Llandaffy. The man I was engaged to was English, and his mother lives there. Stephen was in the R.A.F., a sort of test unit of some kind, using American bases—that's how we happened to meet. He was killed in an experimental flight almost a year ago."

"I see," said Glentower sympathetically. "That kind of thing can be awkward. You'll be wept over, and all of it fetched back and sentimentalized."

She grimaced. "How right you are. Just one of those things."

One of the maids came up to ask if they'd have the cold beef and fried potatoes or sausage and eggs. They both shuddered at the notion of cold beef and settled for the sausage. "You've given me too much sherry on an empty stomach," said Pat. "I've been talking too much about myself."

"Not a bit. Come on, let's kill the bottle. Just another glass apiece. Not that it's especially good sherry, but at least something with a little kick in it. If I had to go traveling to get away from my public," said Glentower sadly, "why didn't I go to France? You always stand a much better chance in French inns of getting really beautiful meals. Especially in the vineyard country. I remember a little place near Aurillac, called Le Chat Noir——" He sighed.

But the sausage was honest homemade sausage, and the eggs beaten beautifully light. There was also fresh lettuce-and-greens salad, and hot muffins with plenty of butter, and a passable apple tart. On the whole, the haven was satisfactory.

The fire was built up, and more men drifted in; the inevitable darts game began. Pat and Glentower sat talking sporadically, rather somnolent with the food and warmth. Presently Glentower reconnoitered, found an unopened bottle of brandy and took it off the landlord's hands. "Just the thing to go down nice and cozy on such a night. Lord, listen to that rain. I wonder if Bob's fetched my car in. I hope somebody remembers to bring up my bag."

About nine o'clock Bob turned up with the bag and said as how Mr. Shipley reckoned the Humber'd need a new battery, that thing in her wasn't worth recharging. "Well, all right, shove it in. Can I have it by tomorrow?"

Bob looked at him scornfully and said it wasn't much of a job, just shove in a new battery, certain sure he could. "All right, then. Thanks very much—here, buy yourself a drink. . . . Damn it," added Glentower, "why *should* I know anything about cars, just because I'm male? Why should everybody expect it and look at me as if I'm a nance when I say something stupid? Talk about the tyranny of sex."

"It's much easier being female," agreed Pat. "People fall over themselves to help you." She liked Glentower; they somehow jibed, and had fallen into the easy conversation of much longer friendship. He was, she could guess, as he'd confessed a shy man; his little poses and didacticisms were cover-up, but almost apologetically delivered. And he had that immense and rare saving grace, a sense of humor about himself. She felt that he was an instinctively warmhearted man who did not make friends easily or often, shied away from people somewhat. But a very self-sufficient man.

The brandy was half gone, and the crowd beginning to thin as closing time approached. Pat yawned and said, "I suppose I'd better get to bed early, if I'm going to get an early start and make Llandaffy tomorrow. I did get off the road, to end up way down south here nearly into Glamorgan."

"Oh, if it clears you should have an easy run. Didn't you say it's somewhere up near Plynlimon? Call it ninety miles."

"Yes, with any luck I should make it by lunchtime. . . . Oh, all right, just one more."

Glentower poured it. "Look," he said abruptly, refilling his own glass, "you needn't stay with the woman more than a couple of days? I'm going to Newcastle to potter around looking at houses—I always wanted a house in Carmarthen, and now I can afford to buy one. Let's see, this is Thursday. Suppose you meet me in Newcastle, say next Thursday, O.K.?—the Black Lion in High Street, they'll do you well—and I'll show you round some of the places you ought to see."

"It's awfully nice of you. I'd like to. The thing is, I don't exactly know how soon I *could* get away." Pat sipped brandy and after a moment said, "I can't tell you how much I'm *not* looking forward to it." The combination of the brandy, and this warm comfortable place after the difficult wet drive, and the peculiar feeling of intimacy with this man only four hours known to her loosened her tongue a little. "I have an idea she's rather a difficult woman. Of course I had letters from her—when we got engaged, and after Stephen was killed. Very stiff formal letters. She's terribly religious."

"Oh, dear," said Glentower.

"Well, yes, you may say so. Stephen never said much about her, but somehow, from what he did say, I got the idea that he'd—oh, sort of escaped from her, if you know what I mean. He was——" she hesitated; no, she really couldn't talk about Stephen to Glentower. Not decent, somehow. Say, I don't think in the end I would have married him anyway. Poor Stephen. Stephen who had been so anxiously earnest—the only phrase for it. Even before he'd been killed, she had been slowly reaching the conclusion that she was more sorry for him than anything else: it had been a—a maternal feeling, which certainly wouldn't have made for a very good marriage. "His father died when he was only a baby, and I think—as mothers will do in that case—she'd rather babied him, you know. Hung onto him, as all she had."

"Yes, I see. Awkward for you now."

"The thing is, she knows—I wrote her when I knew I was coming—she knows I've got lots of time in hand, no reason to make it just a courteous flying visit. Of course, for all I know," added Pat thoughtfully, "she may not want me to stay long—to remind her of him. But the letter I had asking me didn't sound like that. More as if she expected me to settle down for a while and reminisce at leisure over every hour of his life. There was something about, You will find our Welsh summer very delightful from June to September, and I look forward to many long talks with you."

"Oh, lord," said Glentower.

"And I do sound very rude and thoughtless to say all this, don't I? Of course I'm sorry for the woman. And of course it's not that I've forgotten Stephen, or—anything like that. But it was over last year, I've—you know—got past it. . . . I'm afraid it's going to be embarrassing and difficult, yes. But I can get away, perhaps with saying I'll come again, and then let it tail off in letters. . . . I might make you an excuse, say I've arranged to meet someone who can't get away from London any other time. Yes, all right, let's say next Thursday then, at Newcastle, and thanks very much. And now I *will* go to bed. Goodness, I hope it clears by morning!"

TWO

But upstairs in the high-ceilinged, chilly bedroom, getting ready for bed, she found herself thinking about Stephen Trefoile, as she had often in the last weeks. It was always easier to look at things objectively from a little distance; and looking at her three months' engagement to Stephen afterward both sobered and slightly worried her.

No, even before he died she was beginning to see that she couldn't marry him. But if he had lived, would she have been fool enough to go on and marry him just because she hadn't the courage to hurt him? Poor Stephen, so like an anxious little boy who'd done something wrong unwittingly, forever asking apology. It looked like a rather attractive shyness, a reserve, until you knew him better. Until you found out that there really was an anxious little boy behind the facade of tall, slim, good-looking fair young man.

He didn't have any close friends among the men he worked with; he seemed vaguely uninterested in his job, which had something to do with plane communication systems. For his lacks and immaturities as they showed up Pat had made excuses. He'd never been to school, he said, but was tutored at home, sometimes by the local rector, sometimes by a hired teacher. She gathered that there was a sufficient income. So he'd never learned ordinary give and take, how to get along with his own kind. And his mother spoiling him—or, never letting him out from under her thumb? He was—malleable.

But she couldn't go on making excuses. She had just about reached the stage of admitting to herself that she couldn't spend her life with this weak and immature man, when he was killed. What made her think now was the fact that she *had* got engaged to him; impulsively and without knowing him long, but still she'd got that far, sincerely. She'd never thought she was the kind of strong-minded woman who preferred a man weaker than herself; but there was always, didn't they say, some unconscious reason why people were attracted to each other. And men like Stephen were inevitably attracted to women stronger than themselves.

It wasn't a nice idea. Pat looked at herself in the speckled mirror of the bathroom and made a grimace. She didn't look like that sort of female. But they didn't, always. And then abruptly she found she was rather admiring Patricia Carroll, with her slender rounded figure and well-brushed crisp dark hair and nice peaches-and-cream skin and hazel eyes. And wondering if Alan Glentower had admired her too.

She burst out laughing at herself. I must be in a bad way, she thought, if I go to imagining every man I meet——But he *is* nice. I like him. And he needn't have offered to take me around, just because I rescued him out of the rain.

However, Pat Carroll, a little older and wiser, meant to be very much more careful about getting engaged again. Which she fully intended and hoped to do, someday, because she certainly didn't want to be one of those women who go on all their lives working at some sterile office job. But neither did she want to marry just anybody, who might turn out to be a weakling like Stephen.

She'd always thought she had better judgment of people.

Never mind. It was over; and she'd go to see old Mrs. Trefoile, and be kind and polite and sentimental with her for a couple of days, and then she'd be free to go on with her glorious holiday. Some of it with Alan Glentower.

And someday—perhaps by next year or the year after—she'd meet somebody just right for her, and be married, and start another sort of life. A bit funny, starting all over at twenty-seven or twenty-eight. . . . Pat switched off the light and got into bed. . . . Have to be careful not to go on behaving as if she'd still only herself to think about, making decisions alone and so on. For that much of her trouble-borrowing was true at least, she knew: like Alan Glentower, Pat Carroll was a self-sufficient person, and for much the same reasons. She'd been alone so long, for Aunt Tilda was a teacher and had treated the fifteen-year-old niece thrust on her much like an adult guest staying in the house. Pat had not been especially popular at school—she was too good a student and liked to read too much, and considered most sports meaningless. She'd learned to find her own amusements with the two or three close friends she had, and then had come two years of college and the job at the bank. . . .

From the little Glentower had said about himself, she gathered it had been much the same story. He too was an only child, and after a long bout of rheumatic fever hadn't been sent to school until he was twelve. And being the introverted, reserved sort he was, probably hadn't been very truly sought after, ever. He'd mentioned Cambridge. And "when I was on the *Herald,*" so he'd been a newspaperman. Nothing about the war, so perhaps he'd been too young for it, though he looked about thirty-five—but those tall dark craggy men often looked older than they were.

Really, what nonsense . . . She had better get to sleep. Longish drive tomorrow. If it went on raining like this, had she better go on? Yes, of course—annoying, and she couldn't make as good time, but she wanted suddenly to have Llandaffy and Mrs. Trefoile behind her, get on to pleasanter things.

She drifted to sleep to the sound of drumming rain.

Happily, the morning was clear. Glentower was down before her, and reported that he was promised his car by nine o'clock.

"Oh, I'll be off before you then, try to make it by lunchtime. What a glorious morning after the rain!"

They sat down to breakfast together, which began with more sausage and progressed to something on a large platter which drew a glad cry from Glentower. "Wafers, by God! I take back whatever I said in derogation of this charming inn. It has a cook of sorts. I didn't think anyone remembered how to make them."

"What are they?" asked Pat doubtfully.

"It's a very old recipe—wafers were being made in England in the twelfth century. Try one. You eat it like toast—slap some more butter on, though they haven't grudged it. You know them quite well under the corrupted name of the waffle."

"Waffles are purely American," said Pat, tasting a wafer. "It is rather like, though."

"They are not. The *Mayflower* contained a good many wafer irons. You simply forgot the correct word and began making your irons too large. Observe the crisscross design pressed in. The oldest recipe I've come across," said Glentower nostalgically, "starts out *Take fine wheaten flour, mix with cream yolks of eyeroun, spice it and beat it, then warming your irons——"*

"You sound like that detestable thing, a gourmet," said Pat. "I don't know that I'll meet you in Newcastle after all, if you're one of those men who knows more about cooking than any mere female and mixes up tasty little messes for himself."

"*I* don't do any cooking—I am the appreciative audience. I collect examples of wonderful food. Fortunately I have the kind of metabolism that can use up as much as I give it—I never gain a pound. Certainly I'm a gourmet. Pass the wafers, please. Aren't you interested in food?"

"Not to that extent—what does it matter what you eat?"

"Good God, you do need educating. Did I recommend the Black Lion? Yes, well, you can get a very acceptable quince custard there, if it is a modern recipe, but the thing they do really well is hot cockle sauce. And I must take you down to Llanelly—there's a little place there called The Drowned Man where you can get a real old-fashioned Haddyanegg."

"Goodness! What might that be?"

"Nice fresh haddock steamed in butter and milk, with a poached egg on top. The egg must be poached in the gravy from the haddock or you don't get the real flavor."

"I'll remember that. And I must be on my way. You can continue the lecture next week!"

He came out to the Jaguar with her and quite suddenly, as she started the engine, he turned queerly serious and urgent. "Don't forget now, the Black Lion in Newcastle next Thursday. I'll be waiting for you."

"All right," said Pat, smiling at him. "See you then." She realized she hadn't been exactly woolgathering last night: he did want to see her again. And she liked him, yes, but inevitably her reaction was, let's not go too fast. So the smile was not the wide friendly one it might have been, but only courteous.

He stood a moment, hand on the door, and then said, "Right—for sure, now. Have a good trip," and stepped back. Pat raised her hand in casual salute and let out the clutch.

She was going almost due north now, for straying off her road yesterday had taken her too far south. In the rather sharp air, still damp after the rain but with bright whitish sunlight, she made good time up to the town of Brecknock, and there turned northwest toward the border of Cardigan. The country was not very exciting—like so much of the England and Wales she had already seen, its charm was quiet. Perhaps it was only the quality of light today, but the greens here merged into grays, and the hills—higher to her left—went on quietly undulating in monotonous curves. She saw occasional small flocks of sheep scattered on them.

Some miles out of Brecknock she slowed to pass through a village. A ragged line of old cottages, of starker lines than those in villages of other counties she'd seen, but each with its patch of garden. A tall stone church, with its house beside it. An inn. A few women were working in the gardens as she passed, and looked up at the gleaming bright-red Jaguar. A small boy stood staring with the nakedly hungry expression of all small boys on all gleaming automobiles and Pat laughed and waved at him and he grinned.

Then open country again, and no more villages for miles. Much of Wales, she knew, was very lonely country—very rural. The same gray shade of hills and pasture persisted.

By any reckoning, she thought when the meter showed she had come almost fifty miles, she must be over the border into Cardigan. She had passed several more villages, all small, and where the road rose over the hills had glimpsed others and isolated farmhouses in the distance.

More sheep, once a whole flock wandering toward her down the road with a black sheep dog importantly keeping them in order and the shepherd trudging behind. She slowed down, knowing how silly sheep can be, and the man touched his cap to her and she smiled at him.

It was eleven o'clock; she couldn't make as good time on these strange roads as she would at home, driving familiarly on the right side. When she saw a village coming up, she decided to stop and get her bearings, perhaps have a cup of tea and take a little break.

The village, the inn landlord told her in the singing Welsh accent she'd heard before, was Rhydor, and indeed she was in Cardigan. Going up toward the mountains north, was she? A fine day for the drive, and nice it was to see a young American lady taking the trouble to drive into Wales. Mostly American tourists stayed around they Midlands, or at the most took a day's look at the Lake Country, and that was all.

Pat asked for tea. "It's very lovely country," she said. As a matter of fact she thought it not very attractive at all. Those endless undulating gray hills, the lonely arch of the sky over them.

"It iss good country," said the landlord benevolently.

She had the tank filled there, and started on. Her map placed the little town of Llandaffy just this side of the mountain of Plynlimon, which was (it added in fine print) two thousand, four hundred and sixty-eight feet high. Well, well, how interesting.

Almost at once the road began to climb, and she could see ahead of her the big mountains looming up, humpbacked black bulks. The sun had gone under now, and when she rolled down the window to toss out the occasional cigarette stub she could feel that the air had turned very cold. She was not far from the sea here.

As her mileage showed that she must be nearly at her destination—the tallest peak, which must be Plynlimon, was looming up quite near—she slowed a little. Finally the road took a sharp dip and led her into a good-sized village all huddled in a little hollow. And the second building she passed bore a faded sign: The Llandaffy Parish Hall.

So she was here. Pat drew in to the roadside and stopped.

She thought she had never seen uglier, more desolate country. Everything was gray, a uniform dispirited gray; it sloped away, either up or down, in great sweeps of ridges and hollows so far apart that in between were monotonous flat plains. The Parish Hall was square and ugly, the cottages she could see the same.

The one street was deserted, and Pat got out, a little stiff after the long drive, to find someone and ask directions. As she shut the car door, dropping the keys into her bag, the door of the Parish Hall opened and a very fat man all in black came out and started down the street. He was bundled up in a heavy ulster; the wind was cold, this high and near the sea.

Pat intercepted him. "Excuse me, could you tell me where Mrs. Trefoile's house is?"

He removed his hat gravely and released fine tufts of thin white hair to dance merrily in the breeze. "Mrs. Trefoile? Indeed I'm afraid I can't, young lady, for there's no one of that name living here."

"What? But there is," protested Pat. "She does live here. I've had letters from her and written her here."

The man shook his head slowly, looking almost as bewildered as she, in sympathy. "Now this is a pity, and you must have had a long drive too. A young American lady you'll be. I'm the minister here, the Reverend Evan Fallow, and you must allow me to help you if I can. We must sort this out. Letters, you say?"

"Yes, certainly, so she must live here."

"Well now," said the Reverend Mr. Fallow, "I happen to know there's never been a Mrs. Trefoile living here—not since I've been here at least, which is fourteen years—you did say Trefoile? But we'll sort it out." He beamed on her benevolently. "The first thing is to get out of this chill wind, you're not warmly enough dressed for our rigorous climate, Miss——"

"Carroll."

"Miss Carroll. I was just about to step into the inn for my pre-luncheon glass of sherry—for I am not one of these men of God who must see the devil's work in all innocent little pleasures, dear me, no. I should be so happy if you'd join me, and perhaps with the help of Daffyd—ah, the landlord, who is a very sensible fellow—we can sort this out."

"Thank you," said Pat dispiritedly, and fell into step beside him. What on earth was this? She'd sent at least two letters to Mrs. Trefoile here—she remembered distinctly writing down the full address, Mrs. G. Trefoile, Abervy, Llandaffy, Cardigan Wales. And the letters had reached Mrs. Trefoile, because she'd answered them. No, more than two. Mrs. Trefoile had enclosed a letter for Pat in a letter to Stephen when they got engaged, and so Pat hadn't seen the return address, and she'd asked Stephen, and he'd written it down for her. She'd written Mrs. Trefoile then. Then the second time after Stephen was killed. And (why *had* she done *that?)* a third time when she knew she'd be coming to England.

Oh, bother Mrs. Trefoile! If she hadn't let her know she'd be in England, she need never have come near the woman. But Aunt Tilda, who'd been old-fashioned, had brought her up to some of the old-fashioned courtesies, and tiresome as she'd known it would be, she had felt it a duty. (Had she also, perhaps, been a little curious to see if her deductions about Stephen's mother were right?)

THREE

The inn was as stark and ugly inside as it was out. The landlord, another fat man, was leaning on the bar talking in Welsh with his sole customer, a little bantam cock of a man with red hair. They both greeted the Reverend Mr. Fallow and looked at Pat with polite curiosity.

"My usual sherry, Daffyd, and I think one also for this young lady. A Miss Carroll, all the way from America, and with a mystery for us."

"A mystery would it be, sir? What sort indeed?"

"Why, she is looking for a Mrs. Trefoile——"

"I *know* she lives here," said Pat. "I've sent letters to her here, and she answered them."

"Well, indeed, that's very strange." Daffyd poured the sherry leisurely. "For there's never been a Mrs. Trefoile in Llandaffy in *my* memory. Eh, Garry?" The red-haired man contented himself with shaking his head.

"What can be the explanation?" wondered Mr. Fallow. "Does anything useful occur to you, Daffyd? You are always so clearheaded."

"I do believe I'll have a bit o' sherry myself," said Daffyd, and poured it carefully. "Well, now, it might just be useful, Mr. Fallow, what comes into my mind." He drank thoughtfully. Pat realized she was shivering; it was almost as cold inside as out. "Mind if I'm not right, when a letter arrives at a place and the Post can't make out to deliver it, it'll be sent back to some central sorting place for 'em to make another try. Eh? Like as it might be, the person writing careless like, they'd first sort it out for Llandovery, when all the time 'twas meant to be Laugharne or Llandaff. Eh? And second time round, like, the sorter'll scribble on it, Try Llandaff—or as it might be, Try Laugharne. And after a bit it ends up where it was meant to go. Eh?"

"That's perfectly true," nodded Mr. Fallow.

"So it just occurs to me as it might be a useful notion if we should ask Morgan the Post does he recall sending back letters for this Mrs. Trefoile to the sorters. Seeing as he'd've been the one to do it."

"Ah!" said Mr. Fallow, beaming. "Doubtless you are right, as usual. You have such a clear head. We must consult with Morgan the Post."

"Indeed," said Daffyd. And then no one said anything for some time. Pat drank sherry in the vain hope that it would warm her a little.

Presently the red-haired man finished his drink, said, "I'll go and fetch him," and went out.

"But she never mentioned the letters being misdirected," said Pat.

"Perhaps she didn't notice. People often simply turn an envelope over and slit it open, you know. Did you not take any notice of the postmark on her letters, Miss Carroll?"

"Well, no, I don't think I did. I just saw it was a letter from England, on account of the stamp, and opened it." Damn. Most of the day wasted, and she'd *told* the woman she'd be there on Friday. How on earth was she to locate the right place now?

But surely Stephen had said Llandaffy, in talking of his home? He hadn't talked much about it, of course, but——

The red-haired man came back with an immensely tall and thin man. "Ah, Morgan," said Mr. Fallow. "Now you must help us sort this out, my good fellow, if you can."

"Garry was telling me. Times there's letters come as are misdirected, sure. Now tell me, miss, what the address might o' *been* on they letters you sent this lady."

"I'll show you," said Pat, and scrabbled for her address book in her bag, and opened it to T. "Like that. I wrote it down just as it was given to me."

The entry read quite plain:

Mrs. G. Trefoile
Abervy
Llandaffy, Cardigan
Wales

Morgan the Post studied this with his head cocked, and then a great light seemed to dawn on him. "Ah!" he said. "Now this freshens my memory, miss. Indeed and I do remember they letters. I remember saying to myself at the time, it is likely by reason of whoever wrote them being an American. For of course I see the American stamp. The first one, I remember I was about to send it back to the central station in Hereford, and then I looks at it again and it comes to me what this American—as now turns out to be you, miss—had gone and done. They'd got the names of the town and the house all backward. I've heard as they don't name houses in America, but here, whiles, we do. And the reason I says that to myself is that while there isn't no house roundabout here called Abervy, there *is* a town called Abervy down south. So likely that's the place as was meant, and you'll find this lady you want at a house called Llandaffy in the town of Abervy."

"Oh!" said Pat. Of all the stupid things to do—how had she come to do it? She tried to remember how Stephen had written down the address —yes, she could see the scrap of paper in her mind——

Mrs. G. Trefoile
Abervy—Llandaffy
Cardigan, Wales

He had put the name of the village first, and Pat, with her logical mind trained to file cards, and knowing about English houses being named, had taken it for the name of the house. Probably Llandaffy was a fairly common Welsh name, and it was just coincidence there was also a town called that. "How provoking!" she said.

"So I writes on it myself, Try Abervy, and sends it back. I misremember was it one more letter or two more like that come, but I did the same then."

"But where is Abervy—how far?"

"It'll be about a thirty-mile run, miss—down in the south part of the county."

Pat was immensely relieved. She could do that easily by mid-afternoon, unless she got lost. "Thank you so much," she said to all of them. "I think I'll have lunch here, then, and get right on."

"You must lunch with me, Miss Carroll—no, no, I won't take denial —we must do the honors for an intrepid young foreigner penetrating into our west fastnesses! So few of you do."

"But I don't want to put you out——"

"No, no, I've a most amiable housekeeper, I assure you. Another glass of sherry? No? Then come to the parish house—dear me, I do trust that Mary has laid the sitting-room fire—and we shall try to make you comfortable. Thank you so much for your invaluable aid—Daffyd, Garry, Morgan! Yes, yes, come along, Miss Carroll."

Alan Glentower watched the scarlet Jaguar out of sight, until it turned off where the main road curved; then he went back to the inn for a second cup of tea while he waited for his own car.

He realized suddenly that he didn't know the name of the inn. It was an important thing to know, to remember. He made some kind of bad joke to the landlord, an excuse to ask: the inn was called the Tregarth Arms.

Really a very extraordinary thing to happen, at the Tregarth Arms or anywhere else. Of course there was always Marlowe, wasn't there?—*who ever loved that loved not at first sight*—but it had never happened to him before, and he was very much shaken. He had no idea at all what sort of impression he'd made on her; indeed, very little clear recollection of what he'd said and done while he was with her.

It was odd how so many people thought of writers as volatile, emotional erratics—and in the old-fashioned phrase Bohemian—given to sudden enthusiasms, fickle, neurotic, and amoral. Like everybody else, they came all sorts. What really shook him about this was that Alan Glentower had never been that kind of man at all.

Like most acutely perceptive and intuitive people, he had insight into himself. Sometimes it encouraged and helped him (awareness that, despite the crassness of the average man-in-the street, he *had* more understanding, greater intellectual intelligence); quite a lot of the time it exasperated and frightened him (awareness that a great many people found him odd, or difficult, or unfriendly, and had no glimmering that he had as desperate a need as any other human being for communication, affection, understanding). He compromised; as all human beings do, he built the shell with the picture painted on it for outside view. All one could do. He got along. He enjoyed life mostly, and he was tolerably well pleased with himself, if uneasily aware of his shortcomings. He had a vast rational contempt for the maundering pretentiousness of the psychiatrists, who seemed to have reached the conclusion that if all humanity were happy loutish extroverts together, shunning solitude as the devil shunned holy water, the millennium would be reached. Considering that most of the worthwhile, the beautiful, the progressive and the useful achievements of *homo sapiens* had been produced by introverted neurotics, he did not fret at all about what any given psychiatrist might say about the state of Alan Glentower's psyche. No.

But because he was that kind of person, his relationships with people had—fallen short. Most of the time. He covered up very adequately, but he was shy of people; he could not give out of himself easily, glibly. He had had a good friend: Bob Clive, who had died in Korea. With Bob he could be himself, there was quick, easy give-and-take of instinctive understanding. He had loved a woman: poor pretty Kitty Morgan, and there too had been an intuitive understanding of each other. But Kitty had died in the T.B. sanatorium in Switzerland, six years ago. A large part of his *Herald* salary for a year had gone for that—and Mrs. Morgan very damned stiff-necked about taking it, for fear it should *get about* and folk think there'd been *something between them.*

There hadn't been, in that sense. He'd wished there had been. There was something more to that than what he'd had, and he'd like to know about it for sure before he died.

Oh, he was a sentimentalist sometimes, an idealist. He dealt with the very stuff of human dreams. Also, being an occasional cynic, he was aware that the majority of the people who'd so eagerly read *Isle of Gramarye* (and the three not-as-successful novels before it) had not done so for the impeccable crisp style, the decisively trenchant characterization, but for the action and the love-making. Absurd to feel bitter about that. People had always listened to stories for exactly those reasons. They always would.

But, yes, he had gone on feeling that there was something else, something better and nearer completion. The way it would have been with Kitty. Communication. And what all the tales tried so fumblingly to say about true loving.

He was a man of strong sensual appetites; fortunately or otherwise, he had had rather an orthodox upbringing. There had been women, yes: most of them earnest young would-be intellectuals in London, dying for what they called Experience. None of them had touched him: none of them had given him that thing he had shared with Kitty. Kitty, whom he had kissed three times and that was all.

And now, Pat Carroll. Patricia Carroll. He didn't know what her second name was. He didn't know where she came from, or, really, much of anything about her. Except that she had beautiful hazel eyes and dark hair and a lovely voice. He had fallen in love with the voice first. So many Englishwomen had such shrill, high, unpleasant voices. As a Welshman, the sounds of things were important to him, the cadences and the tonal quality. It was a reason he detested London: all London women had voices like parrots, grating on the ear.

She had a lovely voice, deep contralto. They laughed at the same things; they understood each other's talk. A very small beginning, one evening and one breakfast; but he felt—excitedly and hopefully and wonderingly he felt—it could grow into something even better than with Kitty.

A very queer and extraordinary thing. Because Alan Glentower, in every facet of his life, was a cautious and long-planning man. Not given to the impulsive gesture or emotion.

But it had been like an electrical connection, last night: the circuit closed, between one second and the next.

If anyone had asked him, he'd have said The last choice. An American girl. Everyone knew what was said of American women. And he'd always rather fancied blondes over dark girls. And blue eyes. And feminine clothes, and the little feminine graces.

She'd had on a very plain cotton shirt-collared dress, dark green, with gold buttons. And only a rather old-fashioned-looking gold lapel watch ("it was my aunt's; I don't like wrist watches") and a ring on her right hand, for jewelry. It had a big green stone, and she said it was a turquoise. Laughing at his surprise: "Oh, yes, turquoise comes green—it's the rarest kind. The Indians and Mexicans who do most of the mining try to keep all the green stones—they value them much higher. It's only when they get very hard up they'll sell one. My father bought this, years ago, in Arizona, from an old Indian." It was a man's ring, with a heavy silver shank.

She hadn't any airs and graces at all.

How easily wert thou chained,
Fond heart, by favours feigned!
Why lived thy hopes in grace,
Straight to die disdained?

That was Thomas Campion. *To die disdained.* She had liked him, hadn't she? Had she? Was she only polite for an evening, stuck with him here? Had she felt any of that at all? He didn't know; he, who always felt the nuances from people. He didn't know much about her at all. Just that he'd suddenly, inexplicably, violently—and, yes, irritatingly—fallen in love with her.

Well, there was something: quite a lot, in fact: she was going to meet him in Newcastle next Thursday. In the process of taking her about——

He wasn't good with people, damn it. Unless there was that *rapport* to start with. *Had* she felt any of that?

A perfectly absurd thing to happen to a man thirty-three years old, not without experience and cynicism.

And it was such a hell of a long time until next Thursday.

When Bob brought the car round, he paid him, paid the landlord, and set out on the west road for the Carmarthen border, across the Black Mountains.

He knew this country; it was his country; always it had the power to soothe him, settle him less at odds with himself—coming home. There wasn't much to come home to now except the place itself. His parents had been in their forties when he was born; his father, a small-town and not too successful solicitor, had died eight years ago, his mother last summer. There had been an annuity which died with her, no more. The house had been leased. There were old acquaintances, and a couple of cousins over in Pembroke; that was all.

It wasn't very sensible, maybe, to want a house just for himself. But it was one of the things this very welcome new money could buy him that he wanted. Not necessarily in Newcastle: in the country, say, between there and Haverfordwest, in an easy drive of the sea. He had a vague idea of what he wanted, what he'd told Davy Farren to look out for. A nice solid house on half an acre or an acre, maybe with its own patch of woods. Modern kitchen and plumbing. He loathed gardening, but if his books went on selling—if that film contract went through—he could afford a gardener; maybe even stabling—he'd always liked to ride, when he had the chance.

Only now, damn it, he couldn't help thinking, If. If Pat——Because —*if*—she ought to have a say about the house too. Where and what kind. An American girl. She probably wouldn't consider living in England at all, with or without Alan Glentower, who was the biggest damn fool on top of earth. Only, *if,* well, he shouldn't plunge ahead and buy a house.

But he'd written to Davy, damn it.

And you couldn't expect her—even *if*—to decide in a week. On a tour round the British Isles: damn it, he could hardly follow her all over, monopolize her all the time. What could he do? Hold her here, near him, on the pretext of showing her around Wales, as long as possible. Find out when she'd be in London, make an excuse to be there too, ask her out. It didn't give either of them much time—him to impress himself on her, her to make up her mind. If.

Come out plain and open, this is how I feel, please give me a chance —think about it, darling. Yes?

A very damned extraordinary emotional experience. He kept seeing the smile in her hazel eyes. The rather small white hands, with nicely-kept pink-polished nails, the big green ring. The way her dark-brown hair with chestnut lights in it waved cleanly back from her forehead. Hearing the lovely low cadence of her voice.

It was as well that he knew the road; he was not in a very normal state. He got to Newcastle at half-past twelve, and took a room at the Black Lion, and sat in the public bar over a sherry. When he found himself unconsciously caressing the glass because next Thursday it might be the one she drank from, he hauled himself up sharply and tried to summon a little cynical common sense.

Will you now so timely depart
And not return again?
Your sight lends such life to my heart
That to depart is pain.
Fear yields no delay,
Secureness helpeth pleasure;
Then, till the time gives safer stay,
O farewell, my life's treasure!

Damn Campion. What business had Thomas Campion, long since dust, to come intruding into Alan Glentower's mind?

And then of course Davy Farren wandered in after a prelunch drink, and spotted him. "Ah, there, Mr. Glentower! I had your letter. It's gratifying to find you wanting to settle down amongst us in your old home place, and you quite famous up in London, so I understand. Been looking out likely properties for you, I have. Tell you about three-four I'd like you to look at—no obligation, you understand, just *look* at——" He sat down across from Glentower with his drink and leaned close, a little foxy-faced fellow with cynical eyes.

"And I will," said Glentower. "Very damn close, Davy. Not dealing with an innocent soft Englishman you are, friend. Don't I know Davy Farren! Talk fast about the lovely view to take my eye off the 1900 plumbing."

"Don't you go slandering me." Davy grinned. "One line o' chatter for English, another for our own breed, man. And well I know I couldn't shove up the commission on a born Glentower either. I'll fix you up with just what you're after. First of all there's this place down toward Carmarthen town. When I had your letter it was the first place

leaped into my mind, I give you my word—acre o' ground, nice stone house, four bedrooms, modern kitchen, lovely old growth o' oak and elm all about—I said to myself, just the kind o' place Mr. Glentower wants——"

PART 2

FOUR

It was past four o'clock when the Jaguar slid downhill and round a curve somewhere very near the village of Abervy, by the map. Pat had not been able to get away from the hospitable Mr. Fallow until after two.

She had been slightly cheered to find the country somewhat pleasanter as she drove south, often catching glimpses of the sea to her right and for a ten-mile stretch driving right along it. When she was twelve, her father had been transferred by his firm to San Francisco, and they had driven out from Chicago, very far north, down the Oregon coast, as a holiday trip before settling into the new place. Dimly this broken coast with its many rocky inlets reminded her of Oregon.

In the end it was (she was to reflect later) rather eerie, how she came to Mrs. Trefoile's house. The road had been very winding, and she had been forced to slow her pace. Though it was June, and England so far north that dusk would fall late, a dark fog was beginning to shut down on the day. And then quite suddenly there was a sharp bend in the road, she stepped on the brake, and there directly ahead of her was a white gate with the name Llandaffy on it.

She stopped the car. The road went off almost at right angles here, presumably into the village of Abervy. The house called Llandaffy stood —or rather the property stood—at the curve. Because there was no sign of a house: just the gate, which she saw now was white-painted iron, and a paling fence stretching away to either side for a little way, and the curving drive inside.

At the moment Pat was conscious only of relief. It had turned very cold; she hated driving in a bulky coat and had on only a sweater and skirt. Her hands, in thin-shaved pigskin driving gloves, and her feet felt like blocks of ice. June! But this was Wales, and not far from the sea. In fact, as the noise of the engine dropped, she caught the sound of the sea, blown in on the wind, very faint.

Thank God she was here, after this long weary day of driving through dreary country. Mrs. Trefoile might be tiresome and embarrassing, but at least she would offer hot tea, muffins perhaps, hot buttered toast at the least, and a fire. Bless Mrs. Trefoile! Pat swung the Jaguar up to the gates, braked, got out and went to see if they were locked. There were English houses (and Welsh?) where there was a lodge, someone whose duty it was to admit visitors: but she had not gathered that Stephen's mother lived in quite that style.

Nor did she. The gates were not fastened; Pat pushed them back, reentered the car and drove in. The foggy gray light showed her a thick growth of trees, she did not know what kind, to each side of a narrow curving turf drive. It led her round a wide left-hand bend a good quarter-mile up to a house.

After the gates and the drive it was an unpretentious house, and not very attractive, or especially old. It was partly of wood, partly of stone, an odd shade of gray stone, very drab; the frame parts were painted the same color. It was flat-fronted like a Georgian or Regency house, without pillars, and not very large. The front door was squarely in the middle of the flat front, and there was a precise row of four windows on either side of it, on the ground floor, and six windows above. It was depressingly symmetrical.

The drive ended in a semicircle beyond the door. Against the house were tidy squared-off beds of flowers; on the other side of the drive a precisely-edged bed followed its curve, giving on a narrow patch of lawn which ran down to the wilderness of random-growing trees.

Pat switched off the engine. In one swift breath uneasiness passed over her, reasonless uneasiness for this utter deadly precision. A breath drawn, it was gone.

So Mrs. Trefoile liked a tidy garden, arranged in planned, uncluttered design. Pat could have guessed she would.

It was much colder out of the closed car. She went up the few steps to the front door and found the bell, stood shivering in the cold wind.

The tourist bureau certainly knew what they were talking about when they said take plenty of warm clothes!

And quite suddenly she found herself thinking, *Childe Harold to the dark tower came——*

Ridiculous.

Especially when the door opened to reveal, in the cold fading light, the kind of servant she had known Mrs. Trefoile would keep. A woman about fifty, a countrywoman, not a scrap of make-up, graying brown hair, uncompromisingly plain face. She had on a homemade gray cotton dress with a black cardigan over it, ugly thick clumping oxfords and cotton stockings. Nothing, but nothing, could be more respectable and prosaic.

"I'm Miss Carroll. I think Mrs. Trefoile expects me. This *is* Mrs. Trefoile's house?"

"Oh, yes, miss." Just a hint of Welsh accent: the "yes" almost "yess." Quite expressionless and correct. "Come in, miss."

Pat stepped into a dark entry hall. "Madam's at tea in the parlor, you'll be pleased to join her, miss." And a door opened, more light slanting out. "Miss Carroll's come, madam."

The Presence rose up to greet her. It was really the only way to describe it, thought Pat, and the anticipatory thought of tea and muffins receded a little in amusement. So people really went on living this way!

It was a smallish square room, with a very small hearth which bore an even smaller fire. If it had contained any such modernism as a thermometer, Pat reckoned it might have registered about fifty-five. The room was cluttered with furniture. At first glance she could scarcely take in everything: she had only a confused impression that every square inch was occupied. Little tables, bric-a-brac, footstools, pictures, wall shelves, curio cabinets, all jostling each other on a very colorful and ugly Turkish carpet.

The first thing she saw in entirety was a large stuffed pheasant displayed under a glass dome on a table squarely in the center of the room. The second was Mrs. Gwynneth Trefoile.

"My dear Miss Carroll! Such a great pleasure to welcome you! I had rather hoped that you would be with me for luncheon and had quite given you up as the day drew in! I trust your escort and servant are accommodated. Anna, you will see to it."

Mrs. Trefoile was a small plump woman, not unlike Queen Victoria in her latter years. She wore an ankle-length black silk dress, very high to the throat, long-sleeved, full; she had thin gray hair drawn back to a thin bun, and very pale china-blue eyes. Her skin, innocent lifelong of any cosmetic, was like crumpled onionskin paper, she had no eyebrows at all and her voice was thin and high.

And her hands like little hot vises, taking Pat's hands.

"I drove up alone," said Pat. "It's so nice to meet you, Mrs. Trefoile."

"Alone! Dear me, how dangerous and foolish. To drive yourself—the horses—no, no, it will be a motor car now, I must remember. You will think *me* very foolish, my dear. Living alone and seldom going out as I do, I have a stupid way of not remembering exactly. . . . Anna, fresh tea for Miss Carroll."

Why, the poor old thing was a little wandery in her wits, as Aunt used to put it. "Yes, I've got my own car," said Pat carefully. "A Jaguar."

"Dear me, what an exotic name. Such a pleasure to welcome you, my dear—do sit down and be comfortable. My dear Stephen's loved one. Yes, yes, I see why he would have loved you. You are a pretty girl, you know, *in* a perfectly respectable and well-bred way, of course. You do not mind that I call you Patricia?"

"Of course not, Mrs. Trefoile," said Pat, biting back a giggle at this description of herself, "please do."

"It is very kind in you to come and visit me whilst you are in this country. I'm an old woman, perhaps you will find me old-fashioned and tiresome, but I am so pleased for you to come and stay with me. Yes, I am pleased with Stephen's choice indeed—the class of young woman he would properly choose, if need be. If need be. Pour Miss Carroll's tea, Anna. Sugar, my dear? Milk?"

"No, thank you." Very much as she'd imagined, Mrs. Trefoile was the Victorian surviving past her time. Pat took a slice of very thin bread very sparingly buttered and sipped tea. It was borne in on her that about now, in any other house, she'd have been lighting a cigarette. Let it go; presently, very tactfully and apologetically, she'd ask permission.

"We have so much to discuss. My poor Stephen. I can only rejoice that he died unblemished. A virgin soul. Always so much more beloved of the Almighty." Her pale eyes fastened on Pat expectantly.

"Oh—yes," said Pat, and sipped scalding weak tea.

"I have prayed for him, and I know you have done so too, Patricia. Not that I hold with Romanish prayers for the dead in ritual form, indeed no. And I have no doubt, I thank God, that he was at once transported to glory. Being the unstained soul he was, as so I trained him up to be. As I have no doubt you know, my dear Patricia."

"Oh, yes," said Pat uncomfortably. Aunt had been nominally Episcopalian, but they hadn't gone to church much. She couldn't even say she believed in all that. Something, yes, but all churches tried to pin it down to such rigid rules. At the same time, if you had to make a creed, she felt it was better and more dignified somehow to make it a set and proscribed ritual rather than the sort of extemporaneous, incoherent kind of thing the evangelistic sects were given to. She suspected that Mrs. Trefoile was rather evangelistic.

"We will," said her hostess, who had shut her eyes for a long moment, "go to the church together, and offer a token prayer. Not at the regular service. I do not approve of the new rector. I would attend the chapel, which I believe to be more rational and devout, but for the fact that only the lower classes frequent it. The rector uses too many habiliments of Rome. Disgraceful. And the bishop has apparently dismissed my letter of complaint without consideration. But it is a Christian consecrated place, and we may pray there without harm, do you not agree?"

"Oh, yes," said Pat. This would be quite as tiresome as she'd expected, but it wouldn't kill her, after all. Patience and sympathy.

"Will you take more tea, my dear?"

"Just half a cup, thank you." It was very weak tea—about a teaspoonful to a pint, she reckoned; but it was at least hot.

"You must offer a special prayer too," said Mrs. Trefoile, "that through dispensation you may thus remain holily virgin yourself. But tell me, my dear, something of yourself. You are of independent means—good family, then—and traveling alone. The Tour, it used to be called—for health, or knowledge? Young ladies are so bold and intrepid these days. . . ."

Rather senile, thought Pat. Be careful. Damn, probably she'd not dare a cigarette. "Oh, I've had a lovely time so far. But I did a stupid thing—I didn't realize I'd misdirected your letters, I thought you lived in the town of Llandaffy and I went there first."

"Ah, did you? How very awkward. The letters? I really don't recall. Yes, Llandaffy. I was born there, you know—that is why when the late Mr. Trefoile bought this house he called it by that name. Where else have you been in England, my dear?"

Pat made polite talk about her travels thus far. The bread was very dry, but she choked down another slice when it was pressed on her. Why *had* she written that letter to the woman? Two days of this . . . a social duty. Oh, lord.

"—Church?" she echoed. "Oh, I'm afraid I don't go to church often. You see, at home—working all week—the weekend's about your only free time——"

Her hostess frowned disapprovingly. "One's duty to the Lord must always take precedence. I am in this unfortunate situation that I cannot reconcile my conscience to attend service under Mr. Grimes—but I do assure you that I try to keep proper service times in my own household. I am surprised, Patricia. You must learn less selfishness in the future. Pray, my dear. I will help you. It is a grief to me, this matter of our church—most earnestly have I prayed that Mr. Grimes be vouchsafed more light, but so far he remains obstinate. Ritual for ritual's sake is deplorable. An altar cloth! A full choir! And now he is asking subscriptions, I understand, for a new organ! Disgraceful."

"Oh, yes," said Pat, as she seemed expected to say something.

"But I am remiss—you have finished your tea. Anna! I will conduct you to your room, doubtless you will wish to rest after a tiring journey and freshen yourself for dinner." Mrs. Trefoile rose effortlessly from her low plush chair.

"Thank you very much."

"Anna, the tea dishes to be washed up at once. Has Hector fetched in Miss Carroll's luggage?"

"Yes, madam."

"Oh—my car," said Pat hesitantly. "If it could be run into the garage ——?" Did this house have a garage? She fumbled for the keys.

"Car? Oh, most certainly. I daresay Hector can be trusted to convey it so far." The keys were regally transferred from Pat to her hostess to the maidservant. "I keep a very modest establishment these days—one must be careful with one's money—but if there is anything you desire, my dear, only ask. My poor Stephen's true love. But I confess myself disappointed in the matter of your church attendance. You must allow me to guide you, Patricia, to better ways."

It seemed half an hour later when Pat was finally left alone with her luggage. She looked around first for something to use as an ash tray; there was a painted china dish on the bureau, and she lit a philosophic cigarette, looking around the room.

It was a small square bedroom on the second floor. It too had a violent-patterned Turkish carpet, and a good deal of solid black walnut furniture—a very high bed whose headboard nearly reached the ceiling, a lowering tallboy, a large marble-topped dresser, two small and uncomfortable-looking chairs. But not a mirror in sight. And it was unheated.

Two days, thought Pat. Why did I write that letter? Oh, well, the poor old thing. It won't kill me. . . .

FIVE

The bathroom was rather primitive, but adequate. And no mirror there either: in fact, no medicine cabinet. Pat came back to her room along the landing, and made up with the awkward aid of the mirror in her dressing case, the lid propped up, on the dresser. She slipped on the new black patent pumps. Slapped on an extravagant amount of her favorite Ginger Carnation cologne. Took down the nylon dress from its hanger. Bless these uncreasable materials: it looked quite fresh. She slid it over her head, closed the zipper, and went back to stoop before the little glass and comb her hair.

Dressed, she sat on the bed and had another cigarette. No need to go down too early and be moralized at longer than necessary. Dinner at seven o'clock, Mrs. Trefoile had said: it was only six-thirty. After that meager tea, Pat hoped for a decent dinner; she was starving, even after the Reverend Mr. Fallow's sumptuous lunch six hours ago.

She'd even have fallen hungrily on Alan Glentower's Haddyanegg. In fact, when one thought of it, rather an intriguing combination—nice white tender haddock, ready to fall apart under the fork, all buttery, and the poached egg resting on top——

She had another cigarette. At five minutes to seven she sighed, put it out, and went out to the landing. The maid Anna was trudging up the stair toward her.

"Oh, beg pardon, miss. I was just coming to see were you ready. Madam's about to begin the service."

"I'm just coming." Service? Evening grace, perhaps. "Oh, Anna——" after all, she had said to ask. "I wonder if I could have a mirror in my room. It's rather awkward, dressing——"

The woman's expression did not change. "There's no looking glasses in the house, miss. Madam won't allow none. For sinful vanity such are."

"I see," said Pat. About all one could say. And of course typical of Mrs. Trefoile. Annoying, but it was only for a couple of days. Already she was thinking of Sunday (or would it have to be Monday morning?) with quite violent anticipation.

Going down the stairs with Anna's clumping feet a respectful three treads behind, she smiled to herself, thinking ahead to telling Alan Glentower about it.

Anna steered her into the parlor again. Here was Mrs. Trefoile, in the same black gown, and two men. The men stood just inside the door, and Anna halted there between them.

"You are a trifle late, Patricia, you must be more punctual. You may stand here beside me. I will read from Deuteronomy." Mrs. Trefoile had a small Bible open in her hands. She began to read in measured thin tones, almost without expression. "Chapter One. 'These be the words which Moses spake unto all Israel——' "

She went on and on. Pat started out with head bowed appropriately, expecting a few phrases and a "thus endeth the first lesson" and a processional into the dining room; but as the thin voice gave no sign of reaching a conclusion, she shifted and glanced up under her lashes. . . . The three servants were standing in a row against the open door to the hall, wooden-faced, staring straight ahead past their mistress. The man on Anna's right Pat took for Hector, aforementioned: Anna's husband perhaps? He was a man of fifty or so, big and broad and grizzled. He had an oddly Slavic-looking face, high-cheekboned and flat-mouthed, snub-nosed, impassive. His eyes were half-shut. He did not look very intelligent, but at least normal: which the other one was not.

The other man stood on Anna's left. He was bigger than Hector, and almost albino in coloring. His head was too large even for his big body, and he bore the unmistakable stamp of the "natural": the loose thick mouth, the vacant eyes, the slouch and stare and slackness. He and Hector both wore faded, nondescript, dirty working clothes.

They all just stood, and the thin high voice went on and *on,* and Pat realized with fatalistic horror that the entire book was to be read.

She shifted position again, and with horrid embarrassment heard her stomach rumble, demanding food.

On and on and *on.*

"Chapter Four. 'Now therefore hearken, O Israel, unto the statutes and unto the judgments——' "

"Amen!" shouted the albino natural suddenly. "Praise ye the Lord! Amen!"

No one took much notice. Anna and Hector remained wooden-faced; Mrs. Trefoile checked and glanced up to give the man an approving smile.

But, the whole *book?* Pat tried vainly to remember her Bible, how long Deuteronomy was. Surely——

The fire on the little hearth had died and it was very cold in the room. Immobile, her feet began to feel numb. Surreptitiously she chafed her hands together.

On and on and *on.*

"Chapter Nine. 'Hear, O Israel: thou art to pass over Jordan——' "

Like a funeral attended of social duty. Like any monumentally boring social occasion you withstood out of common courtesy.

She could not feel her feet at all, now.

"Chapter Twenty-four. 'When a man hath taken a wife, and married her, and it come to pass that she find no favour in his eyes, because he hath found some uncleanness in her——' "

Pat wondered vaguely how they could go on standing like that, still and straight. Of course they must be used to it.

"Amen!" shouted the natural. "Praise ye the Lord!"

" 'Ye stand this day all of you before the Lord your God——' "

"Amen!"

Yes, undoubtedly the whole book. Her stomach rumbled again, embarrassingly. She squinted down unobtrusively at her lapel watch. It was ten minutes to eight.

"Chapter Thirty-three. 'Give ear, O ye heavens, and I will speak——' "

Magnificent language, the Old Testament; but just before dinner was not a very good time to appreciate it. Probably the theory was to mortify the flesh.

"Amen!" cried the natural. She saw that these interjections were quite automatic: his expression never changed.

" 'And Moses was a hundred and twenty years old when he died. . . . And Joshua the son of Nun was full of the spirit of wisdom . . . in all the great terror which Moses shewed in the sight of all Israel.' "

Incredibly, the book was shut. It was over.

Mrs. Trefoile took six steps and laid the Bible on the table beside the stuffed pheasant. "Anna, you may serve the meal." The servants turned and went out. Pat wondered if she could move without staggering or falling down, but obediently followed Mrs. Trefoile's straight back across the hall to the dining room, and sank thankfully into a chair.

The dining room was smaller than the parlor, and dim. There was electricity, of course, but everywhere she'd seen only very low-wattage bulbs used; this room was lighted by a single small fixture overhead. A rectangular table, no cloth on it. Hard little Windsor chairs. A heavy dark sideboard. Big dark paintings in dark frames: she could just make out that the one facing her had an armored knight on a white horse as the main subject.

Anna came through the door at the rear with a tray. Food.

It was thin clear bouillon. Pat took up her spoon and saw that it was plate long unpolished—dark streaks and marks. But she'd have drunk out of the bowl if necessary, she was so hungry. She took a spoonful, seeing her hand shake slightly, and discovered that the bouillon was lukewarm and quite unsalted.

"—A very modest establishment," Mrs. Trefoile was saying. "For some strange reason, one's money does not seem to go as far these days as it should. But I should not be ungenteel."

Pat made mechanical responses. The bouillon was removed and in its place appeared a queer unadorned salad of leaf lettuce and anonymous greens, without any dressing. There was no salt, pepper, vinegar or any other condiment on the table. She munched lettuce unsatisfactorily.

Mrs. Trefoile talked about the principles of vegetarianism. It seemed that she subscribed to them wholeheartedly and had not touched Flesh in years, which increased Pat's depression. New plates were served: a synthetic meat loaf compounded of bread, oatmeal by the taste, and heaven knew what else. A plate of this afternoon's dry bread was offered.

"Fish I will accept," said her hostess placidly. "It is not the same thing."

Next to appear was obviously the final course, and Pat regarded it with joy: a great round of cheese with the knife in its center, and some sort of thin crackers. At least something to get one's teeth into. She helped herself liberally, and was taken aback at Mrs. Trefoile's sharp reproof. "You should not be so greedy, child. One of the seven deadly sins. Nothing matters less than the body, nothing!"

Well, even stiff Victorian old ladies forgot their manners when they began to grow senile. Pat said grimly to herself for the dozenth time, Two days.

"Put half of that back at once, Patricia. While you stay with me you shall not be allowed to fall into sensual error."

Pat stared at her; but it was, of course, impossible to refuse, to make a scene. She expended momentary sympathy for the servants, who were doubtless rationed as strictly. How on earth did she *keep* any servants? The days were long past when there were a dozen domestics scrabbling for every job. The near-idiot, of course, would not be in much demand; but the other two could surely get better jobs, certainly more comfortable ones.

When Anna brought in two cups, Pat hardly knew whether to hope it was more weak tea or the awful British version of coffee, perennially boiled. It proved to be the former. She sighed gloomily, and was unprepared for Mrs. Trefoile's agitated cry as she set her cup down.

"Anna, come here at once! Disgraceful! You have not washed up properly, there is a mark on Miss Carroll's cup! I will not tolerate carelessness!"

"Oh, no, Mrs. Trefoile, it's only my lipstick, see." Pat smiled. "It does come off, even when they guarantee it won't, you know——"

"Lipstick! What is——You wear—*cosmetics?"* Oh, lord, thought Pat, I might have known. Her hostess rose up in a flurry, came round the table and bent over her close, peering. So close that Pat felt her quick breath, caught a faint musty smell from old clothes and old woman. "This is more sin and vanity and sensuality! I am surprised at you, Patricia. Surprised and disappointed. Such grievous error—the body is *nothing!* Wash it off immediately, all this devil's paint—go upstairs and wash it off!"

This was really too much. "Mrs. Trefoile," began Pat reasonably, politely, "everyone does nowadays, you know. It doesn't mean we're—" what term would she understand? "—fast, or immoral. It's quite accepted——"

"And you have used scent also—the devil's incense!" The old woman drew back and wafted her handkerchief rapidly before her face. "I had not expected such grossness of Stephen's——Did you not hear me? I said go and remove this filth at once!"

Pat got up uncertainly. Mrs. Trefoile was gasping, panting, her white face turned even whiter, and there was a little line of foam at one side of her mouth. She fell back to her chair, a hand at her side.

"Better go, miss," muttered Anna behind Pat. "Regular fit she'll have, don't you."

But it was absurd. Senile or not, one didn't give orders like that to guests—or if one did, the guests took no notice. Pat was very angry and at the same time rather wildly amused. "But it's silly——" A fit? She could imagine what that was: pure temper at being crossed.

"Better go an' do like she says, miss!" Anna looked her up and down a little scornfully. "Why for should you care? No handsome gennelmen about to see you!"

Even the woman's servants rude. "Oh, for heaven's *sake!*" said Pat, and ran out. Upstairs, she scrubbed her face with angry thoroughness. Social duty and common courtesy be damned, she couldn't be expected to put up with this sort of thing. She'd leave in the morning.

She combed her hair again; resigned to spending a few more hours with this absurd old soul, she tried to achieve the philosophical attitude. People! It was to be presumed that Mrs. Trefoile brushed her hair and took baths: what was the precise difference, in religious implication, between a comb and a powder puff? Pat wondered. Or bath soap and cologne? She supposed a psychiatrist would say of these people that there was a tendency to masochism.

Tomorrow, she vowed, I'll get away.

She came downstairs slowly, feeling naked without lipstick. The dining room was empty, the dishes removed. She turned into the parlor.

Mrs. Trefoile was sitting in the little low plush chair, with the closed Bible on her lap. She sat very upright, facing the door. When Pat came in, she beckoned her across and rose to peer at her face again. "Very well. Very well. But I still detect that devilish scent."

"It's very strong," said Pat coldly. And expensive.

"Sit down. We shall pray."

Pat sat down opposite her, in what, when these suites of furniture were new, was called the gentleman's chair. Mrs. Trefoile began to pray aloud, ramblingly. She went on for quite a while, and as she prayed with closed eyes, Pat was able to look about the room. This stuffy, cluttered, dreadful room. All the Victorian monstrosities were present: the bird under glass, the tortured framed landscape made out of sea shells, the marble clock, the countless cheap porcelain figurines and vases and candlesticks, the dried flowers stiffly sprayed to an everlasting bouquet. She knew that even by day this room—all the rooms in this house—would be dark, with heavy curtains in layers obscuring the windows.

She thought of Stephen growing up here. Any child. With compassion she thought, A wonder he was as normal as he was. Half-formulated little random guesses flitted through her mind as to how this woman would have reacted to a small boy's misdeeds and noise and occasional rebellion.

And it seemed quite, quite impossible that the woman could be anyone's mother. Could have been young and desired, could have been loved and borne a child. How old was she? She couldn't be much more than sixty, unless Stephen had been born to her late: he had been just Pat's age. But people didn't start going senile at sixty, did they? Some people, perhaps; but not Mrs. Trefoile. She wasn't senile; she must have been this way for a long time. Just getting worse, more fanatical, with time.

Pat tried, and failed, to imagine what kind of man Mr. Trefoile had been.

The woman suddenly stopped praying and opened her eyes. "We must talk," she said. "I must talk with you, Patricia. You should not be angry with me that I try to teach you the errors of your ways. Stephen's true love. Stephen . . . Oh, I feared for him! I prayed for him! He should not have left home, there was money enough. He would come back, then, a little while, and he was troubled and afraid—I had known how it would be—and then he came back less and less. . . ."

She went on talking incoherently about Stephen. He had been trained up in the right way, but who knew what dreadful temptations would beset him, away from home and alone? She had prayed. He knew what sin was, in all its guises; she must trust him. But to ally himself with the military, so notoriously a rakish and devilish crew——They had quarreled. He had gone away and not come back for a long time. Until he was to go overseas. And then——

With growing comprehension of his background, Pat was wondering how he had ever summoned the courage to ask a girl to marry him. And a poor prospect for his building any kind of marriage . . . For she also realized that his mother's teaching had, as the phrase went, taken. If he had really escaped and rebelled cleanly, he'd have talked about it—bitter, or humorous, or resigned, he'd have talked. But it had all stayed inside. He had still felt, uneasily, that he rebelled against truth. Poor Stephen.

"Now again am I fearing for his soul. Oh, God, I fear! When he chose you, so deep in error and sin! And yet looking so innocent. I will not believe it is too late to redeem you, gather you into the fold——"

Pat had set herself to endure all this in silence; it was useless to argue with the woman. But she was trapped into futile protest. "Please, Mrs. Trefoile, this is silly. I'm not——I have every respect for anyone's religious views, but this is quite ridiculous—just because I don't go to church regularly and so on, I'm scarcely immoral. Really——"

"*Such* grievous error, my child. But I will labor to reclaim you—for Stephen. I must believe that Stephen was not contaminated, that he remained pure and undefiled." Well! thought Pat. "I must pray, I must have faith." Slowly Mrs. Trefoile rose. "It is late, we will retire. Most earnestly I urge you to pray for light, Patricia."

Pat followed her out to the hall. One thin little clawlike hand darted back inside the doorway to switch off the light. The hall was dark, only a faint slanting light coming down the stair from the dim fixture at the upstairs landing. They went up toward it in silence.

On the landing, in more light, Pat called up her courage and tact. "Mrs. Trefoile," she said firmly, "I must leave tomorrow morning. It's been very nice to meet you, but—I should have explained before—I've an arrangement to meet a friend who's on holiday. I'm sure you understand."

Mrs. Trefoile turned and looked at her. She had to look up, for though Pat was not tall the old woman barely topped five feet. "You were to stay—for a little visit."

"Yes, I know, but I thought—I've made this arrangement, you see—perhaps I could come back later." Anything to get away decently.

The hand came to rest on her arm. "No. No. You are fleeing from truth and right as I expound it to you. You must not. I must not let you."

"Really, I must keep my appointment," said Pat. These single-minded fanatics never knew when they were rude. "I can come back." Any promise.

"You would? You will? You will promise me on your oath? My dear, indulge me, will you not? If you will promise faithfully to come back to me within a few days, I will let you go tomorrow, but not before midday. You will come to the church with me, in the morning, and we will pray together for Stephen's soul and yours. Will you do that, Patricia?"

"Yes, certainly," said Pat, relieved. Jesuitical, she thought wryly, making a promise with reservation; but anyone would do the same. This nightmare of a house . . .

"Thank you, my dear. Do not forget your prayers. I shall see you in the morning, then."

"Good night, Mrs. Trefoile." Pat escaped into the stuffy little bedroom thankfully. She lit a cigarette, took a few deep grateful draws; then she went to her dressing case and put on lipstick, smiling at herself. Silly: a gesture. Be taking it off in a few minutes. Or would she? It was only ten minutes past ten.

And she was hungry. That frightful meal . . .

Tomorrow at noon (no, she would *not* stay for lunch!) she'd be driving away from here, and she'd stop at the first place she came to and have a decent meal.

A perfunctory tap at the door, and Anna came in. She looked at Pat, and at the cigarette, expressionlessly. "Was there aught else you want, miss?"

Anna not very friendly—whether impersonally to any guest, or personally to Pat. Which didn't matter. "Yes," said Pat frankly, "there is. I'd like something to eat. If you could bring me up some of that cheese, anything——"

Anna said woodenly, "Sorry, miss. Every door in the larder's locked up after meals, and madam's got the keys."

Well, really, thought Pat. "All right, I suppose you can't, then. Do you think I could have an extra blanket?" There was only one on the bed, and it would be cold here at night.

"I'll find one, miss."

When Anna had brought the blanket, Pat went along to the bathroom, washed and brushed her teeth, came back and got undressed. Defiantly she put on her best nightgown, the frivolous red nylon one with all the lace, climbed into bed with cigarettes and ash tray at hand, and propped herself up on the pillows. All she had with her to read was a recent *Tatler,* picked up a couple of days ago. She began looking through it. Every other advertisement was about a restaurant or somebody's fine wines, and all the photographs seemed to be of people eating and drinking. Damn.

At a quarter to eleven she got out of bed, struggled and heaved to raise the window a couple of inches, and switched off the light.

SIX

"I will read," said Mrs. Trefoile, "from Joshua. Chapter One. 'Now after the death of Moses the servant of the Lord it came to pass that the Lord spake unto Joshua——' "

It was seven o'clock in the morning, and Pat stood beside her hostess, the three servants facing them across the room, and shuddered with cold. The philosophic attitude, she reminded herself: another few hours. After it's over, this will be quite an experience to look back on.

"Amen!" cried the simpleton automatically.

She had been wakened by Anna at six, suddenly and without tact. "Service and breakfast at seven, miss. You're not to be late." She knew what the service meant now; whatever breakfast might offer, she wouldn't see it for some time. Fog was thick beyond the window. Pat had got up shivering and scrambled hastily into her warmest clothes; she'd meant to have a bath this morning, but it was far too cold to risk the quality of hot water in this house. She put on a tweed skirt and her thick cable-knit scarlet pullover, and at that sat huddled under the blankets again to smoke a cigarette before she went downstairs.

But little good it had done her. Mrs. Trefoile had exclaimed in outrage at the scarlet pullover and sent her back upstairs like a naughty child to exchange it for something of a proper subdued color. Escape so near, every new absurdity was striking Pat as rather funny now, and she went off meekly. "And make haste, Patricia, for it is seven o'clock now —we will fall behind in the day's routine!"

She had nothing so warm as the pullover; she substituted a sweater and cardigan set of pale beige. In the little mirror of her dressing case she looked ghastly without make-up, she thought. Her almost-fair complexion had not lost its California tan, but it had little natural color at the best of times and needed the touch of rouge, the bright lipstick, to look its best.

She stood shivering beside the old woman now and wondered what sort of breakfast it would be. Ten to one on oatmeal porridge, she decided.

Praise be to God there were only twenty-four chapters in the Book of Joshua.

It was over. The Bible closed and laid down. "Anna, you may serve the meal." And Pat won the bet with herself: it was oatmeal, served plain, with no sugar or butter, only a very small jug of skim milk.

Evidently the pullover incident was to be forgiven if not forgotten for the moment: Mrs. Trefoile was describing her contrivances to maintain proper service to the Lord, even in the face of the obstinate Romanish rector who in effect closed the church to her. "Anna and Hector, of course, have sufficient free time upon the Sabbath to attend the chapel service, but for myself it was different. There is also Joseph, who—as if his sad handicap were not enough—had never received proper religious teaching. I am pleased with how he responds—you notice how enthusiastic he is at the readings. But it is never amiss that one should attend two services instead of one—indeed, doubtless it is of great benefit to Anna and Hector. I took thought, you see. Obviously it would not be proper that I contrive some service alone, for it distinctly says, 'Wherever two or three are gathered together.' With the three servants, it is thus quite proper and orthodox. I read a book of Scripture each night and morning, and when the entire Book has been read, we begin over. This, naturally, aside from my private prayers. Since I have stopped attending the church, we have read the Book through nine, no, ten times and are now embarked on the eleventh."

Pat tried to remember how many books there were in the Bible. She also felt extremely curious as to why Anna and Hector stayed on here. Unless, of course, they were the same breed of fanatic as their mistress; that could be the only explanation.

Breakfast, such as it was, was over within half an hour; they had not sat down to it until nearly eight. "I will fetch my coat, Patricia, and we will go to the church at once."

"Why don't we take my car?"

"Oh, dear me, no, most unsuitable," said Mrs. Trefoile.

She must remember to get the car keys back from Hector. She'd never thought of them again last night. Pat went upstairs for her own coat, thinking that, and put it on. She'd had the sense not to wear any jewelry; the old woman was quite capable of confiscating it. The thing had its absurd side, but she felt horribly plain and naked without any make-up or ornament, going out—more or less—in public.

A little Welsh village, a church. What did it matter, for an hour or so? Well away afterward in the car, she'd stop and put on lipstick. . . . They went out the front door and down the curving drive. Hector was kneeling beside one of the beds against the house, weeding. He did not look up as they passed, but Pat had the feeling that he looked after them. Mrs. Trefoile looked as if she'd been lifted entire from an illustrated Victorian novel: she wore something that looked like a bonnet, and mittens, and her heavy black coat reached her ankles. She tripped along at a nervous little walk, quite fast.

Almost to the gates, they met the natural. He dodged out of the trees in front of them, and froze as he saw them. "Joseph! Come here. What were you doing in the trees? Mischief?"

"Nothin'." He came up with a dragging step.

"Look at me and speak the truth, Joseph."

He raised his vacant colorless eyes slowly. Why, he's afraid of her, Pat realized. "A-lookin' for tootleberries," he said, triumphant, sly.

"There are no such things, and no berries here. Go and help Hector. . . . One must be tolerant of such poor souls," said Mrs. Trefoile as he slouched away. "The air is sharp, is it not? But the sun will break through later."

Past the gates they turned left along the road. Not a car passed them. Pat had not realized how close the house of Llandaffy lay to the village; round the sharp bend where the property stood, two hundred yards on, the village of Abervy began. A longish narrow street lined with cottages, a few larger buildings. A dreary enough little village, not very big, but modern civilization of sorts. There was a woman sweeping her doorstep, at the first cottage they came to; she straightened and stared as they passed. Here was the inn, its sign newly repainted: The Dog and Gun. A stout but not unhandsome middle-aged man was straddling the threshold: he had a thick crest of wavy gray hair. He said in a subtly amused tone, "Good morning, Mrs. Trefoile."

She did not glance at him. Past the door, she said primly, "A most lewd man, the publican. People grow extremely lax and decadent these days. I had some occasion to complain to the local magistrate about him—he would allow Hector to charge strong waters—but Mr. Morecambe is scarcely better and paid no notice at all. I have strictly forbidden Hector to enter the place. Unfortunately I have no way of knowing if he should lie to me, but I pray for him often, that he may be released from such bondage to the flesh."

Another woman was staring at them now, up ahead, from another doorway. Yes, Pat could easily imagine what the village thought of Mrs. Trefoile. If she'd been eccentric in some other way, perhaps the village would be proud of her as the local oddity: if she'd collected African masks or gone butterfly-hunting or smoked cigars. As it was, they would only laugh at her—until she tried to tread on their toes, as with the complaint about the publican, when they'd be irritated.

"The lower classes," said Mrs. Trefoile, "have no longer decent respect for their betters." And was immediately confirmed.

The woman in the doorway, watching them approach, said boldly, "Morning, Mis' Trefoile. Don't say as you've a visitor. You're looking spry as usual." She was a scrawny middle-aged woman, in a very bright-colored print cotton housedress; her gray hair had a cheap permanent wave, a little frizzy, and she had slapped on too dark a shade of lipstick, but she looked eminently sane and twentieth century. The house, Pat saw, was not a cottage but the general store.

Mrs. Trefoile said with freezing politeness, "Good morning, Mrs. Evans."

But Pat stopped, purely on impulse. Perhaps only of random relief at talking to someone who knew what year it was. "Good morning," she said pleasantly. "Do you mind, Mrs. Trefoile, if I buy a postcard or two? It won't take a minute. And as I'm leaving today——" She went into the shop, and Mrs. Evans followed her with alacrity. The usual general village store. Everything you could imagine, if not quite as catholic as its typical American counterpart. The postcards were on a rack at the back. Pat twirled it absently, looking at highly-colored photographs of the Teifi pools, the waterfall at Cenarth, the banks of the Teifi, the ruins of the castle at Cardigan, the lake of Llyn Berwyn.

"You'll be an American," said Mrs. Evans.

"Yes, that's right," said Pat. She picked out two postcards at random. Souvenirs. She was suddenly, unexpectedly in high spirits. In a very little while she'd be away from this place; and she sensed a bond between this woman and herself—that they both stood on one side opposite Mrs. Trefoile.

Who had come just inside the door and was watching disapprovingly.

"Now isn't that inter*est*ing," said Mrs. Evans brightly. Pat marked her without much difficulty as the village gossip: those avid little black eyes. "It's not often at all that we get American tourists in Abervy. What part of America might you be from, miss?"

"California," said Pat. Spread charity as you go, she reflected. "I was engaged to Mrs. Trefoile's son, you see."

"Ah, you're *that* young American lady! A terrible thing that was indeed, to be sure, you've my sympathy, miss." Both perfunctory sorrow and curiosity in the eyes and voice.

"But I'm leaving today."

"Ah, *indeed,* miss, it's to be hoped you've enjoyed your stay," said Mrs. Evans, straight-faced. Pat knew quite well the woman was aware why she was leaving; probably Mrs. Trefoile's foibles were thoroughly familiar to all the village. She might as well have said to Pat, No wonder you're going, who could put up with it?

Pat's back was to Mrs. Trefoile. Outrageously, but unable to resist it, she winked at Mrs. Evans and said gravely, "I've an urgent appointment."

Mrs. Evans very nearly winked back; she gave Pat a broad smile and said, "That'll be fivepence, miss."

Pat rummaged in her bag, paid her and tucked the postcards away. "Thank you very much."

"Good morning, miss," came Mrs. Evans' unctuous voice after them.

Mrs. Trefoile said nothing as they walked on, but her silence continued disapproving.

The church stood at the north end of the village. It was a Victorian building, bastard-Gothic in style, with a good deal of bad stained glass. Pat had brought a scarf for her head; Mrs. Trefoile had expressed dislike of this lax modern custom, but had not positively insisted on a hat. Tying the scarf hastily, Pat reflected that it was the last touch needed to make her really dowdy. She followed the old woman up the steps. . . . Not a very interesting or attractive church. She must remember to look for the offending altar cloth.

"Is your hair entirely covered, Patricia? Please be sure."

Following her up the center aisle between hard wooden pews, Pat wondered about these puritanical Christians. St. Paul, she thought vaguely: mostly his fault. Dogmas. It certainly said, quite plain, So God created man in His own image; and if you were going to accept that, then what could there be sinful about the human body? These people, these illogical, fearful, masochistic people . . .

Mrs. Trefoile veered aside and went along to the left of the altar, and

knelt before the first row of pews. "Now we will pray most earnestly together, Patricia."

Pat knelt beside her a little unwillingly. What nonsense it all was. Something—yes, there was—but too vast and all-tolerant and immense a power to care about what little rituals men devised. That did not matter. The important thing was recognizing good from evil. . . . The Mrs. Trefoiles, in their narrow creed, nullified life itself, which was the ultimate sin.

Pray. Pray? Pat did not believe much in it, as mere supplication. She felt vaguely that if *she* were God (or Whatever) she'd only feel annoyed at these greedy human creatures forever mouthing Give me, give me. What was due, you would receive. But she did not either believe that dying was the end of everything; and so—for what it was worth—she began thinking a rather incoherent prayer for Aunt Tilda, that she should be happy and content wherever she was. Dear, precise, sardonic, shyly affectionate Aunt, who'd never had what she wanted of life . . . After ten years of correct, standoffish companionship, it had all come out as she lay dying painfully, clutching for Pat's hand. "You're prettier than I ever was. . . . Don't dawdle, child. You want to take care—choose a good man, a reliable man—but don't be—capricious. Particular . . . Such nonsense they talk about one's own life, a career, money. Meaningless. One has pride—one says, my own choice. But it never is, it never is. . . . It's not a woman's life . . . made the way we're made. . . . Don't let them tell you, Pat—the strong ones, yes, we are, one way—because of the children, we have to be—but *they* have their own ways of being stronger than we are, men, and we need them. Oh, God, we need them! It was not my choice . . . never wanted anything else really—than a man and the children . . . but it came down to being—other people's children. Don't let them lie to you, Pat. Take your own man and be happy. . . ."

Aunt Tilda hadn't needed to say all that to her; she knew it. But it had nearly broken Pat's heart, listening and stroking the hot dry hand and saying over and over, "Yes, dearest, I'll remember."

And so if there was—Anyone—there, she offered a prayer now that Aunt was somewhere happy and safe and maybe had another chance to make things more as she wanted them. . . .

But it was forever she had been kneeling here. The stone was very cold under her knees. She glanced sidewise at the little bowed crumpled figure of Mrs. Trefoile, motionless beside her.

It seemed an age later that the little figure moved, and got slowly to its feet. "Very well," said the old woman in a whisper. "Very well." And moved toward Pat, toward the center aisle. But meanwhile Pat had discovered that in the west wall across from them were a number of bronze plaques set into the stone, and with the random interest of the tourist she made for them.

"This way, my dear," said Mrs. Trefoile almost sharply.

"Just a moment, I want to see——"

She had time only to see the first plaque, at this side of the first row of pews. It was not old; this was not an old church. The raised lettering was modern:

In remembrance of
John Sheringham Ffolliott
of the manor of Rhydenn
b. 1889—d. 1955
also Joan his wife b. 1891—d. 1930
also Marian his wife b. 1900—d. 1953
Hic Jacet

"Not this aisle, Patricia," said Mrs. Trefoile, and took her arm with an astonishingly strong little hand.

"Why not?"

"It is a consecrated Christian place, but the church, I fear, is becoming debased. There is actually a wicked person entombed there. You have prayed sincerely, I trust. Come away. I daresay the rector will be arriving soon with the choir for the Sabbath rehearsal, and I do not care to meet him."

The sun had come out briefly; it struck sharp white against the eyeballs. "What kind of wicked person?" asked Pat on the church steps, and it was an idle question, amused.

"A person who forswore his marriage vows. We will not discuss it, my dear." Mrs. Trefoile stepped aside as a little fat black-clad man came up the steps. He gave her a "Good day, madam," but she did not reply. "Mr. Andrews, the master of this dreadful choir," she murmured through tight lips. He brushed past and went into the church. "We were only just in time to be alone."

Pat took off the scarf and folded it. She was in the fatal grip of flippant curiosity. "Marriage vows? Did he—the wicked person in the church—keep a mistress? How horrible."

"That is not seemly. Religion has sadly deteriorated in principle, it is no longer the true, simple creed of the earliest disciples. I reprimanded the late rector, Mr. David, upon that matter, but he did not seem to understand me at all. He had the effrontery to explain to me that the church recognizes second marriages. As if I were not aware of that!—and a disgraceful state of affairs it is. It only proves how sadly corrupt the church is. This gross and wanton person, actually interred within the church! That was bad enough, but his wicked mistress also—disgraceful."

"Mr. John Sheringham Ffolliott?" murmured Pat. "But I don't see—all churches *do* allow second marriage, when it's death and not divorce."

"Quibbling and corruption. We are assured of resurrection. How inconceivable, on that Day, to meet two! But quite aside from that, a most unchristian grossness and sensuality, to desire——! Never mind. You must not burden your mind with such thoughts. . . . Patricia?"

They were out of the churchyard now, into the village street again. "Mmh?"

"Patricia, you do not subscribe to this? You are mistaken, you have erred in some ways, but innocently so, I must believe! Not so to contaminate Stephen beyond redemption, I must believe."

Pat did not ask what complex theology this might refer to. She paced at Mrs. Trefoile's side, hands in pockets, and all her thoughts were fixed half an hour ahead, when she could in decency get away.

She heard the old woman only vaguely, overlaid by the other voice.

"Hi, miss. You got a norful pretty car, ain't you?"

Pat stopped. A boy, about ten or twelve: sandy and freckle-faced. Boys were boys, no matter the country or language or anything else; and she liked them, so she grinned back at his impudent grin and said, "How'd you know that?"

"I seen you drive in t' gates," he said triumphantly. "Yestiddy. It's a Jaguar you got. I know all the cars, every model they make. You got a XK 152 Fixed-Head Coupé, you got—newest sports model. Ain't you?"

"That's right," said Pat, laughing at him. "You're a smart boy."

"Well, I seen you drive up."

"If you watch close, you'll see me drive away again in a little while." He was walking alongside, sometimes backward to see her expression.

"Where you going?"

"Newcastle, but not right away."

"That ain't far. Just over t' border. You could get t' Lunnon in maybe fower hours. She'll do a hundert and ten, book said, your car."

"Well, but I don't drive so fast. It isn't safe. What's your name?"

"Garry Evans, what's yours?"

"A very impudent dirty young rascal," said Mrs. Trefoile distantly. Neither Pat nor Garry took any notice.

"Pat Carroll."

"You're an American."

"That's right."

"You know any gangsters?"

"Goodness, no. America isn't like all the films, you know. Not a bit. Just ordinary people, like anywhere."

"Oh," said the boy. "Haven't you got a million dollars?"

"I wish I had," laughed Pat. "Not many Americans have, Garry."

"You got a *Jaguar.*"

"Yes, but not an awful lot of money."

"Go away, little boy," said Mrs. Trefoile. Garry dropped behind, not before Pat caught the hideous grimace he made at the old woman. They were almost up to the gates of Llandaffy. "Patricia."

"Yes, Mrs. Trefoile."

"I am troubled. You trouble me. It is not only for yourself, but for Stephen. You would condone such a thing? I heard it in your voice—you would *jest* about it!"

"About what?"

"The—the sin of the flesh. Such as that person—and others—commit."

"What d' you mean, people marrying twice? Well, it's their own choice," said Pat.

"It is against God's law! You are fallen into deeper error than I imagined!"

The sun was gone under now; it was still quite cold. But a thin watery white light, as the sun struggled to break through again, slanted down through the trees to either side of the drive, as they walked up toward the house. Pat drew a deep breath, savoring the clear dry air. Hector was still weeding, farther down the bed. He glanced up briefly.

"—As it might be, for example, a wedded woman like yourself! No matter what the church may allow, in its degraded creed, it is wanton sensuality——"

Pat had stood back, politely, to let Mrs. Trefoile precede her into the house. She had paid only surface attention to what the old woman was saying, and caught those words with surprise. "Like myself? But I'm not married——"

"Patricia! My dear, you cannot mean you do not *realize——!* You *are,* my child—you are Stephen's wife. A betrothal, a marriage, it is all the same in the sight of God. Do you not understand that, Patricia? Mistaken and strayed in some matters as you are, I had thought you understood this—this fundamental fact. You are Stephen's wife! You must only feel grateful—you will never conceive how *very* grateful you must feel!—that by the will of God you may thus escape any gross bodily consummation of the marriage, and live out your life as a pure virgin until it shall please Him to call you. Patricia——"

Pat looked down at her there, in the dim entrance hall of the house, with amusement, bewilderment, pity, a very little anger. (Escape so very near.) "Why, Mrs. Trefoile," she said, "I can't agree with that, no." One couldn't say anything about Stephen; and it was quite useless to argue with the Mrs. Trefoiles; but Pat's essential forthrightness made it impossible even to imply acceptance of an irrational principle. "Stephen is dead," she said gently. "I wasn't married to him, but even if I had been, I'm only twenty-six, you know. I want a husband and children, and I hope I'll have them. It doesn't mean I've—forgotten Stephen. It's just—life." But Mrs. Trefoile's creed was a nullification of life. "You mustn't mind," she said awkwardly. "We—we all have different ideas about these things, you know."

The woman just stared at her, her crumpled mouth working. "I must get my things together," said Pat, and ran up the stairs. Poor silly earnest old soul. And poor Stephen. People!

She packed rapidly, efficiently. She didn't bother to do a complete make-up job, just delicately touched on a little rouge and powder, a lot of lipstick. Snapped the cases shut, checked her handbag. The man Hector still had the car keys, she must——

She froze, with her hand on the door.

It was locked on the outside.

SEVEN

Pat's first reaction was, But this is impossible. Quite impossible. Such things don't happen.

Just what did you do, ostensibly a guest in a private house, when you found yourself locked in your bedroom? What was called an unprecedented situation.

A mistake, of course. Perhaps the rooms were all kept locked when they were empty, and Anna had thought she was gone.

So she banged at the door, and after a while when that brought no response she went to the window.

The window overlooked the side garden of the house, a narrow strip of flower beds and lawn. When she first looked out it was empty, but in a few minutes the simpleton Joseph slouched into sight, round the corner of the house.

"Hi!" called Pat. "Joseph!" She fought to raise the window higher, and got it another six inches up. "Joseph!" He looked up vacantly. "I'm locked in. Go and tell madam. *Locked in,* Joseph. Tell madam!"

The second floor, where her room was, was only about twenty-five feet above the ground. He heard her; he came over interestedly, just below her. "Hello," he said tentatively.

"Hello, Joseph. Go and tell madam—*locked in!"* But surely someone would realize it soon?

Joseph went on looking up at her for a few moments and then lost interest and wandered away. "Damn!" said Pat. Of all the ridiculous things——

Time went on. As the civilized, cultured human being one hesitated to raise a fuss—bang on doors and shout—but that seemed indicated.

She had said she was leaving, and Hector still had the car keys; surely they must realize——?

Pat banged and shouted again. Through the door and out the window.

It had been about ten o'clock when she and Mrs. Trefoile returned from the church, and perhaps ten-fifteen when Pat had found her bedroom door locked. At ten-thirty, when a good quarter-hour of banging and shouting had had no result, Pat sat down on the bed and lit a cigarette.

Think about it calmly, she told herself. Reason it out. Anna could not have thought she had left, for all her baggage was still here. It was the old woman who had deliberately locked the door. For whatever reason. Mrs. Trefoile was mad, as mad as a hatter; that was now quite obvious. But there were three other people nearby, in and out of the house. Well, discount Joseph and say two. Anna and Hector must have heard her shouts and knocks. Why had they not responded?

The explanation was simple, of course. She knew Hector was within hearing; he'd been weeding that bed round at the front of the house. But she'd never exchanged a word with the man, and it now seemed probable that he was deaf. Anna, without doubt, had gone into the village to shop.

Pat couldn't conceive why these servants stayed with such a woman; but they were not insane. Perhaps they were religious fanatics of the same kind, but even so they would be aware that it was against the law to keep someone confined against her will. The old woman was mad, had some crazed idea—considering that last little exchange—about keeping Stephen's wife safe from any marauding male. Undoubtedly that was it, for up to then she'd been willing—if reluctant—to let Pat go. She hadn't thought beyond that, or she'd realize the impossibility of keeping a prisoner in the house for any length of time.

Anna would let her out as soon as she knew. Anna must have suspected that the old woman was more than a little mad, and this would prove it.

Pat considered her situation. No use to go on shouting until Anna was once more within hearing; and she had no way of knowing when Anna was back from the village. (No other place Anna could be, and she obviously wasn't here or she'd have come before.) However, expecting the guest to be gone by noon, very likely when Anna came back she would come straight to this room to strip off the used bedding and so on. In any case she was bound to be in the house by noon, in order to prepare whatever nameless mess Mrs. Trefoile would lunch on. Therefore, thought Pat, if she doesn't come here first, wait until she must be home and then make another row for her to hear.

It seemed a very long time to wait. Pat smoked another cigarette; she could feel her hands shaking, and she was growing angrier and angrier. One shouldn't be angry at the antics of lunatics, who lived by private logic, but right now it was impossible not to be, at this one.

She had just put out that cigarette when a key rattled in the lock and the old woman came in. Pat immediately sprang off the bed, took up her handbag and two cases, and made for the door. "Let me by," she said coldly; she could no longer summon politeness.

"No. You are not going away," said Mrs. Trefoile rigidly. Her crumpled-onionskin face was whiter than ever, her pale eyes blazing. "I have prayed, I needed this time to pray and be certain what is best to do. I have received God's word. I must save you from your baser self, Patricia, for Stephen's sake. For Stephen. You were lying to me—this is revealed to me—you never intended to come back. There is no way I may persuade you, and so I must keep you as I can. It is my Christian duty, both to God and to Stephen. You must——"

"Get *out* of my way!" said Pat loudly, walking toward her. "I'm leaving now!"

"No!" said the old woman, and put both hands on Pat's chest and shoved her back. She was surprisingly strong; Pat staggered back a step, caught her heel in the carpet and fell sprawling. You read about these things in the books picked up for an evening's amusement: physical violence. The ordinary person might live a whole life without experiencing that. With outraged shock Pat found herself thinking childishly, She knocked me down!

"You must be made to understand! Since there is no other way, I must keep you here until you do, until you are saved from these devil's temptations! I will——"

"Oh, don't be ridiculous!" exclaimed Pat contemptuously. "Let me out, damn you!" Up on her feet again, she snatched up the bags. Only an old woman, smaller than she was—if physical violence was the only way, well, she had started it!

But before she'd taken a step, the woman was at the door and through it. Pat flung herself at it, too late; the key snicked in the lock.

"Well, of all the——" Pat vented her feelings with a little bad language. All *right,* said her logical mind crossly, it can't be long before

Anna is back and this absurd farce is over. No matter in what uproar of a scene, I'll be let out. Eventually.

And so far from getting as far away as possible at once, she would find the village police station and complain. The woman was a menace; she ought to be shut up.

It was five to eleven. She went back to the window. The strip of garden below looked very peaceful and pretty, the quiet garden of a quiet British country house. Pat did not much appreciate it at the moment. The sun had come out now and melted away the thin fog, and the air coming in felt warmer.

Patience, she thought. Neither Mrs. Trefoile nor anyone else could keep her imprisoned very long, with two servants in the place. As soon as Anna knew——But even in this relatively short while, the walls of the little room seemed to be closing in on her; it was not a pleasant feeling. Pat shivered. There was Joseph again. He did not look up. And Hector might be deaf, but if he were to see her making gestures out the window, obviously asking help, he'd realize——

"Joseph! Joseph!" The simpleton looked up. "Go and bring Hector! Hector, understand? Bring Hector *here!*"

Joseph gave her a wide grin. "You're pretty," he remarked conversationally. "Ol' Hector, he's a-weedin' they sprouts."

"Go and bring him *here,*" said Pat distinctly.

"Good-bye," said Joseph, and wandered away out of sight.

Really. At home you wouldn't be allowed to keep one like that loose. Suddenly, clutching at her sense of humor, Pat laughed. All the crazy ones were wandering around loose here, while she was shut up.

But Anna would let her out, as soon as she knew.

She stayed at the window in the vague hope of seeing the servant; she had no idea where the rear entrance was, perhaps Anna would come along this side garden to reach it. Some time passed, and then Hector came in sight, slouching along at the stooped walk of the gardener. Hector must be deaf or he'd have heard her before, but nevertheless she shouted at him out of the window. "Hector! Hector!"

She thought he checked slightly; but he never looked up. He must be stone deaf. *Had* he started? In a moment he was out of sight around the corner of the house.

Pat sat down on the bed again. She felt very shaken suddenly: for the first time in this hour since she'd been locked in, she felt—for a terrible moment—frightened.

Hector *had* started, as one does at an unexpected shout. He *had* heard her. And he'd deliberately paid no attention.

Nonsense. That really was nonsense. Because Mrs. Trefoile was mad, it didn't follow that her servants were.

But suppose they were? Suppose they agreed with her that——Oh, *nonsense.* However fanatically religious they might be, they would know the dangers of a criminal charge of kidnaping—which Mrs. Trefoile, in her madness, evidently didn't know or care about.

It was twenty past eleven. Pat went back to the window and began to shout. She called Anna's name over and over. After a while she left the window and banged and shouted at the door again. She kept it up for about ten minutes, and heard her voice growing hoarse.

She stopped then and leaned on the door a moment, trying to hear if there were any sounds of rescue on the way. This was not one of those very old houses where doors were three-inch oak planks and walls solid stone; nor was it a very large house. They must be able to hear her everywhere in the place.

She didn't hear Anna's clumping tread on the stair. She heard, just outside this door, an agitated whispering, and Mrs. Trefoile's sharp voice.

"That is no matter, it will be quite all right, I have thought for everything. Unlock the door."

Pat fell back as the key rattled in the lock. She was to think later what a fool she had been; if she had stood her ground, to take the advantage of surprise, and fought past and run, never bothering about her bags——But lifetime habits of courtesy are not easily broken, and she was still suffering astonishment that this could be happening to her, Pat Carroll. . . . She took two steps back, and Mrs. Trefoile came in as the door opened. She held a pistol in one hand. Anna was behind her.

"This is," said the old woman surprisingly, "a most disgraceful and —and undignified situation."

"I couldn't agree with you more," said Pat steadily. For some reason the pistol had put all this into the realm of fantasy, where anything can happen but one need not fear any actual harm: just a silly dream. One would as soon expect to meet Mrs. Trefoile with a banjo or a boa constrictor as a pistol.

"I don't like it," said the servant. She was pleating her apron nervously.

"Do not be foolish. It is necessary. Patricia, I cannot tell you how grieved I am that it must be this way. If you were not so firmly in the grasp of the devil, it would not be needful—if you would place yourself in my hands for proper teaching. But I see that for the moment—until you can be made to see reason and accept the truth—you must be forced to stay here, in order that I may save you. Please believe me, do nothing foolish, the firearm is dangerous. I know nothing of such dreadful things, but Hector has prepared it."

"It's loaded all right," muttered Anna. "Madam——"

"You understand, Patricia?"

"I understand that you're mad," said Pat bluntly. But—Anna? "You must know you're committing a crime—you can be sent to jail for this. Anna, *you* know that if she doesn't! The woman's mad——"

Incredibly, Anna did not even look at her.

"You must be brought to see God's truth, and this duty is laid on me, for Stephen's sake, as I have explained. Do not struggle against it, Patricia. When I spoke with you before, I saw that in your blindness you would use physical force against me, and at once I thought of Mr. Trefoile's firearm. Providential. One must fight fire with fire. If it must be so, and no other way, then it must."

"You can't keep her in this room," said Anna sullenly. "I'm not goin' to empty no slop jars for her nor fetch water."

The little blue pistol was quite steady in the old woman's hand. "No, quite true. It will be the closed-up room—Mr. Trefoile's room. I have told Hector to unseal and unlock the door. We may take her there now."

"You're both mad!" said Pat incredulously. "Anna, why are you doing this? You can't—you must realize what——"

The woman snapped out at her with something like a snarl, "None o' *my* idea, but no choice!—think I want see my man back in t' Moor for life? Ten year she've held us on that, you think we'd stay else? I got no choice——" And one rough hand went to her mouth. "Oh, Gawd, now *you* know——"

"I don't know anything," said Pat. Her mind had never worked so fast in her life. "It doesn't matter to me, that——I'll forget I ever heard it, Anna, if you go into the village now, right now, and tell the constable about this. You know you can't hope to keep me here, I'll get away somehow, and then you'll be sent to jail as accessory. But if you go now——"

"Anna knows better than to do that. You will *not* go away, Patricia, until you have been brought into the fold of truth and righteousness. We will take you to the other room now."

"You can try!" said Pat, losing her temper as Anna's hand fell on her arm. She fought quite instinctively, kicking and biting and scratching. From somewhere outside, one part of her looked on in horrified surprise at this desperately undignified display; she'd never in her life done such things—she wouldn't have imagined she *could*. And that outside part of her realized almost at once that she was making a mistake: the moment she struggled against that grasp on her arm, struck Anna the first wild blow, the other woman's grip tightened and she fought back. This was a thing she understood, physical force: her instinct was working too, to protect herself. And she was the stronger: taller and heavier than Pat, and all her muscles toughened by a lifetime of hard work.

After the first incredible moment of finding herself in a no-holds-barred physical fight, Pat threw herself into it wholeheartedly. She remembered little of it afterward: striking out wildly, falling, feeling the woman's hard hands wrenching at her arms—flailing about with her legs to trip her—even at one point sinking teeth in flesh——

But the other woman was stronger. In five minutes Pat was nearly spent; her breath came in gasps. She felt she was being hauled up to her feet, and then Anna slapped her hard across the face. "Why can't you—be sensible, little fool?" she asked harshly. "It's no choice!"

She was being pulled out, along the hall, half-carried, feet dragging. Now, she thought, now—out of the room—get away, and run! The stairs—down the stairs, and out——

She made a great effort to summon the strength, and struggled again briefly, and was shaken hard, her head snapping back. Too late—too late, she was pushed forward, and fell, and heard a door shut behind her and a lock snap.

She knew she was lying on a carpet somewhere, a carpet that smelled very dusty, as if it hadn't been cleaned in years. For the moment she hadn't the strength to get up; but after an unknown time she felt a sneeze coming on from the dust, and turned on her side.

She was just inside the door, and as she sneezed the door was thrust halfway open and her suitcases and handbag were shoved in, one case falling over against her leg, and the door pulled to again.

None of this, of course, was really happening to Pat Carroll. It wasn't the kind of thing that could happen to anybody, in this sixth decade of the twentieth century. It was even a little funny as well as frightening: and real terror couldn't ever have a funny side, could it?

Stephen's wife . . . any gross bodily consummation . . . Yes, of course the ones like Mrs. Trefoile always felt that way. *Until you are saved from your baser nature.*

Undoubtedly a little funny. Pat giggled weakly against the carpet.

Not very funny. Because Mrs. Trefoile was mad.

And Anna——

Anna Fields went into the guest bedroom again and leaned on the marble-topped dresser, still breathing hard from the struggle. Little fool, if she hadn't gone all out like that I'd never have hurt her, she thought. She didn't like this much, the old woman'd never done nothing like this before; Anna reckoned the girl might be right to say she was mad. Or going that way. But there wasn't no choice. Cross her any way, she'd go and tell the police about Harry—Hector—she never could remember to say Hector instead—and they'd come and fetch him back inside. And no asking parole now, even after fifteen-twenty years in, when he'd broken out and stayed out eleven years, after serving only one.

A lifer, he'd got, just for knifing that fellow when he was in whisky. Because they made out he'd threatened him afore, sober.

Out eleven years—and much good had it done them! Anna sobbed for breath and pounded one fist on the marble impotently. How clever they'd planned it—get off somewhere quiet, take a job awhile as servants in the country, nobody'd look at such—somewhere right off the map. Well, that they were anyhow: Anna's old village, that she'd got away from as soon as she was grown. But safe, they'd thought. Quiet. Because nobody knew here that her husband was the Harry Fielding as broke out of the Moor. She'd never been much of a one for writing, and there was only her sister Marian left anyways. She'd let Marian know when she got married, fifteen years back, but Marian died a couple of years after and the kid, Gloria, wouldn't remember names. Hadn't seemed to think nothing of it, Gloria hadn't, her dead ma's sister turning up as a Mrs. Hector Fields eleven years back—still just a kid then, acourse, only nine. And Gloria's dad Jim Llewellyn had married again and wasn't interested. Gloria was a nice girl, kind of girl Anna'd like to have had—a pity——

Said as how Hector had a chest, the doctor told him country air, so they wanted a man-and-wife place for a bit. God, they'd been that pleased, get the place at Llandaffy with this funny old woman! Only her and the boy, fifteen he'd been then, and a little white rat of a youngster. Easy work. Stick it a year, they'd said, until the heat cools off——

And then when they went to leave, her coming out so cool that she knew. Seen a picture in the paper awhile back, when they'd still been hunting him. The sly old bitch. . . . Some of her crazy religious talk, how she didn't believe in prisons, there wasn't any attempt made to *reclaim* criminals, way she put it, and he'd be a deal better off here at honest work, and getting instructed in religion by a godly woman. But they must realize that if they ever tried to go away—doubtless back to more sin and wantonness—she would be compelled to inform the police . . . ah, bitch, bitch. . . . Ask Anna, mostly to get servants at a miser's wage. . . . Talk about them needing to embrace righteousness for its own sake!

Eleven years . . . Anna looked down at her roughened red hand on the marble top of the dresser. A clerk at a nice department store in London, she'd been. Harry—Hector—wasn't a bad man, a real crook. It was more an accident, like. They'd meant to get a little house of their own when they could, have a family.

Never done anything like this before, hadn't she, the old woman? What else had she done to Anna and Harry Fielding for eleven years? Only difference, they could come and go a bit, between this house and the village.

No question, she'd got queerer since the boy had left home. These five-six years. Funny he ever got up the guts to do it. But she'd not been the same since. She'd stopped reading any papers on account they were full of sin, she said, and there'd been the fuss with the rector—she'd got a lot more religious even than she'd been before. And trying to get Davies the publican to stop selling drink to Harry. About the only little pleasure he had left. . . .

A poor excuse for a man the boy had been, all right. Anna had been a little surprised at the girl—why she'd ever looked at such a one—maybe him being in uniform fooled her. A pretty girl, she was.

There wasn't no choice. They couldn't do aught else but do like the old woman said. By now, this long time, Anna knew the village stories about her: knew, or guessed, what else she'd done. Her husband. . . . Besides everything else, she was afraid of the old woman.

A pretty American girl. *Damn her!* thought Anna. No odds, do her good to suffer a little. As other people had. Never wanted for aught. That red car that Harry said cost maybe two thousand pounds. Her pretty clothes and fashionable-cut hair and lipstick and thin nylons and high heels and scent——

It had been a real downright pleasure, that few minutes of getting her hands on something to fight. Anna hadn't anything against the girl, except that she was pretty and young and Anna Fields wasn't any more; but she hadn't any especial liking for her either. And fighting her like that, it was like a chance to fight all the injustice and frustration she'd known the last eleven years—almost like fighting the old woman she was afraid of. It had been good.

She saw that there was something extraneous beside her hand on the dresser. A ring. The girl had used the hairpin tray as an ash tray, it was a mess of ashes and stubs, and there was the dresser cloth, and one of those old-fashioned covered dishes for loose hair, and the rest of the dresser set. The ring didn't belong, it was hers; she must have meant to put it on and then forgot.

Anna picked it up. It was a big ring, looked like a man's ring, silver with a big dull green stone. Suddenly the ring was to Anna all that Patricia Carroll had and was that Anna had ever wanted and now could never have, and thus an object of hate.

She walked across and threw it as hard as she could out of the window.

EIGHT

After a long while Pat stirred. Better take inventory, she thought weakly. See where she was and try to make some plans.

She sat up, and felt pain here and there. She had wrenched one ankle, there was a long bloody scratch down one arm, her head ached, she had runs in both stockings and a rip up one seam of her skirt.

"That'll teach you to be a tomboy and go fighting," she said aloud, shakily, and tried to laugh.

It was a larger room than the other, and immediately she realized that—strangely—it was a man's room. One wall was paneled in a dark wood, and on it hung six hunting prints. They were very dim, for they were framed under glass which had not been washed for years; but she could see a hint of the bright colors, the lively action—find, view, yoicks-and-away, the chase, the kill. There was a solid high walnut bedstead against the opposite wall, with an ugly walnut commode standing beside it. On the same wall as the door, a big walnut highboy; the walls were papered in an ugly dark-red Victorian paper, and over the highboy was a large lighter-colored rectangle where obviously a mirror had once hung. *For sinful vanity are such. . . .*

In the paneled wall were two windows, velvet-hung, with a small solid-walnut desk between them. In the rear wall of the room was an inner door and a long low chest. The carpet she was sitting on was a drab faded brown.

She realized, looking about the room, that everything here had been neglected for a very long time. There was a thick gray film of dust over everything. The carpet was packed with dust. She remembered the old woman saying, Mr. Trefoile's room. He had been dead since Stephen was a baby—over twenty years. Had the room been shut up and never entered since? It looked like it.

Pat crawled over to the bed on hands and knees and dragged herself up by the footboard. After a moment of dizziness her head cleared and she could stand. She went across to the door in the rear wall and turned the knob. It resisted, and then opened with a long squeak. A bathroom. Old-fashioned, a claw-footed tub like a coffin, a queer-shaped washbowl. She wondered if the faucets worked, and tried one. It was very stiff to turn, but turned at last and a rusty stream of water began to flow. She watched it until it began to run clear.

She staggered back to the bedroom and got her dressing case. When she opened it, her face in the little mirror in the lid startled her: a scratch down one cheek, a bruise on the other cheekbone, showing dark —her hair in wild disarray, her lipstick grotesquely smeared.

"Goodness, that must have been some fight," she murmured weakly to herself. There were no towels or face cloths; she washed her face with her hands, and let it dry of itself. The water was cold; probably she'd have to let it run forever to get warm. She took off her torn skirt and the cardigan and sweater, substituted the dark-green cotton frock and a brown cardigan. Stripped off the ruins of her nylons and put on fresh ones. When her face and hands were dry she applied new make-up, covering the scratch and bruise with foundation cream, taking pains with rouge and mascara and lipstick. She slapped on cologne.

It was surprising how much better she felt. Morale—feminine armor. She looked like the usual Pat Carroll in the mirror now: hair crisply brushed, make-up nicely in place.

And so, what now?

She came back to the bedroom and found an honest-to-goodness ash tray on the desk. Rummaged for cigarettes and lit one, and sat down to think.

The situation was fantastic, but there it was. It was no good wasting time and energy thinking. Impossible. Wondering why and how Anna and Hector could be coerced into conspiring——Anna had implied, some crime Hector was guilty of, and Mrs. Trefoile blackmailing them, which did *not* fit with Mrs. Trefoile's earnestly pious character, but let it go. For this or that reason, incredible as it seemed, the servants were aiding and abetting in this ridiculous kidnaping. Or whatever you wanted to call it. Count them out. Also Joseph, for obvious reasons.

It appeared that she had only herself to rely on.

Presumably the woman intended to keep her here until she was convinced that she was saved—probably, then, no actual physical harm was contemplated. Shouldn't have attacked Anna like that . . . all the more difficult now to win her over, if that was possible?

Pat told herself that in time to come she'd be telling this story as an amusing personal experience.

Because of *course* she would get away and—what did they call it?—lay a complaint. This kind of thing just couldn't happen these days, but when it did the police liked to know.

Even in a remote Welsh village.

Easier, of course also, in a remote Welsh village, to get away with it. For a while.

Think about it. This house was, she knew, a good three-quarters of a mile from the village, counting the long drive to the road. Apparently the two sane servants were prepared to go along with the madwoman in whatever she did. The other nearby human being, Joseph, couldn't be relied on for anything. She couldn't yell loud enough to be heard in the village, and doubtless Mrs. Trefoile and Anna would take care to approach her together now: no chance of another fight. Oh, they could keep her here all right.

Not forever, but for a long time.

It was odd how quickly the mind adjusted to conditions of violence. Pat thought quite coolly, If Mrs. Trefoile comes in alone, even with the gun, I can handle her. I think. Try, even with the gun. Anna is stronger, I daren't tackle her again, but the old woman——And if I got past her, and out to the stair, I don't *think* Anna could catch me, stop me. If Hector was round the front, he might—have to chance that. If the opportunity came.

Was Anna reluctant? ("I don't like it.") And she knew that now she was legally a conspirator, an accessory. Could she be won over, bribed?

But if the other chance came, Pat would bet that once out of this room her youth would tell against Anna's middle age, that she'd be faster if not stronger and get away before Anna or Hector could catch her.

She stubbed out her cigarette and went to look at the door. It was an ordinary inside door, finished in dark walnut, with a brass knob (long unpolished) and a simple-looking keyhole, no Yale lock or anything like that. The only unusual thing about it was that it had a bolt on this side. An ordinary brass bolt. She tried it; it was stiff and immobile.

The bolt told her, amusedly even in the midst of her own unenviable situation, something about the late Mr. Trefoile. Twenty-odd years ago.

. . . It came to Pat with a little shock that Mrs. Trefoile need be no more than fifty. Stephen had been not quite twenty-six. Oh, poor Stephen. . . . And perhaps another man, this one, only thirty or so? Another weak man like Stephen, or different? Anyway, finding himself married to this woman. Why? Had she ever been pretty, flirtatious, young? Impossible to imagine. But here he was (of whatever kind) married to her; and putting a bolt on the inside of his bedroom door. It should have been funny. It struck Pat as a little pathetic.

However, she wasn't concerned with the character or personal troubles of a dead and gone Mr. Trefoile. The lock. In books it was always a hairpin you used. She didn't have any hairpins; she kept her hair cut short, in casual style. She did have some aluminum pin-curl things, two-pronged, for putting it up. She got one of those from her dressing case, and kneeling before the door to try it, hesitated.

Use some sense about this. As the only sane person in the house, she thought, I'd better use sense.

The woman didn't mean her any actual physical harm. Probably meant to spend time arguing at her, converting her. So she'd see Pat was fed. It was one o'clock now. It could be expected that very soon Mrs. Trefoile and Anna would appear with a lunch tray. And she'd better not be caught trying to finagle the lock.

Also, if the lock could be finagled, the sensible time for it was late tonight. When everyone was in bed. If she could get out of this room, slip downstairs—damn the front door, if its bolt was hard or its key missing—break a window, get out, run to the village. You turned left from the gates. Run. Knock up the first house you came to, demand the constable, tell the story.

That was the sensible thing to do. After lunch had been brought, perhaps the old woman delivering a lecture with it, and she was left alone, *then* try the pin-curl thing on the lock and see if she could turn it.

So she waited. For two hours she waited; because just so soon as she decided they weren't going to bring her lunch, and started to see what she could do with the lock, that was the time they'd come in and find her. And probably confiscate anything she could use on the lock. It mustn't occur to them that she'd try.

Surely it must occur to them? The obvious thing. No, use sense: neither of them was experienced at this sort of thing.

By three o'clock Pat confessed to herself that she'd be very pleased to see anybody, providing they brought her some food. Her last really solid meal had been the Reverend Mr. Fallow's lunch a bit over twenty-four hours ago, up north in Llandaffy village. It seemed much longer, and not only from the standpoint of meals. . . . He had given her another glass of sherry, and a cream soup with delightful little bits of chives and mushrooms in it, and a lovely slice of Dover sole with lemon and butter, and a quite passable imitation of American coffee. As fat as he was (dear Reverend Mr. Fallow) he definitely knew how to eat.

Alan Glentower the gourmet and his beautiful food. Pat wouldn't be at all particular what kind of food it was, so it was edible, right now.

But it was a quarter past three before there was a sound at the door. It took her unawares; she was sitting on the bed smoking, and had no time to get the door, try another desperate push past them, before they were in.

Mrs. Trefoile still clutched the little pistol, incongruously. And Anna did not carry a tray.

Be damned if she'd *ask,* thought Pat. She said coldly, "Well, what now? Am I to have my first lecture on primitive Christianity, Mrs. Trefoile?"

Mrs. Trefoile stood just inside the shut door; for the moment she did not look at Pat, but around the room. Her thin, shrunken little mouth worked slightly. "So odd," she murmured. "So odd. After all these years. I have not been in this room for twenty-four years. Julian's room." Literally and visibly she shuddered, down her whole body. "Julian," she said. Her pale eyes were very bright.

And Pat saw Anna, for some reason, shrink a little away from her. Anna, like the simple Joseph, was afraid of her—why? Just a little old woman, old before her time, insignificant really. But her eyes were not on Pat, and neither were Anna's——

Pat slid off the bed and made a wild dash for the door. Instantly they both moved; she was caught between them and thrust back.

"You will *not!*" said the old woman. "Before God, as I have vowed, I will preserve you for Stephen—my duty as a Christian—I *will* save you! The only way—the only way! Anna——"

"Yes—madam."

"What I—what we have come here to do . . . Patricia? Patricia—you are—you use this devilish narcotic of tobacco? I might have suspected! Oh, I am right in thus being instructed by God—I see clearer and clearer how right it is that I do this! So sunk in deep error. . . . Anna! Go and look—find it all—all these damnable artifacts of Satan she has with her!"

Pat had thought she hadn't any more physical fight in her, after that bout with Anna before and the hunger gnawing at her now, but when she saw Anna opening her fortnighter case a righteous wrath possessed her. "Leave my things alone! Take your hands——"

"You will stay where you are, Patricia. This is needful and overdue destruction. I pray you, I pray you, accept it with good grace as the first step to salvation! I only seek to save you!"

The first thing Anna brought out in her rough hands was the scarlet nightgown with the lavish lace. Even in the midst of her fury, Pat saw how those hands turned it and felt it, wonderingly, caressingly. A lovely, delicate, feminine thing.

"Anathema!" said the old woman. "The devil's very color! I knew there would be such things—I knew she would possess much of sinful vanity! Destroy it, destory it—all such vanity and vexation of spirit!"

The other woman reached into the pocket of her dress and brought out a large pair of shears. Fitted her right hand into them slowly, almost reluctantly.

"Don't you dare!" cried Pat. "Take your hands off my things!" She forgot the pistol, everything but the prying hands and those hideous gleaming shears; she lunged across the room at Anna just as the metal slashed into the shimmering cloth, and caught her arm. *"Take your hands off——"*

Anna jerked back, and the nightgown tore between them, all crooked down its length where the cut was begun. "Damn you!" panted Pat. "My things——"

"And why should *you* have *things* 'n' nobody else, anyways?" snapped the other woman suddenly. "You——! Never lacked for aught, did you? Never went hungry in strike time, hadda go 'thout a warm coat account t' new babby! Not t' likes o' you!" She slashed at the nightgown viciously, flung it aside, reached into the open case for the next thing—Pat's newest nylon slip, deep-bordered with Chantilly lace. "You think *I* never wanted nice things?" She ripped it apart in her strong hands, one savage gesture.

"Take your hands off my things!" Pat tore the poor ruined thing from her furiously, made a grab for the hand holding the shears; Anna did not step back, but unbelievably, snake-sinuous, the pointed shears came up and almost of themselves entered the flesh. Pat felt nothing but rage and astonishment; she looked down, she stepped back, and saw the closed shears draw out of her flesh as if it was someone else's. There was

a little thin red blood on the point. She saw Anna move back away from her: Anna, wetting her lips, her eyes queerly bright.

She felt the pain, then. Felt blood coming wet down her shoulder, inside her dress.

"All these appurtenances of the devil," said Mrs. Trefoile harshly. "All! You will go right through all her possessions, and destroy what we see is of the devil!" She did not seem to have taken in what had happened; she was still staring at the torn clothes on the floor.

Pat thought numbly, I *will* not faint, here, before these two, to seem so weak. I *will* not. She turned and with immense effort got across to the door of the bathroom, and pushed it half shut behind her. She collapsed onto the stool, thinking, Hurt, I'm hurt, must look and see how and where. Pain. She fumbled at the buttons of the dark-green dress. It buttoned all the way down: easy to get in and out of, but it was a little struggle to get the cardigan off first. She got both off at last. There was blood on both dress and cardigan. Nothing to do about the latter, but the dress——Cold water to take out bloodstains. Painstakingly she arranged the stained part under the faucet in the bowl and turned on the water.

The shears had made a fairly deep puncture midway between her shoulder and breast. There was blood on her slip too. She didn't think it was a dangerous wound, but it hurt. Nothing to wash with; she hadn't a first-aid kit in her bag, that was in the glove compartment in the car. She felt faint again, and sat on the stool with her head down until the giddiness passed.

None of this was happening, could happen.

Nothing to bandage it with. She leaned over the bowl, slapping on cold water with her hands. It had almost stopped bleeding. She hoped the stain would come out of the green dress; and then she thought, But there'll be a tear in it where the shears went in. Maybe it could be mended so it wouldn't show. She liked that dress. She'd paid a good deal for it, more than she should afford.

She did not know how much later it was that she leaned on the door of the bathroom and looked out at the havoc in the other room. She'd taken off the slip too—the slip not torn, but blood on it; better get it out right away—and stood there in just her bra and garter belt and panties, looking; but she wasn't conscious of that. Only of the havoc. Mrs. Trefoile still standing there rapt—yes, the very word—and Anna ripping and cutting and tearing insanely.

Pat was a little faint from loss of blood and shock, but her mind was quite clear; and watching that scene, she knew that Anna cared not a damn for what straight-and-narrow dogmas Mrs. Trefoile subscribed to. Anna was taking savage pleasure in destroying these things because they were things she wanted so desperately and could never have. Pat saw it in her face.

To the old woman these were habiliments of vanity and sensuality. To Anna they were dearly coveted things owned by those with money, leisure, freedom; and if Anna could not have them, she was taking furious pleasure in preventing anyone else from having them.

The second-best apricot-colored lace and nylon slip. The beige and chocolate nightgown and its matching peignoir. A dozen pairs of new nylon stockings. The nylon lace brassières and panties; her best garter belt; the apricot half-slip; the one full dacron petticoat she'd brought, in its umbrella-like plastic carrier. The tartan skirt she paid thirty dollars for. The green cashmere sweater set, the brown cashmere set. The beige drip-dry shirtmaker dress, so practical for traveling. The sheer Georgette evening blouse. The offending scarlet pullover. The black crepe evening skirt, so well-cut and so becoming. (She'd rather planned to wear that if Alan Glentower took her anywhere where evening dress would be appropriate.) The blue dressmaker suit with the silver buttons.

It all lay in slashed shreds about the musty carpet, ruined.

And the big fortnighter case was empty, and Anna was starting on the smaller one. The shears driven with savage strength into black patent high-heeled dress shoes, the frivolous linen sandals; the lilac-print afternoon dress, the——Anna, breathing hard, looking around for more to destroy.

Pat thought dully, Damn her, damn her.

In an odd sort of way, it was possible to absolve Mrs. Trefoile, who—whatever one thought of her—adhered to principles. Of a kind. But Anna—Anna enjoyed this destruction for its own sake.

All my lovely things, Pat thought. Things she'd saved for and planned for. And she had not, right now, the strength to move and do the slightest harm in retaliation to this vindictive, ugly woman ten feet away.

"This is God's work," said the other woman. "All these trappings of vanity!" With dim surprise Pat saw that she had been rapt in the destruction, had not realized that the subject of it had ceased obstruction, had gone from the room. But now she looked up.

"Patricia," she said. And the hand holding the little pistol was lax; the pale eyes were glazed. But Pat hadn't the strength to seize any opportunity there was. "Blood," said Mrs. Trefoile. "You are hurt—you are bleeding."

"Her make-up stuff somewhere," muttered Anna. "Her perfume and all that——" She reached out and pulled Pat away from the bathroom door, and shoved past her.

"You have been hurt," said Mrs. Trefoile. Her pale eyes were fixed on Pat's shoulder. Pat looked down at it. Not a very deep wound, it would heal; but another little sluggish line of blood was straggling down toward the top curve of her brassière. It looked very red against the white skin.

"I do not *want* to hurt you," said Mrs. Trefoile, "that way. Indeed no. But you must be brought into the fold. You must be saved. It is the duty laid on me, for Stephen. You must understand." Suddenly she reached out her left hand and touched the wet red blood. "Sacrifices. It is always necessary to make sacrifices. . . . Sometimes it is the only way. Yes. . . . Cover yourself immediately, Patricia! You cannot go about like that! Anna! Anna!"

The other woman came out of the bathroom clutching Pat's dressing case. "I've got it all, madam."

"Sacrifice. . . . We have done what is needful thus far. Now I must pray. I must pray more, to receive insight as how best to save her."

They went out, and the key snicked in the lock.

NINE

Pat lay on the bed and summoned all her courage and common sense.

She needed to, after that nightmare this afternoon.

When a first bad bout of impotent fury died a little she had told herself that it was senseless to waste emotion on what had been destroyed. But it was impossible not to. Not only most of her clothes; all her cosmetics, of course, and her jewel case as well. Not that there was much of value, but her aunt's trinkets, some things that had belonged to her mother. . . . What would be done with them?

Don't think of that; it's too late, and they're only things. Think of yourself.

She thought of Mrs. Trefoile's light eyes on the blood, and Anna's savagery on the clothes—and on herself.

She'd examined the cut again; it wasn't bad, but she'd lost a little blood, and it hurt. She had done what she could for it. It had stopped bleeding now; it would heal.

Pat lay in the dark and thought very coldly and calculatingly of what her chances might be, between these two women. The man Hector was an unknown; she must discount him.

Whatever absurdities the psychiatrists might promote, they did know pretty well about some definite types, didn't they? Masochists and sadists, a very thin line between, they said.

That avid, rapt look in Mrs. Trefoile's eyes, on the line of blood from her shoulder, seven hours ago . . . And Anna, jealous, savage Anna.

Oh, it was the kind of thing that couldn't happen. But it had happened, it was happening to Pat Carroll, and she had better use her intelligence and think about it.

Because after this afternoon, she was by no means sure that no physical harm was meant her. The way the woman had looked; and her mutter about sacrifices. There was precedent, wasn't there? The Inquisition . . . and beating, starving the devils out of the insane, in Bedlam —all in the name of God. The woman was mad; but Anna—surely Anna, even in her savagery, wouldn't let her go so far?—knowing the dangers of being found out. . . . Anna, God knew what devils gnawing at her, might stand by and enjoy it. Or join in.

Pat had realized quite coldly since that scene that her situation was more serious than she'd admitted. In half an hour she meant to have another try at the door; she'd tried it once, after they'd brought her food at six o'clock. A serving of the synthetic meat loaf, a lettuce salad, a thin wedge of cheese. She'd eaten every scrap, knowing it was needed strength. When the tray was taken away she waited, listening, and tried the pin-curl thing on the lock; by the grace of God it had been in the pocket of the green dress, and overlooked. Patiently trying to remember all the meager hints gleaned from detective stories, she'd worked at it. Entirely without success.

And then she had heard steps on the stair and the faucet turned on in the main bath, out there along the hall; and she'd stopped, lest she be heard, to try again later.

No, it was not at all unlikely—Mrs. Trefoile being what she was, and Anna what *she* was—that physical torture would be used on her. To elicit whatever meaningless oath or confession. God knew what fantasies would come into the old woman's mind.

And it might sound easy, to get away—from an ordinary house within running distance of a village where perhaps five hundred people lived and had their being. It wasn't, Pat was realizing, so simple as it sounded.

She'd wandered around the room, opened one top drawer of the bureau and found it filled with masculine trivia—cuff links and so on— that were no use to her. The second drawer was locked and probably contained nothing useful to her. Nothing in a bedroom would be of much help to her in this situation, would it? She'd tried the lock. She'd try it again. But suppose trying the lock was no good: what then? She was beyond hearing distance of the village, and it could be guessed that the queer Mrs. Trefoile of Llandaffy had no gentry acquaintances to call on her. Probably long ago she had removed herself from village affairs. Not going to the church, she wouldn't be involved in the perennial social affairs connected with it. Who from outside might be coming to the house? In these postwar days, not the butcher's boy or the bakery van. The postman? Not often, probably; and Pat had no idea what time of day he might call.

In a sudden nightmare of despair, she thought, Why, they could keep me here for years. Nobody to ask; nobody to suspect.

Unless she goes so very mad that it's noticed and reported, and people come to take her away. Unless Anna gets an attack of conscience (faint hope!) or lets out something inadvertently.

Don't be silly. Something would happen. She would manage to finagle the lock, get out some way.

It could be a long time.

Pat tried to think of all the things that might happen. All the chances she might have, which she must be expecting and ready to seize if they came along. The postman. This room was at the side of the house, the other side from where she'd slept last night. The two windows were at the side; she did not think it was very near the house front. Never having observed the house carefully, she had no idea how deep it might be. The postman would come to the front; she'd probably have no way of knowing when, but she could listen—mornings, they usually came in the morning, didn't they? And if she did hear steps on the invisible drive, shout out the window. Listen always for any unusual noises in the house, which just *might* mean a caller, someone from outside. And think of plans for trying to get in touch with outside . . .

There were a few people in the village of Abervy who knew that Mrs. Trefoile had a young lady visitor from America. That Mrs. Evans. And the publican had seen her, and the little boy. But she'd told Mrs. Evans that she was leaving at once—oh, fatally Mrs. Evans was the village gossip, wasn't she?—and there was no possible way for anyone to know she hadn't. She was gone, they'd assume she'd driven off the other way. She wasn't even sure that anyone there knew her name—it didn't seem likely that either Anna or Mrs. Trefoile, a year ago, had indulged in any light chitchat to the village: "Young Mr. Trefoile's engaged to an American girl, her name's Pat Carroll and she lives in Santa Rosa, California." No. In the rather unlikely event that there was ever an inquiry about Pat Carroll, who in Abervy would recognize the name?

Unlikely? She realized how alone and unimportant, in the sum of things, was Patricia Carroll of Santa Rosa, California.

There were her closest friends. Betty Kelly. Alicia Carson. Liz Anderson. Marjorie Mackay. All but Marjorie married, and she was newly caught up in the flurry of an engagement and preparing for a September wedding. Betty and Liz both had small children. They had their own routines and daily lives to think about. They knew she intended to wander around the British Isles, perhaps over to the Continent, as long as the money held out. They might say, "Funny Pat hasn't sent any postcards since she left London," but they wouldn't *worry.* They wouldn't dream—for a long time anyhow—of contacting Authority and saying, Pat Carroll's been in England for so many weeks and hasn't been heard from, find out where she is.

(And if they did, Authority might trace her here and be told she'd gone away, and look for her elsewhere.)

The bank. Mr. Morrisson had been nice, helping her about the visitors' permit, her passport, traveler's checks. But he wouldn't be surprised to receive no postcard from her. The girls she'd worked with mostly—Fran and Cheryl, a couple of others—just like her closer friends, they'd be surprised but not at once worried.

Traveler's checks. Well, if they weren't cashed, so what? Banks wouldn't check up for a long while.

The visitor's permit. But it was for six months. Not for six long months would Authority realize that Pat Carroll, American citizen, was unlawfully within Great Britain on an expired permit, and come hunting her.

No relatives. She dimly remembered saying that, "Our family doesn't seem to acquire them"—quite true. There were second cousins somewhere, a brother of her grandfather who'd married a Catholic and naturally been dropped from the family lists, a horrid crime: she had no idea where that branch of the family was living.

There wasn't, when you came to think, anyone at all to *miss* Pat Carroll for quite some time. It was a sobering thought. It was frightening. Even though it wasn't going to make any difference, because nothing could really happen—it would be all right, she'd get away, she'd establish outside contact and be rescued. But it was frightening.

And not true. There was one person who'd miss her quite soon. Only one person who'd been what was called in personal contact with Pat Carroll since she'd been in England. That was Alan Glentower, met casually by chance, in a rainstorm, his car breaking down. She'd promised to meet Alan Glentower in Newcastle next Thursday. When—*if*—she didn't turn up, he'd know something had happened to her.

Wouldn't he? Next Thursday. Oh, God, she must be out of here by *then,* unthinkable that she could be prisoned here another six days. . . .

Would he? Wouldn't he just think she'd decided to skip it? That she'd just been polite, and never meant to meet him at all? No, of course not; he knew she wasn't that rude or thoughtless, if she hadn't wanted to meet him there she'd have said so, made some excuse.

Alan Glentower was the only person who knew where Pat Carroll was. And that only by accident. And actually, now she thought about it, Pat reflected dismally that he didn't know. She'd told him she was going to the village of Llandudno. And she didn't think she had once mentioned Mrs. Trefoile's name to him.

"I can't say as I like it," said the man known as Hector Fields. "Ask me, she's barmy. What's she mean to do with the lass?"

"Just preach at her, I reckon," said Anna. "I don't know nor I don't care! No business of ours. Only we got to do like she says. What'd she want with you?"

He sipped tea. Not that weak stuff *she* had, good strong tea made proper. Anna had to buy it and keep the packet in their room, but at least they had decent tea. "I'm to put a bolt on the door. I said I reckoned I got 'un in the shed I can use, old 'un but still good. That please her, didn't it. Anything t' save coin."

"To save money," said Anna suddenly. Every once in a while she realized how far downhill they'd come. It was all coming back to Abervy, this damned backwater place. Up in London, that ten years, she'd taught herself to speak nice, got a good place in a store, waiting on ladies. Harry'd been selling kitchen gadgets house to house, on a commission; sometimes he made thirteen-fourteen pounds a week; he was a good salesman, not that he had any gift of gab but folk believed him, he talked so honest. They'd been on the way up. And then just because he got a grudge on Jim Harvey, had to go and get nasty in a pub . . . This God-forgotten backwater. She'd got out of it soon as she could; and then, have to come back. *Stay.* You couldn't help it, seemed like, old ways and habits got a hold on you again. Every once in a while she realized how she'd fallen back into the old slipshod country talk, and tried to remember to do better; but she never remembered long. Why, only the other day she'd heard herself saying, *Rhy ddrwg* instead of "too bad" to that Mrs. Evans. Bad as her old folks, or any of these sillies hadn't ever had sense to get away to a real town.

He didn't take any notice. "It's not right," he said.

"You want t' go in and hunt up Griffiths the pollis?" she asked sharply. "Tell him: Please, sir, Mis' Trefoile's a-holdin' a young lady against her will? An' Mis' Trefoile turnin' 'n' sayin': Yes, an' here's

Harry Fielding as broke out o' t' Moor eleven years back, now you can have him again!"

"I don't want that," he said. "All I'm sayin' is, it's not right. She's a pretty lass. That's a funny bee the old woman's got in her bonnet, folk shouldn't marry more 'n once—an' figurin' engaging same as marrying. Don't make sense."

"Oh, trust *you* to notice she's young 'n' pretty!"

"Don't bite my head off," he said mildly. "I don't reckon t' risk my neck for her nor nobody else. It's no kind o' way I'd choose to live, this beant——"

"Isn't," said Anna.

"—But a damn sight better nor the Moor. But the old bitch won't live forever, Anna."

"We've said that afore too. Why, she could go on for twenty years! She's nobbut sixty, about."

"I s'pose. I'm just thinkin', Anna. Just thinkin' about this."

"How d'you mean?"

"I'll tell you when I've thought," he said. "Gimme another cuppa, will you, lass, there's a good girl."

On Tuesday morning Joseph found a Good Thing.

He was not aware that it was Tuesday; he knew the names of the days, if you asked he could rattle them off obligingly, a lesson learned, but he never knew which was which in relation to actual sunup and sundown, a different and quite unconnected thing.

He woke up at dawn, in his nest among the roots of the alder tree up from the road this side of the gates. He was supposed to sleep inside, in the little room over the old stables, but walls fretted him. It was no good to a man, sleep under a roof.

Other folk thought Joseph didn't know much, but he knew a deal of things. Like crossing water confounded witches and fairies, and where the first mushrooms'd be, and where the old badger lived.

Time was all now. There had been a time he was in a Place, and people shouting at him, swearing at him and saying fool. A name for that Place, there was—school. It didn't matter any more. Other Places. Where they tried to teach you queer things, like knitting. It was shepherds knitted, out on the hills watching sheep: Joseph knew that: and he wasn't a shepherd. And that Place was inside too. He didn't like inside.

He seemed to remember he'd run away from that Place. It didn't matter.

This Place was easy. There were only two hard times, just after sunup and just before sundown, and they weren't really bad times. You had to stand still and straight, inside walls and a ceiling over, and listen to the Lady talking. The Lady talked a lot, and one time—a very long time ago—he'd found that if he said over some of what the Lady said, she would smile at him and praise him. Not everything. But some things. What she liked him to say best was *Amen* and *Praise ye the Lord.* Funny words. He didn't know exactly what they meant, but after the first time he'd said them he'd had a fine supper, sprouts and beans and thick soup. And so he remembered. He remembered the important things good.

It wasn't much to do, say the funny words two times in one sunup and sundown, for good thick soup and nobody saying Do this, Do that. Except just now and then when he couldn't get away from ol' Hector.

Joseph had a Place of his own, for keeping Good Things. It was in the little hollow of the fourth oak from the gates on the right side. He kept the Good Things carefully wrapped in a piece of cloth that had once been a shirt, only it got torn and dirty.

He had had ten Good Things. A knife with a black handle that he'd found in the woods. A watch, he knew its name, with writing around a circle and a leather strap; he'd found that in the road. A shiny silver sixpence. A dried badger's foot, which was the finest of good luck to have. The old witch woman up the hill had given him that afore she died. A big gold button with a blue stone in it; he'd found that in the road too. He mostly found his Good Things. The big horse brass piece he'd found in what used to be the stables; there hadn't been a horse there in a long, long time, you could smell, but that had been there, the piece of brass with a horse's head on it. A queer-shaped Thing he had too, like a Thing Mr. Davies the publican had, you pushed it and it clicked and made a fire. This Thing didn't any more, but once in a while Joseph tried to hear the click and see if it would do like it was supposed to. A real snakestone, smooth and round and white, that was good luck too, the witch woman said the snakes spit them out in the spring, on what she called Beltane Night. An old twist of dried snakeskin where one left it last season, crawling out of old into new. A pink shell off the beach, little and curly.

But this was the best Good Thing he'd found in a long while. He found it right after the hard-time-after-sunup. As always after standing stiff and straight so long, just listening to the Lady talk, he felt right joyous, get out in the sun and air again. He skipped out ahead of ol'

Hector and got his bowl of porridge off the kitchen table to take with him, and ate it on the kitchen steps. Anna didn't care, if he remembered to put the bowl back. He ate fast, so as to be off afore ol' Hector came out and caught him, set him to some job like cutting grass or trimming hedge. When he'd put the bowl back inside he went round the house to the sunup side of the yard, where they'd set out sweet peas and stock along the grass. There was a little old clump of wild clover a-growing in there, far into the farthest bed, and he meant to look for a four-leafed one. But instead he found the Good Thing, right in the middle of the clover.

He turned it round in his hands, admiring it. It was a ring, a ring you were supposed to wear on your finger. It was silver, part shiny and part not, and it had a big green stone, smoother than the snakestone and heavier.

He'd have liked to put it on his finger to wear; it went about halfway down his littlest finger, no more, but it looked nice there. Only he was afraid that ol' Hector or Anna would see it and take it away.

All the same, he wouldn't put it with his other Good Things right off. The latest Good Thing he found, he always carried it around a while, for the luck and feel of it; and he felt that this was a Best Thing, a lot of luck in it, and he might like to carry it around a long while.

After a few minutes' earnest frowning thought he tore a piece out of the bottom of his shirt, wrapped the ring in it, and put it carefully in his shirt pocket.

It was nice, feeling it was there.

Garry Evans picked his way through the trees onto old Mrs. Trefoile's land very cautiously. He didn't go there very often, none of the kids did, though it'd be a good place to play, in all those trees. Some people didn't care if you played on their land—Mr. Morecambe never did, up at Rhyd Llws, or the Cadys either—just so you didn't do any damage or kill birds or aim your catapult at cats or some such. But old Mrs. Trefoile was what Mr. Morecambe called Eck-something and Garry's ma called Barmy, and she didn't like anybody coming on her place. She'd run you right off, or that Hector would.

The reason Garry came now was not to play. It was that Joseph, the loony. He knew Joseph picked things up sometimes; he'd seen him, mooning along the village street or the road, stoop and pick up a pebble or a lost button or something. Garry's ma said you couldn't expect loonies to know what stealing was, you did ought to be sorry for them was all; but if Joseph had picked up his new compass Garry sure would count it stealing and get it back somehow. He wasn't sure where he'd lost it; he'd found out afterward there was a hole in his pants pocket. Might have been in the road or right in the village. The thing was, he'd already showed it to a lot of people, and they'd know it was his; and nobody *but* Joseph'd find a brand-new compass, solid brass, just lying around, and not ask who'd lost it.

It wouldn't be any good asking him, of course. He'd just look silly and not answer, or say something crazy. But if Garry watched him, maybe he'd see Joseph playing with it, or something, and know for sure.

He came up toward the house through the trees, silently; and around the side of the house, still keeping to the shelter of the trees. Presently he saw Joseph. Joseph was just sitting on the grass, half-turned away from Garry, looking at something in his hand. Garry couldn't see what it was, and he couldn't get much closer *to* see.

In a minute Hector came up, and Joseph put whatever it was into his shirt pocket, quick. Looked like something he wanted to hide, all right. Even Joseph'd know good and well it was wrong to steal something good like a compass. He wasn't that loony. Hector said something to him, and Joseph got up and shambled off behind him. Gone to weed or cut grass, some job.

Garry said a grownup swear word under his breath.

If you asked him, they were all loonies at this place. Old lady sure looked it, and Hector and Anna not that much better. Even that young American lady come visiting in the Jaguar—a liar, she'd been.

He'd wanted to see that car again, a brand-new Jaguar, and he'd watched like she'd said, but she never come out of the drive. Not before he had to go home for supper, anyways.

Oh, well. He'd just have to keep watching Joseph, that was all. If it was anyhow possible, Garry meant to get back his new brass compass.

TEN

Pat sat on the bed, with her face turned toward the windows. She thought by the sun it must be about three o'clock. This was the west side of the house, and she could watch the sun go down. On a day, and another day, and another day.

Only they had daylight saving in England too. She didn't know if it had begun in June, or if they had what they called Double Summer Time now, two hours instead of one. It was funny how it bothered her, not knowing the time. The sun's time was the real time, wasn't it? Appurtenances of civilized life . . . It didn't matter.

People safe at home in free places never could realize fully the horrors of being shut up in prison. Just *shut up,* never mind anything else. As prisoners go, she supposed she was a good deal better off than many. She was being fed, she was reasonably comfortable, with a bed and blanket, she had clothes—of a sort—and even her own private bath. Luxury. But *shut up.*

There were people who'd been shut up for years, in much worse places than this.

Of course, you never stopped thinking of ways to get out.

Right now she was thinking about the British Post Office. Whether it was going to be the key to unlock the door. It seemed a very unlikely one, but maybe—maybe. She could hope, anyway, couldn't she?

There was a bolt on the other side of the door now. Since Saturday night. In sudden panic she wondered, This *is* Tuesday, isn't it? She hadn't lost count of the days so soon, had she? No; Saturday, Sunday, Monday and today.

One of the worst things, and that was quite irrational, was being without decent clothes and make up. That didn't matter either, when she might be in danger of her life—or sanity; it couldn't matter less. But anyone female couldn't help feeling that way. They had not left her any clothes but the torn green dress, the slip, the brown walking pumps she'd had on—that day—the brown cardigan and her topcoat. Whether Mrs. Trefoile considered everything Pat had possessed representative of sinful vanity, or more likely had got caught up like Anna in the exultant work of destruction, she hadn't asked. That didn't matter either now. She felt she could have borne that now, if she had so much as a lipstick and some way to put her hair up in its usual loose waves. She couldn't see, but she could feel it straggling all round her face, and by the way the comb went through it she knew it was limp and straight. Eventually she'd have to wash it, when it would of course be worse.

Ridiculous to mind, when so much worse could happen.

Oh, she hadn't given up; she never would.

After the bolt was put on the door, she had thought first of the windows. They both overlooked another strip of side garden, and all of it she could see except the actual flower beds was paved with what the English called crazy-paving. That must be the path round to the kitchen door, then. She was on the second floor, and she thought not more than twenty-five feet from the ground. . . . She had waited until the middle of that evening, when the women had come and gone. . . . For Mrs. Trefoile now conducted four services a day instead of two; with a dumb, sullen Anna beside her to guard the tray of food until the reading was finished. That it was stone-cold by then, presumably, was all to the good. "And you shall fast one day a week, Patricia, it is excellent for strengthening of the spirit." Quite a bit of Pat's days was taken up with Mrs. Trefoile, now. She was with her morning, noon and evening, exhorting, praying aloud, demanding confession, listing all the sins according to her own gospel.

(Oh, mad in several unpleasant ways . . . "Do not be afraid to tell me, my dear, confession is good for the soul. You have been wickedly sinful, have you not? All your vanity, all your error . . . Tell me of it, Patricia, tell me. How have you sinned?" And avid expectation in the eyes fixed on her.)

Anna probably found it very tiresome. . . .

A mistake, was it, trying force again the once Mrs. Trefoile came alone? *With* the little pistol, but nevertheless Pat had tried. Waiting until she seemed off guard, lunging for the hand that held it. Luckily she'd got the wrist, and turned it, or the bullet might have gone into her instead of the wall. But the old woman was surprisingly strong; she'd struggled, calling for Anna in a high shrill voice, and Anna had come in before Pat had got away to dash for the door. All she'd got out of that was a wrenched wrist and another slap, and Mrs. Trefoile's deepened conviction that she was a stubborn sinner. And hoping that someone from outside would have heard the shot, come to investigate, she realized that it hadn't after all made enough noise to carry to the road, the village. It was a small pistol. And anyway, people were always shooting in the country.

And Mrs. Trefoile had never come in alone after that. Yes, Anna must find it very boring.

The day after that was fast day. Even one day without food, she found, was weakening, even to a young healthy woman.

Anna, dumb and sullen . . . When they'd come in the evening of that day, Pat had said instantly, cutting across the other woman's opening stiff greeting, "Anna, I'll give you a thousand pounds if you can get me out of here."

"Do not speak foolishness, Patricia. Sit down and listen quietly."

Anna looked past her, expressionless and silent. "I've got it, you know," said Pat. "I promise you'd have it. On any terms, Anna."

"Anna knows better than to listen to you! Stop talking and sit down." And Anna had never opened her mouth. Any good? Would she rise to the bait? Perhaps slip up at night and open the door? The old woman blackmailing them for some reason; she would know who had done it. . . . And no one had come; the door stayed locked and bolted. But Pat would renew the offer whenever she saw her; perhaps one day she'd believe it and begin to think about how she could do it safely.

But there must be active steps she could take herself to get out. She had thought, Listen for the postman, for callers; but the old woman was there so much of the time, and faint steps on the drive an unknown distance away . . . At no time had she heard the bell or the knocker. The added difficulty there was that both windows were tight shut and all her strength could not move them. The only air she got came from the tiny window in the bathroom, a casement opening inward, scarcely bigger than an arrow slot.

But windows could be broken. If she had something to get down by——

She looked at the bed. In books, you knotted sheets together. It would take time, and she mustn't risk being interrupted. . . . So she had waited, that night, until the house settled down, a couple of hours after the old woman had left her. Then she'd got the sheets off the bed and began knotting them together, as securely as she could; and as she worked she figured sums. Were English sheets the same size as American? A hundred and eight inches. But the diagonal length, corner to corner, would be different; how did you work that out? She'd forgotten. It ought to be longer, but with the knots taking up much of each corner —Well, call it a hundred and eight. Nine feet. Eighteen feet—quite long enough to slide down without risking a long drop. No, less, because she'd have to tie one end to something here. The desk between the windows; any other heavy piece of furniture might be pulled across the room by her weight, and make a noise. The window-breaking would do that, all right; she'd just hope against hope that everybody here slept sound. Wait until just before to break the window; the small chair would do for that.

You noticed noises more at night. Have to risk it, and once she was down run as fast as she could—keep her sense of direction—turn right, for the curving drive, and *run.*

She had just got the sheets knotted to her satisfaction and was about to begin tying one corner to the desk leg, when there was the rattle of the bolt——

"I *see,*" said Mrs. Trefoile from the door. "How providential I could not sleep for my thoughts of you, and saw your light still on. You persist in your obstinacy—you do not realize that I mean you only good, only good."

The other woman was with her, a shabby dressing gown huddled about her, heavy-eyed from sleep. It was no use at all to protest or struggle; Pat knew what it would earn her. She only said steadily to the servant, "A thousand pounds, Anna. It wouldn't make any difference what she said about you or your husband—she's quite mad, and nobody would believe her. Think about that, Anna." She got up from where she knelt over the knotted sheets, and went into the bathroom.

To fail before she'd even tried . . . But they shouldn't see her humiliated, or crying. And it was only the first of many tries.

When she came out, hearing the outer door close, the sheets were gone. They had not brought in others the next morning.

So she had looked at the curtains speculatively. They might serve the same purpose. And last night she had waited again, and tried the curtains. . . . She still felt, at the memory, the sick disappointment that had swept through her when she'd climbed precariously onto the desk and reached to the curtain-rods—must be careful, they'll be heavy, don't make a noise——And at the first tug, the left-hand curtain almost dissolving under her fingers, the old rotten material sleazy to begin with and collecting dust and mildew here for years . . . They would not support a child's weight.

It was not the only way. Think. Get in contact with someone outside. . . .

But how—how? The woman was not a fool. Little shrewdnesses she had, and this would be such an obvious way to attempt escape.

A message. An S.O.S. It was a melodramatic idea, and seemed quite impractical at first thought.

She had sat up in bed in the dark, last night after the abortive attempt on the curtains, shivering a little under the one blanket, which would not be long enough to let her down that long drop, and thought very hard about it. The standard procedure of scribbling an S.O.S. and dropping it out a window was just silly—no one here to find it, who'd act on it: Joseph probably couldn't read. It had to be something much subtler.

And in a hurry, because——

Suddenly, from hunger and panic, she felt faint, and lay down flat, hearing her heart pound. Remembering the old woman this afternoon.

A very thin line between, they said. . . . The old woman abruptly breaking off some rambling prayer, saying, "Patricia, you were—hurt. Open your dress, let me see. Has it bled again?"

The wound had formed over; it did not look very big, but it still hurt. "It—no longer bleeds, I see. Is it painful?" Pat did not reply to her. "It is good for the spirit to suffer pain, you know. One should not rebel against it. That I know well. My own terrible sufferings have greatly strengthened my soul. Do not refasten your dress——" Quickly the little hand darted out to the red mark, pressing it hard, fingers digging; Pat jerked back involuntarily. Mrs. Trefoile was breathing hard. Without looking down, Pat knew that some of the formed-over tissue had been pulled loose, and the wound was bleeding a little again. She turned her back and buttoned the dress with trembling fingers, seeing the pale eyes rapt on the blood.

She could guess that this had put the woman right over the edge. Mrs. Trefoile had been a little mad—and then more mad—for a long time: God knew what had driven her. The husband, something to do with the husband? It was possible to guess that the key to Mrs. Trefoile was her need for power—power over people. If a passive one. Keeping Stephen chained to her as long as she could. Keeping these two servants here, under threats. She would make some pious rationalization about that to herself ("Being a godly woman I know what is best for you, you must do as I say"?) but the power was what she craved. Up to now, probably, her craving had been satisfied in little, indirect ways. But anything like that—it was like dope addiction: the user had to have more and more.

And now for the first time she was using direct physical force to keep someone in her power. And savoring it: a little taste of the stronger satisfaction——She was wanting more of this more potent drink.

"The blood will let flow the evil spirit from you," she said.

Angry, frightened, shaking, Pat turned back to her, fumbling at the top button. "You're mad, you can't keep me here forever, you know it! There are people to miss me—hunt for me—when I don't keep my appointment on Thursday, they'll come looking—and you'll all be put in jail then! You can't——" It was a childish, incoherent outburst, meaningless.

Now, alone in the dark, she thought, Meaningless?

She could send no message of her own volition. There wasn't a chance. But—but suppose she were *forced* to send a message? Suppose she——?

One thing she realized at once. This was a desperate and very long chance, but if it should work out as she hoped, not only must the actual message be subtle, but it would need to be apparently scribbled off very unwillingly at once. No time to work out a code of some sort, any subtlety, in the moment. She must have the message worked out in her mind, ready to be scrawled down if the chance was allowed her.

Think. Think. What could she write to look innocent to any inspection—and it might be close inspection—yet convey an urgent S.O.S.?

A code. The simplest. First letters of each word. But after her first excitement at that idea, she dropped it reluctantly. . . . The message, if there was to be one, had to go to Alan Glentower; and the little she knew of him, Glentower was a thoughtful and intelligent man, but receiving a brief note or postcard telling him that she was unavoidably detained (a certain grim humor there) he would have no reason to look beyond the surface meaning. He certainly wouldn't suspect it of containing a code.

Think. Something odd in the surface meaning to catch his attention. Something that *he* would realize was odd for Pat Carroll to say, but something that would pass with Mrs. Trefoile? Would he even then divine anything so extraordinary as a simple code and look for it?

All too easily she could see such a message reaching him—if it ever *did,* if there ever *was* one—and being read, and tossed into the wastebasket.

He didn't know Pat Carroll well. They'd spent about six hours together. And it seemed a very long time ago, now. . . . She had liked him, there had been a certain instant feeling of friendship, of understanding; they were, as the phrase went, the same kind of people. But he didn't really know her. As, for instance, people six thousand miles and more away knew her: little mannerisms of speech, of thought.

But, she thought, that morning I left he was so—urgent. Serious. I knew it at the time, I knew he really wanted to see me again, that he was attracted, as they say. He was looking forward to it. Would he so casually toss away a note of excuse? He'd be disappointed. . . . He knows, for instance, that I'd be polite about it; if I was very rude in making some flimsy excuse, would he think, That's not in character, and——

No. And suspect something as fantastic as that she needed help, that she was a prisoner? It had to be some kind of concrete message. *Help imprisoned Abervy Trefoile,* something like that.

Perhaps it was the incessant prayers and Bible-reading, in the thin expressionless voice, that started the stately Old Testament language weaving through her head the last few days. It had been Ruth and Samuel today. All about David and a great many battles . . . *O God our help in ages past*—they used to sing that at the Sunday School when she was a little girl. And *Gentle Jesus meek and mild. A mighty fortress is our God*——

Maybe it wouldn't do any harm, at that, to offer up a few prayers. In case Anyone was listening.

Code. *Not* a code. He'd never look for such a thing. And it wouldn't, in the event, be a long message.

It was then she had her inspiration, perhaps as a direct answer to prayer. Not a code, but a directive. A reference. If she could write, say, something like "I have been enjoying *Isle of Gramarye,* especially chapter fourteen"—when there was in that chapter a direct reference to a damsel in a dungeon——Oh, a crude example, but that *sort* of thing. Telling him in effect, Look *there* and read my real message!

But what book of reference could it be? She was an inveterate reader, but she couldn't think of any book she knew well enough to say what was on which page. Who did? And any familiar book, even a piece of poetry, might be available in several editions, the pagination not agree.

If she had time to think—and, she thought ruefully, a library at her disposal! She had only one book. A very ancient little Bible which the old woman had given her, earnestly recommending that she study it much.

A Bible. No matter what edition, what number of pages, Bibles were all the same in text, that is, the familiar King James translation.

And she had not slept at all this night: light was beginning to come in the window, the pale light of dawn. On Tuesday. In a while she would be able to see to read without turning on the light. Not that it would matter if she were found peacefully reading the Bible.

Pat got out of bed and went across to the desk, where she'd put it. Her handbag was there too; they'd left that, after ransacking it of all cosmetics and cigarettes. . . . Don't think about how much she'd like a cigarette. They said you lost the taste after a while . . . She took up the Bible hastily, and knocked the bag to the floor, spilling its contents. With an annoyed exclamation she gathered them up. Not much. A couple of handkerchiefs, old sales slips, a forgotten letter from Marjorie, a snapshot of herself and Liz, her address book, her fountain pen. And two postcards. The postcards she had bought in Mrs. Evans' general shop on Saturday morning.

Whatever message it was, it wouldn't be any longer than would go on a postcard.

The light was growing by the minute. Pat looked down absently at the card in her hand. The back was uppermost. The few lines of printing across the top said: "At the southern border of Cardigan runs the Teifi. Its origin is in several small lakes, the delight of fishermen, called the Teifi Pools."

She laid the cards on the desk and sat down there, oblivious of the dawn chill, to catch all the light on the Bible. There ought to be some very appropriate quotations: a lot of people got into a lot of trouble throughout, especially in the Old Testament. . . .

ELEVEN

It was nearly eight-thirty, the sun long up, when the two women came in that morning. Pat said to Anna, "Have you been thinking about that thousand pounds?" and got no reply.

"You must also learn manners," said the other woman. "That is rude, to make me no greeting. You will——"

"I don't speak with mad people any more than I can help. And I shan't be speaking to you much longer—or be here to speak to you, Mrs. Trefoile." She made her tone contemptuous, turning back to Anna. "And you can stop thinking about the money, if you have. I don't know why I offered it, when it's not necessary. I just wanted to be out of here sooner, that's all. . . . You've probably forgotten, Mrs. Trefoile, that I told you I have an arrangement to meet a friend in Newcastle Emlyn on Thursday. When I don't turn up, he'll know there's a good reason, and he'll come here to find out why."

Perhaps characteristically, the first thing that seemed to penetrate Mrs. Trefoile's mind in that little speech was the pronoun. "A *man,*" she said. "You were going to meet——"

"Yes, a *man,*" said Pat mockingly. "A big strong young man, Mrs. Trefoile. He'll come straight here, looking for me."

"I have been only in time to save you then—or have there been *others?* Tell me, Patricia——"

"I needn't tell you anything except that I'll be away from here in two days, when Alan comes looking. I don't know why I worried about it, really—except that I don't exactly appreciate your idea of hospitality!"

"Be quiet. I will read from Second Kings."

"Quite mad!" said Pat. "You don't even understand plain English!"

"Be quiet." The expressionless voice began to read. Pat flung herself down on the bed, ostentatiously paying no attention, smiling to herself.

There were twenty-five chapters in that book.

" 'And changed his prison garments——' " came the steady voice, drawing to a close.

"Which is what I will do, thank God," said Pat, "in two days. It's a long time in this house, but it'll come eventually. And all of you will be arrested on a criminal charge and you'll go to jail. I'll enjoy giving my testimony about you, *how* I shall enjoy it!"

Mrs. Trefoile read the few words to end the book, and said, "You may have your breakfast now."

Pat was starving, even for the gray gelid mass of cold oatmeal and the nauseating weak tea; but she contrived to eat slowly. And once in a while she looked up to smile confidently at them. She didn't think she had to be very subtle with Anna, and she was putting faith in Anna, somehow, to be her unwitting co-conspirator in this. "I don't think I'm very vindictive as a rule, but, you know, I'll take great pleasure in seeing you all arrested and sent to jail. And you may be sure, Mrs. Trefoile—" the locked-up larder and so on, she could guess the woman was a miser too—"I'll put in a bill for damages to collect the cost of all my things you destroyed. It'd come to around five hundred pounds, I think. Of course they'll send you to a mental home, not prison." There had been a quiver of emotion in Anna's expression. "And as for you," said Pat, looking back to her, "as soon as you're arrested they'll take Hector's fingerprints and find out he's a wanted man, won't they? Very gratifying."

"You are speaking very foolishly and obstinately," said Mrs. Trefoile, rising. "Anna, take the tray."

Would they believe her, believe in her new confidence? When she'd made several such desperate attempts to escape on her own? Yes—anyone would try, unable to face even a week of this, even when certain rescue was coming then. That was rather subtle. Would they think, a bluff, when she had said nothing before? She had, in a way; thank God she had mentioned it before, if only vaguely. . . . Pray God Anna had risen to the bait and might influence the old woman.

"Madam——"

"Yes, Anna?" Mrs. Trefoile turned slightly from the parlor door.

"Madam—if what she says is so, an' somebody comes looking——"

"Do not be foolish. Anyone inquiring would be told simply that she has left."

"Don't you think it," said Anna, in sudden panic forgetting some respect, "if 'tis some young chap sweet on her 'n' expectin' she's to meet him somewheres! He'd be like a leech—madam. *You* dunno, but *I* can guess! She's downright sure in her own mind, 'n' that sort knows her young fellas, that I know. An' besides, what's *she* doin' t' while he's at t' door axin'? Or any'un at t' door for any reason—madam? You thort o' that? Screamin' her head off for help, that's what. An'——"

"An *appointment,*" said the old woman fastidiously. "An *assignation!* Some low-class rake——"

"Oh, for Gord's sake see it! Not with *her,* 'twouldn't be that kind! An' if he knows where she is——"

"You are impertinent!"

"Madam—axe pardon—but you got to *see* it! It'll be some chap all on fire t' get on her track, way she's talkin' and smilin'—*she'll* know him! We can't——"

Mrs. Trefoile gave her a cold stare and turned away. "Control yourself," she said rigidly, and went into the parlor.

Anna stood in an agony of indecision for a moment. The girl sounded almighty sure of herself. Not without rudimentary shrewdness of her own, Anna might have suspected all that for bluff, the desperate efforts the girl had made to get away these four days; but she remembered her saying about that before. The Friday night, on the landing—she'd been up turning down the beds and heard them talk there, the girl saying as she had to leave tomorrow, she'd an appointment. Excuse to get away then, certain—especially if it wasn't until Thursday—but—but——

The old woman *was* mad, think she could get away with it forever. Suppose——

Garry Evans spotted Joseph from his cautious prone position in the fallen leaves under the trees. Lucky this wasn't term time and he had all day to stalk him, if need be. Garry had all a Welshman's patience and capacity for grudge-holding, and if it was humanly possible he meant to have his compass back.

Joseph was crouching down among the flowers in the bed, peering around like he looked for something. Presently he sat back as if disappointed and fumbled in his shirt pocket. Took something out and looked at it. Garry was nearer today, and Joseph was facing him. He couldn't see what the thing was, but it was too small to be a compass. He muttered a bad word.

"I will *not* listen to all this nonsense!" said Pat loudly. "You can go on and preach if you like, I can stop my ears. It won't be for long—only until Thursday. Or Friday at the outside. Then *you'll* be listening to the police—and a prison doctor, probably!"

The old woman closed the Bible on her lap and sat quietly for a moment, her eyes narrowing. "This is foolish. Any who comes here asking for you will be told you have gone away, and look elsewhere."

"Now you do sound silly," said Pat. "Don't you know—I expect Anna, who has just a trifle more sense, has suggested it to you—that I've been listening for the bell or the knocker all this while? And the minute I hear it I'll put that chair through a window and scream as loud as I can!—whoever's there'll hear me all right! And on Thursday, it'll be Alan out there. And if I know him, he'll be up the stairs in thirty seconds and have that door down in another thirty!"

Quietly, "Is this young man so strong, then?"

"Oh, a regular Samson!" said Pat a little wildly. "And what's more, he's *madly* in love with me——"

"As I suspected, a wicked assignation!"

"Of course it is—why not? He'll be raging mad—because you see, he'll know nothing could keep me away from him but force! He'll know——"

Mrs. Trefoile got up and went away, and the other woman followed her out. Pat flew to the door after them and put her ear to it hopefully, but heard nothing. . . . Oh, God, she had overplayed it then, with all that. When she'd been the polite, well-brought-up lady at first. But not since, exactly; of course you could say that. Fanatic as the woman was, perhaps one needn't be so awfully subtle—and Anna single-minded if not fanatic——

And then when the moment arrived, two hours later, she felt not so much triumphant as a little sick at the anticipation of the acting and doubtless the physical pain she must go through if this wild and desperate plan were to succeed.

It was at one o'clock they came back. They had brought her no food.

"Patricia. This further wickedness you confess——"

"Worries you?" Pat laughed. "And well it might!" Had the fish taken the bait, or was it to be only a lecture?

"I do not know whether you are lying to me, but it will be better to have no trouble over it. So you will write a note to this man making some plausible excuse that you will not keep your assignation."

"You're madder than I thought! I'll do no such thing!" And hysterical laughter welled in her throat. They were not so shrewd at all; the fish had risen.

"At once," said the old woman. "Merely to avoid trouble."

"Oh, don't be silly," said Pat. "You don't really think I'd do that just for the asking? You can't force me——"

"You will do it—by force or otherwise." There was sudden, frightening, real madness in the pale eyes. "Anna!"

The remembered rough hand on her arm. She had invited this, expected it—reading them both, these two different women. Mrs. Trefoile for perhaps the first time savoring the pleasure of inflicting physical as well as mental power over another person: using it as always for cruelty, never admitting that or knowing that consciously. Always an incipient sadist, able to practice it for the first time. And finding it a sensation much to be enjoyed. Anna less complex. Yes. Anna blurting it out—"Ten year she've held us . . . think we'd stay else?" Ten long years of bitter frustration, unable to fight back. Yes, the other one a miser: so, the poor insufficient food, the (probably) inadequate wages. And never able to rebel, for fear——That had been the real reason Anna had so enjoyed destroying Pat's things—and hurting her physically. A chance to work off some of the helpless, held-inside rage—hurt someone even more helpless than herself. Anna was probably not a sadist in her right mind, but after those long years, maybe Anna wasn't quite in her right mind. Anna, the victim, enjoyed the struggles of a greater victim.

She caught hold of Pat's left arm and began to force it back cruelly, wrenching the shoulder. "You *got* to! You go to do like she says——"

"Stop—you're hurting——" She must hold out, to make it look as if she resisted to the limit of her strength. She waited until the pain was just short of bearable, and then screamed convincingly. She who never screamed. *"Don't——"*

"Open her dress," said Mrs. Trefoile. She was leaning forward, watching almost greedily.

"No——!"

The dress was ripped open. A hand at the wound on her shoulder: she felt it torn again, and the blood trickling down. Heard the old woman say suddenly, vaguely, in a blurred tone, "There were saints and martyrs—mortifying the flesh for greater spirituality—I have read—the flagellations, and wounds pricked open day by day——"

Pat screamed again, struggled. Quite genuinely then, for the other woman had her left hand now, bending back the little finger ruthlessly. "Don't—oh, God——"

"You!" panted Anna. "Come here—make trouble—you, as never wanted or suffered aught—fine Lunnon clothes an' scent an' paint on your face——" It was grotesque, irrelevant, random fury. "Folk like us less 'n dirt to you, I know *your* kind! No odds! You do like she say, see —you got to——"

She thought she felt the bone snap. Too soon—too soon to give in. Sickly she thought, Must not make it too soon—they'll suspect—how I *want* to write it, oh, God, how I must have the chance——

Such a very slender chance. That he'd understand, do more than glance at it.

Keep her mind clear, remember the message she'd worked out, word by word, so when the time came——

"The blood," said the old woman's voice. "The blood."

Pain somewhere else now, she wasn't sure where. Pain forever——

At that moment Alan Glentower was sitting on a stone wall round the front garden of a house five miles this side of Haverfordwest, and thinking half about the house and half about Rupert Brooke.

It was embarrassing and annoying that these damned poets should keep invading his mind, out of his undergraduate days fourteen years ago. Only the callowest of young men in love quoted poetry.

For the uttermost years have cried and clung
To kiss your mouth to mine;
And hair long dust was caught, was flung
Hand shaken to hand divine——

"It's a nice bit o' land," said Davy Farren.

Glentower grunted. "House wants a new boiler in the kitchen." If she —could she——It was wild, she didn't *know* him. And absurd that cautious Glentower shouldn't have recovered from brief madness overnight, and trying futilely to think sanely about it, shouldn't care a damn that *he* didn't know *her,* really. Whether or not she had a temper. Or went to bed covered with cold cream. Or had funny American ideas about ordering men around. You shouldn't jump into things; but he just didn't care. Only that she was Pat.

Academic, anyway. She never would. On six hours' acquaintance. Damn it, even two weeks or a month. No sensible girl——

He liked the house, but *if*—if she *could*—if by some incredible chance she too had felt——

And Life has fired, and Death not shaded,
All Time's uncounted bliss,
And the height o' the world has flamed and faded,
Love, that our love be this!

The hell with Brooke. And all the rest of them.

"I'll think about it," he said, sliding off the wall, and Farren sighed.

"All *right*—all right, I'll—stop, please, for God's sake——"

Cessation of sharper pain. Things swimming back into focus. Pat felt faint and sick, but one part of her mind told her coolly that she'd made it look plausible, all right. With a vengeance.

And a moment later, the world in place again, their faces so close, staring, she felt an unexpected panic, sharpening all her senses. Their expressions . . . What had she done, inviting this? The other times it had been random impulse with both of them, and a little excuse possible to find for themselves—offered struggle. This they had planned—and enjoyed to the full after planning.

Two house cats, she thought dimly, claws sheathed for being fed; now, with the taste of live blood enjoyed fresh after a hunt—tigers. Knowing what they wanted.

She shut her eyes and leaned back in the chair. She heard them vaguely.

The old woman, vexed over a trifle. "But how could I be so forgetful? No paper—no pen—I meant to bring . . . I—I am upset. That was the most necessary——I cannot conceive how I should have forgotten. . . . This terrible affair has so disturbed me. Stop. The desk. Nothing was taken from here. Julian's—Julian's desk. I cannot touch it—any of —*his*—possessions. Go and look, Anna. Paper—a pen."

It was there, waiting, in the left-hand top drawer, Pat knew. She had found it early this morning; she needed paper to work out her message, see how it would look written. She had flushed it down the drain afterward. . . . But no sound of a drawer opening.

"There's—postcards here," Anna's voice curiously muffled. "And her fountain pen."

"That will do, that is good. Get up!" A smaller hand on her arm, but strong. "Get up, go to the desk and write!"

"No——" mumbled Pat.

"Get up! You have said you will do so!"

"D'you want some more, my fine lass?" Another hand, harder.

"All right——" She pretended to be much weaker than she was, let them half-drag her to the desk, head down, as if thoroughly cowed and beaten.

"It will be—listen to me, Patricia!—it will be an ordinary message, do you understand? There will be nothing in it that may arouse this man's suspicion. He knew you were here, you said—you will tell him you have left this place. Do you understand?" Pat had reckoned on that condition, allowed for it. "You will write this over and over if need be, until I am satisfied."

Oh, God, let her pass it. Let her think it ordinary phrases between young modern people these days. Remember—remember every word as she'd planned it out.

"Your own pen—here!" And Anna thrust it into her hand.

Pat waited a moment, to control the involuntary shaking of that hand, bent and addressed the postcard. And she took a long chance there too. She did not know where he'd be staying. He'd recommended that place, but he might be staying with friends for all she knew. But Newcastle wasn't a very big town, and if it was his home country surely someone would know him, where he was, and deliver it. Especially as his name was well-known now, and probably more so in his home place. . . . Mr. Alan Glentower, The Black Lion (inn or hotel?) Inn, Newcastle Emlyn, Carmarthen.

Remember just how you decided it should go.

Pat bent lower over the desk and wrote her message.

That had been four hours ago. She sat here now, watching the westering light out the window and wondering if that postcard had been mailed as yet, was perhaps even now being collected from some pillar box by a deliberately efficient postman—or was on a sorting table. Postmark. She put some faith in that; but did Mrs. Trefoile have enough cleverness to send Hector or Anna to post it somewhere away from Abervy?

Sometimes the old woman seemed quite wandery, other times shrewd.

Her own damage might have been worse, she supposed. The little finger was badly sprained but not broken, she'd decided; although it was considerably swollen it hadn't turned black. The wound in her shoulder had been opened again; she hoped it wouldn't get infected. That shoulder was badly wrenched. At one point, though she didn't remember it clearly, she must have been struck on the head; there was a dark bruise on one temple, another on her right cheekbone, and she had a headache.

But after that scene, it came to her mind that it might be useful, later on, if she could bolt herself into this room and keep them out. It could happen that she would have to do that, if possible—even at the risk of starvation, of jumping from the window. . . . And the bolt seemed to be immovable. She had struggled at it with all her strength, but it was rusted into its socket. . . .

If the card was to be posted away from Abervy, it might not be collected until tomorrow. But he must have it by Thursday.

The British Post Office was very efficient.

TWELVE

*The man known as Hector Fields came back to Abervy late on Wednes*day morning, off the bus from Devil's Bridge. He went into the inn and bought himself a whisky. The publican Davies said genially, "Take a day off, eh?" The bus stopped at the door; he'd seen Hector alight.

"Not likely. Errand for the madam," said Hector. "Women—arrgh!" He drank. He and Anna had never been very communicative with the village folk; first for fear someone'd seen the police pictures, later from habit. Except for that niece of Anna's, Gloria Llewellyn; and Hector didn't approve so much of that. Good enough girl, but Anna was fair silly over her. And that likely came of having none of her own, poor woman. He sighed, finishing the whisky.

"I know what you mean," said Davies with a wink; but there was covert curiosity in his eyes. Hector was aware that the village had found its own explanation of why he and Anna stayed on at Llandaffy, where previously a series of girls and by-the-week gardeners had not stayed on account of the impossible conditions and poor wages. The village surmised that the old woman had promised them a substantial sum in her will. Everybody knew she was rich as Croesus; that kind usually was stingy. The village speculated with amusement as to whether the canny old lady was having them on and wouldn't leave them a shilling. Well, let them talk; that was safe enough.

He was neither overfriendly nor rude to Davies, but left the inn and started up the high street for home. Opposite the general store he met Gloria.

"Hi, Uncle Hector. The old terror let you off lead once in a ways?" she asked cheekily. Gloria had a good deal of ash-blond hair, a pert pretty face, a film-star figure, and a collection of random Americanisms, but was possessed of far more common sense than you might expect. She was, in fact, the jewel-of-a-domestic-help Mrs. Morecambe prized almost above rubies, and she was walking out with young Jim Evans, who had a good garage business up Tregaron way; she'd do well for herself there.

"Just an errand," said Hector.

"Same as me—matching yarn for Mrs. M. Uncle, you tell Auntie I'm ever so much obliged for my birthday present, will you? She said to save it, so I did until yesterday. Likely I won't see her till the weekend, so you tell her. She didn't ought to've spent so much, it must've cost a lot, it's imported. But I'm ever so obliged."

"I'll tell her," said Hector, and went on. He wondered what Anna'd given the girl: didn't recall her saying, or saying she'd taken money from their joint savings in the steel box under the bed. Anna was honest, she'd say if she had.

But he was a little troubled about her, all the same. Way she'd looked two-three times lately, since this business: sort of wild and heated up. She hadn't said as how they'd got the girl to do the postcard, but not being a fool he didn't reckon she'd have wrote that for the asking. . . . The old woman hell of a lot queerer than usual these last few days too.

He trudged up the drive, went round to the kitchen door. "Home again, girl," he said. Anna was at the stove; she turned quickly. They were not demonstrative, but he knew she was glad to see him.

"Where'd you go?"

"Up to Welshpool on the bus. Too late to get another un back, like I figured, so I stopped the night an' got first one back 's morning. You got a cuppa for me?"

"Kettle'll boil in a minute. You—posted it."

"What I went to do, certain. I met Gloria just now. She says tell you thanks ever so for her birthday present."

"Oh——" Anna smiled. "She like it? That's good. I'd just a half-hour Monday, run over, an' I told her keep it till next day."

"What'd you get her? She said must've cost a deal."

"Oh, not—s' much," said Anna. "Liddle bottle o' scent, 's all. Not much."

His mind wasn't really on that. The kettle boiled, she made the tea and poured him a cup, good and black and hot. He rubbed a hand over his jaw. "I been thinking. I don't half like this business."

"There's no way get out of it," she said, back turned at the stove.

"Well, there might be. What the hell're we doin' here, anyway, eleven years?" he said suddenly, violently. "One li'l old bitch of a woman! Think neither on us had any guts at all! An' now this bad business—crazy she is safe enough, do this. I been thinkin', there's no two ways about it, I don't see but what soon or late it's bound to get found out. Don't care what she does or thinks for. It might be now or it might be next year, but it'll get found out."

"Not—not if——She's kep' fast as can be, Harry. If that card keeps her fella off——"

"There's all sorts o' things can happen, all I'm sayin'. Only needs some'un comin' to the door for summat and hearin' her yell—like that. And she's American—there's permits, like, for foreigners, an' soon or late some government office lookin'. Like I say, the old woman's crazy. 'Specially since all this—you must've noticed she's got funnier."

"I reckon. Her talk don't make sense sometimes." Anna was bent over the stove; her tone was uneasy. "What you gettin' at?"

"Look, girl. It's bound t' happen—this gettin' out—an' then we're for it with her, see. Accessories like they say. I don't want no part o' that. Were we O.K. rest o' the way, I'd say go 'n' tell pollis right now, an' they wouldn't hold us on it if we were the ones see the girl got free. But that we can't do, on account they'd know me right off. What I'm gettin' at is what we shoulda done years ago. Get away."

"There's no way," she said flatly; she turned on him in sudden passion. "You think *I* haven't thought? Look at me—only forty-one, an' I look ten year older—you too—this dead-alive hole—slavey's work, 'n' can't fix myself up any or she's preachin' at me! I wasn't so bad once—was I? Was I? I——"

"You could be again, girl," he said gently.

"Oh, could I? Could either of us, after all this time? It's no *use*—certain sure, we can run away—an' her settin' the pollis on right away after she knows——"

"Maybe not," he said. "There's that car, see."

"What car?"

"The girl's car—in the garridge." He jerked his head. "I got the keys. I figured it, we could get off at night, 'n' go straight up to Lunnon. I used to know a chap'd take a car off your hands, even if you didn't have papers—we'd try that, but if he's gone, we can't—just have t' leave it. Anyways, we got almost two hundred fifty pounds saved. Get ourselves all smartened up like, wouldn't know either of us, see, an' get passports 'n' that in another name, take ship for Canada or Australia."

She stared at him. "An' what's t' old lady doin' all that while? They'd be on us——"

"Not if she was dead," he said harshly. "God, I shoulda had the guts afore!"

Her eyes widened and she made a smothered exclamation. "No—Harry, you couldn't! Harry—you're crazy yourself, think o' such a thing! Listen——"

"Might's well be hanged for a sheep as a lamb," he muttered.

"And hanged's the word. You think I don't know that? They can't hang you for one any more, but they do for two! An' they'd know right off 'twas you—'twas us."

"Didn't know as you knowed that. . . . It's got t' be finished *somehow,*" he said desperately. "I got the feeling this crazy thing'll do for her in the end, Anna—bound to—an' they'll take us too, any old way it finishes. Damn the odds, we oughta try make a break."

"Not *that* way."

"Well, all right, you tell me how, then!"

"I dunno," she said miserably. "I dunno, Harry."

Pat had wakened very early as usual. The lack of exercise lessened her need of sleep. And as usual she was desperately hungry; in the last days she had had only about a quarter of the amount of food she was used to.

She lay for a while half-waking, thinking vaguely that there was something she meant to do today. Presently she remembered what it was, and forced herself out from under the blanket. She had to sleep in her slip; she felt dirty and disheveled, though she did her best with the trickle of lukewarm water in the bathroom. She was stiff this morning, the wrenched shoulder hurting, the little finger still badly swollen, and her head ached dully. The wound in her shoulder looked red and angry.

That locked drawer, she thought; was it really? And she'd given up too easily; just because one drawer was locked, it didn't mean everything was. She should have looked before—there might be something here, in this room, to help her escape. She remembered the old woman saying, Nothing was removed. . . . Something about the husband, Stephen's father, there must be, behind that: the curious shudder that shook her when she spoke his name. Never mind that; the point was, had he kept anything here which might be of use to Pat Carroll now, twenty-four years later?

Such as fishing line, say. Good line would be tough and strong; several thicknesses of it might bear her weight.

It would not be easy to search, with the two women intruding on her so much of the day; she must use what time she had, and be careful to put everything back as she finished looking, not to let them suspect what she was up to.

She splashed her face with cold water and quickly slipped into the wreck of her dress and the cardigan. It was just dawn. She decided to start with the desk.

Whatever else he had been, the late Julian Trefoile had not been a tidy man. The drawers were in the careless muddle of a man with little sense of order. And he had not used the desk much as a desk, she surmised. The thin pile of plain stationery she'd found before, and envelopes, several pens, old-fashioned nibs as well as two fountain pens, paper clips and a bottle of ink completely dried up ended the expectable inventory of a desk. The other drawers were stuffed with odds and ends of surprising objects. Pat went through each methodically, putting everything back before attacking the next.

She stared at the first two she opened, the middle and bottom left-hand drawers. They held a cache of liquor. Incredulously she counted the bottles: at least a dozen each of brandy and Scotch whisky, and in the bottom drawer wine—mostly Burgundy. She lifted out a few. All but three were full, seals unbroken.

"Well!" she said to herself. "If things get too bad, I can always get drunk and try to forget this mess! *Stay me with flagons,* very appropriate." The picture emerged of a genial fellow who liked his drink (maybe a little too well) saddled with a teetotal wife, secreting his supply in his sanctum. Yes, that bolt on the door: solid reason for it.

The top right-hand drawer was filled with books. She took out the top one, a thin black volume, and opened it where it naturally fell apart, to be confronted by a distinctly obscene line drawing. The title was *Joys of Paris.* The one beneath it was titled *Raptures of Rome.* Cheap pornography. At the very bottom of the pile were the two volumes of a famous edition of the *Memoirs of Casanova;* both were fresh and stiff as from the shop, and temporarily Pat found herself highly amused. How disappointed he must have been in Casanova after *Joys of Paris!*—all that tedious commentary on the culture of the period, and improbable journeys, with only a few scattered anecdotes (so elegantly and vaguely phrased, too) for spice. Inadvertently, Julian Trefoile assumed character. She could see him sitting here, leafing over the *Memoirs* and muttering, "Damn dull stuff!"

At least I've kept my sense of humor, she thought; and sobered. Once before she'd thought that terror could not be juxtaposed to comedy. But it could, and be all the deeper for it. . . .

In the middle drawer were a few more books, all the same except for a textbook on dog breeding. A rusted stiff old dog collar with a brass name tag dangling from it; the tag was inscribed, *Dandy, Capt. J. Trefoile, 10 Stowe Square, Shrewsbury.* So he hadn't come from around here. A sentimental man, keeping the collar of a loved dog. She wondered what kind of dog Dandy had been: it was a big collar. And took herself to task. Get on with the job. Another half hour and they'd be coming in on her.

A dog whistle. A tarnished silver model of a plebeian-looking little squat dog with big ears, not a breed she knew—yes—she'd seen pictures: the Queen kept dogs like those. Welsh Corgis. An old photograph album, half full of faded bad snapshots. A handful of miscellaneous brochures about automobiles, circa the mid-thirties. How odd they looked now. A pack of cards in a leather case. A larger leather case with more cards, poker chips, a dice cup. A tarnished silver whisky jigger with his initials on it. And that was all.

In the last drawer she found (ear cocked for the sound of the bolt being pulled back) a box of very dry cigars—"Damn, why didn't he smoke cigarettes? but I haven't any matches anyway"—a can of lighter fluid, an old pipe, and a fat black book stamped *Diary.* She riffled through it disappointedly and had time to see that it was filled in only here and there before she heard a sound at the door. She dropped it back in the drawer, shut the drawer silently and got quickly to her feet.

When they came in she was leaning on the desk facing the door.

The thought of that liquor was demoralizing. A little something to warm her internally—the house was very cold, though she could see that the sun was out and perhaps it was warmer outside. A little something to cheer her up, however falsely and temporarily. But she must be careful, on a practically empty stomach. The temptation wasn't to be resisted. When she was alone, near noon, she got out a bottle of brandy—French brandy it was—and after a struggle succeeded in opening it with the aid of the single pin-curl holder left to her. About to raise the bottle, she stopped and admonished herself.

"At least I can drink like a lady——" and she found the silver jigger, washed it in the bathroom, and filled it.

The brandy was grateful fire in her stomach. She put the bottle back and turned to the long chest. . . . An old-fashioned house, no walk-in closets. The chest held folded suits and odd trousers, neatly laid out to hold their press. Probably full of moths now; there was no odor of camphor. She didn't know what men had been wearing twenty-four years ago, but some of the clothes struck her as rather gay. That purple heather-tweed mixture, and the black-and-white plaid plus fours. Jodhpurs. Gray flannels. She lifted them all out and went through the pockets, but found nothing more useful than an odd sixpence and several handkerchiefs. There was a long drawer in the bottom of the chest; this held several pairs of shoes, low boots, dress pumps.

Disappointed, she shut it. It didn't seem that she was going to find anything useful—except, of course, the liquor. The one small drink had put new confidence in her, however, and she turned to the highboy. . . . What might be expected—shirts, socks, underwear. Again, the latter rather gay patterns. In the first of the two small top drawers she found a large gold pocket watch, and wondered if it would run; it was irrational, but a ticking watch would be rather comforting. But she'd never know what time to set it to. . . . Handkerchiefs in a pile. A watch chain. Three pairs of cuff links, one monogrammed. She turned to the other top drawer, the one that had seemed to be locked, and tugged at it again. It resisted and then suddenly moved; something had been caught in it, it was stiff, that was all. A pile of neckties, one all crumpled where it had been crushed all these years between the drawer and the top of the highboy. Folded suspenders—no, he'd called them braces. A large Benares brass jar; it rattled when she picked it up and, curious, she lifted the lid. It was half full of the big English pennies.

Odds and ends, odds and ends. He hadn't been a sportsman, evidently. But of course all that would have been kept elsewhere anyway—guns, fishing tackle, that kind of thing. Silly to expect it here. Nothing of any use to her.

She shut the last drawer disconsolately. All she had found was the ghostly image of Julian Trefoile.—And some explanation of his widow? (If that mattered.) A hearty straightforward masculine man, earthy and simple; and—her. How had they ever come to marry?

Which was of no consequence to Pat Carroll a quarter of a century later.

And very soon the old woman would be coming again. Pat had maintained her pose of cool contemptuous confidence before her, this morning, but it hadn't been easy. Afterthoughts had told her just how very long a chance that little postcard was. . . . Gamble on it against the odds that he'd decipher the message: then what? He didn't know where she was. Very likely it had been posted in another town, maybe a distance away: and it said in surface meaning she had left Llandaffy. Llandaffy village, Llandaffy house; he didn't know there was any difference. Oh, why hadn't she put in a return address? Not thinking straight . . . Would he go to Llandaffy up north? If he did, by the grace of God he'd meet the Reverend Mr. Fallow or Daffyd in the pub, or Morgan the Post, and ask, and they would tell him, Abervy. Or did they remember the name—any of the names? And even if he came, what——

No use being pessimistic; you just had to hope.

Her hands were dirty from grubbing in the dusty furniture; she went to wash them. They had belatedly brought her a small cake of kitchen soap and a thin towel. In the bathroom, she tugged the little window wider for more air; she had to stand on tiptoe, for it was above the washbowl, its lower sill on the level of her chin.

The sun had come out; it looked to be a pleasantly warm summer day, and a very faint scent of stock drifted in. Wistfully she leaned over the bowl, pulling herself up by the sill, and looked out. The window overlooked the rear of the property. She hadn't noticed when she drove in, but evidently the drive branched somewhere to reach the garage; she could see just a corner of that from here, off to the right. About a hundred feet away from the house was another belt of trees, and in the foreground was what looked like the kitchen garden: several big wired-off plots with unidentifiable green sprouting in tidy rows. They gave on the far side to wind grass growth running down to the trees.

Hector was working at some job along the edge of one plot, and Joseph was doing nothing, sitting in the grass beyond. Everything looked very still and peaceful.

Suddenly she exclaimed in excitement. There had been movement out there in the trees. From this higher vantage point she could see where Hector and Joseph probably wouldn't; neither seemed to have noticed. But there was someone else there, and moving furtively too——

For one ridiculous moment her heart beat high with hope. Someone knows!—someone has come——And then common sense told her that if anyone *did,* they wouldn't go about rescue that way, but march up to the front door with a policeman.

A moment later she saw him plainly. A boy. Just a boy. He darted from the shelter of one tree to another and was almost lost to sight, but she could still see a little edge of his tan jacket showing.

Just a boy from the village, like that one she'd met that day, cheeky young Garry Evans. This was summer holiday, he'd be out playing. Playing Red Indians or something here, pretending to stalk the oblivious Hector and Joseph.

But somebody from outside, to hear and carry tales back to the village. Could she make him hear?

She heard the bolt rattle behind her on the bedroom door, but ignoring that she drew herself up as high as she could to the window and shouted lustily, *"Help! Help!"*

And heard the desperate cry drowned in the overhead thunder of a low-flying plane.

In another moment Mrs. Trefoile had grasped her arm and pulled her roughly around.

PART 3

THIRTEEN

"*—Until you understand fully, and accept God's laws. I cannot conceive* how anyone finds them difficult to understand——"

And of course that was a way: was it? Pat thought about it drearily, trying to shut her mind to the thin old voice talking at her, to the pain in her shoulder, her finger, her head. Yes, Mrs. Trefoile, I understand, you have explained it to me; I believe and will do all as you say, I promise. *Now let me out!* A fine idea.

It couldn't be done quite like that, after all this rebellion and contempt. Just out of the blue. Even mad little Mrs. Trefoile wouldn't be taken in by any sudden capitulation. If it came to that, all other resources closed to her, it would mean a long time of acting and pretense before the woman was convinced. If at all. Did she want to be convinced? Was this means to an end, or an end in itself—now she knew (kitten grown to tiger and hunting-hungry) what pleasure this was? . . .

Honestly, thought Pat. She looked back to last Saturday morning, that little exchange so thoughtless on her part which had started this nightmare. *As it might be a wedded wife like yourself.* If she had not had that small impulse to honesty—if she'd had any common sense whatever—she'd have made some vague soothing polite answer to satisfy the woman, and none of this would have happened.

Would it?

Six days. It felt like six years.

"There are *ways.* Good ways, for realizing God and His truth. Mortify the flesh—mortify the flesh. Sacrifices. Pain can be very helpful."

Pat raised her eyes just as the small hand darted out. "Let the blood flow—every day—from it, the bad blood." The hand had ragged nails, uncared-for and a little dirty. Every time Pat tried to jerk away, knowing it was useless but unable to help it; there was the other woman behind her, holding her—and the pain, and the blood flowing.

It will get infected, said her mind. It looked much worse yesterday—if feels worse. If it's a much longer time here—infected, and spread, and the whole arm——Don't borrow trouble. I'm young and healthy, it'll heal. Suddenly—how had she been so stupid not to think of that before?—she thought of the brandy. Gratefully she thought of Julian Trefoile's cache of liquor. Antiseptic—alcohol. They used to wash battle wounds in whisky, didn't they? Something she remembered reading——A half-hysterical laugh rose in her throat; she bit it back.

She opened her eyes and looked at the old woman steadily. Mrs. Trefoile was staring at the fresh blood and at that moment she looked, and was, beyond all doubt a madwoman. The little froth at the corner of her mouth: the fixed stare of the pale eyes. Whether these days of new power, of first savoring of physical power, had wholly and suddenly turned her mind—or whether without that she'd have gone so far mad now or later. Or whether——

For the next moment she rose abruptly, and the light eyes were almost wild. "This room—this room! Why must you be *here,* in this place? Full of evil always——" It was nearly as if she fled in panic.

Pat did not move for a moment, left alone; then she got up stiffly from the chair and went across to the desk, a little uncertain on her feet from pain. Got the opened bottle of brandy, took it into the bathroom. She had stopped bothering about the bloodstains on the dress; three of the buttons hung by threads, the top one was off, and the original tear had widened beyond repair. She took it off, leaned over the bowl; opening the bottle, she poured brandy into her cupped palm, slapped it on the raw wound. It burned like fire, and she clung to the bowl against faintness; but she forced herself to do it again and again.

Then she splashed her face with cold water. Without refastening her dress, she sat down on the stool and drank brandy neat from the bottle. Set the bottle down carefully, and laid her head on her knees.

After an unspecified time she began to feel stronger; the alcohol was reaching her. She thought with small attempt at humor, If I stay here long I'll turn into a drunkard.

It can't be long. I'll get away. Something will happen.

Today is Thursday, Thursday, Thursday. Thursday morning about eleven o'clock, I think, and please God Alan Glentower has the postcard—and please God he reads it twice and sees something odd about it

—and looks between the lines. But if he doesn't—if he doesn't? Only myself to rely on.

This madwoman. Anything—anything might come into her warped mind. But Anna—browbeaten, bitter, but sane—Anna would not let her go too far, of fear for herself? How far was too far?

There were voices under the bathroom window. Pat lifted her head. She felt better; the brandy rose slightly over the sudden dark despair. She got up and leaned to the little casement, listening.

Thursday, Thursday, Thursday. Perhaps not this morning, but by this afternoon. Perfectly ridiculous, a grown man. He hadn't felt like this since he was a kid promised some very special treat.

Glentower didn't go out looking at houses or just driving. He wandered around the town a little, killing the morning, never too far from the Lion. Came back and had lunch. A good lunch: they always did you well here. But the perfect *rissoles,* the cheese dressing, the light scones might have been good, bad, or indifferent for all he noticed. He consumed them absently. And then it was one-thirty.

Then it was two-thirty. She hadn't come. But soon, now.

He had a glass of Burley's excellent claret. Three o'clock. He gave up the pretense of trying to read the *Herald* on his lap and just sat there, inwardly tense, outwardly relaxed, waiting. There in the comfortable public lounge.

The hands of the mantel clock crawled to three-thirty, and he heard the house door open and got up, dropping the paper. It was an hour to opening time, so it must be someone coming in to book a room. He went out to the hall.

A uniform just disappearing out to the street again. Burley the landlord stood there with a thin sheaf of letters in his hands, sorting them, before the mail rack. "Afternoon post, Mr. Glentower. Half a minute, sir, I'll see is there aught for you. . . . One card, sir, here you are."

Glentower took it. He was suddenly afraid to turn it over, and looked at the too-highly-colored photograph on its face with absurd care: the Teifi Pools. Slowly he turned it and read the message.

"Bad news, sir?"

"No . . . No, nothing." Glentower put the card into his inside breast pocket and started for the stair.

Well, it was what he'd half-expected, wasn't it? Just too good to be true. Especially if she too could have felt——But he might have been given a *chance.* Damn it, damn it.

He shut himself into his room and paced it awhile, swearing. But that was cover-up—even alone, cover-up. He wasn't angry, except at destiny. He was sick at heart, savagely sick and bitter and hurt.

She couldn't know what this meant to him, of course. She couldn't have any idea that this—this absurd and violent thing had happened to him, so that this casual putting-off of their appointment was like a little death.

Because he could never find her again, now. She had gone on—somewhere. In her new gleaming red car, blithely on holiday—somewhere. Anywhere. Side-stepping him neatly, driving away from him without a back look.

He took off his jacket and tie, lay down on the bed. For a while he felt appallingly sorry for himself; he could have wept like a frustrated five-year-old. That was senseless: ought to have learned better than that long ago. And then he tried to summon a righteous healthy anger that this girl only six hours known should have such terrible emotional power over him. He tried to summon hope that it would go as quickly as it had come. Now it was irrevocably finished. Just a chance encounter, and courtesies exchanged. Pass by.

And awhile after that he tried to tell himself that it was as well; because—those flip airy phrases, the bold *Darling*—they sounded like a girl he wouldn't really like much. Americans tended to scatter *darlings* around, didn't they? She hadn't, in talk; she hadn't been that way. . . . So, he'd seen and heard her in a rosy haze of infatuation, he hadn't seen her true. . . . No! She *was* what he'd felt, she was——

Lucky escape, whispered his mind, trying to summon cynicism now. You don't know her. What she's really like.

Yes, I do, and she's mine. All I'd ever want.

Damn fool.

And it's no good now, whatever you feel or want to feel or ought to feel about her, because she's gone. She says she can't meet you and she's gone on somewhere else, and she doesn't say where, and so that's that. *Kaput.*

Why? She'd said——Don't be callow. She had second thoughts. All right. She saw something in your eyes that morning, heard something in your voice—remember how her farewell smile was just polite, nothing more?—and she doesn't want to get involved.

She knows I wouldn't have—the old-fashioned phrase for it—made unwelcome advances. If only because she'd know *I* know it wouldn't be any good.

It didn't matter why. She'd gone. There was no way to find her.

All *right,* be a damn fool. The postmark on the card. Go there, wherever it was—he hadn't noticed—and ask, find where she'd stayed, where she'd been making for. If anyone knew. Chase her. What kind of reception would he get if he found her?

Irrationally and frighteningly, this was the worst thing that had ever happened to him. Maybe because he was getting older, more set in his own emotional routines. Because the times his best manuscripts had been rejected coldly, he had always known they'd be sold eventually, one day he'd have the recognition he'd earned, and he'd write better. He had had a long time to get used to the idea of Kitty dying; he'd known she was dying as everyone knew, and the actual end was in a sense a release. Nothing had ever dealt him quite so violent a blow as this. It was easy to think, such a small thing: irrational, yes. Human beings were not made like clockwork, forever rational.

He did not get up to look at the postmark on the card; he didn't want to look at the card again. When he got up, a long while later as the dusk came down, it was to ring for the maid.

"Tell Mr. Burley I don't want dinner until later—maybe not at all. I'm—I've got a bit of a headache. Ask him to send up a bottle of whisky, will you?"

"Yes, sir."

She wasn't worth it. It wasn't reasonable. All this violent emotion expended on something so ephemeral——

Whisky usually relaxed him, loosened all those inhibitions and shynesses so that something nearer the real Glentower showed through. This didn't. He sat brooding over it alone, drinking too quickly. He killed more than half the bottle and stumbled into bed dead drunk.

The voices beneath the little casement were Hector's and Joseph's.

"I'm—I'm—I'm—goin' town."

"You're goin' t' weed out this bed afore you go anywheres, see. Oh—reckon I forgot—Thursday, so 'tis. You got your pocket money, eh?" The man laughed.

"I—I—got, I'm goin'——"

"My Lady High 'n' Mighty give you your li'l arf-crown, certain, an' you're goin' in to Mis' Evans' to spend it all on peppermint creams, like allus. But not till after we eat, Joseph—see? Then you can go. Right now you set to 'n' get all the weeds outta here."

"I—I can go—atter?"

"Certain sure—like allus."

Joseph, thought Pat—things were different here. Oh, well, different in all remote country places from cities and towns. There, the remorseless wheels of bureaucratic efficiency picked up the Josephs and deposited them in supervised surroundings. Places like this, they could wander. You could guess that he did a little unwilling slow work here, helping Hector: not much. For his food and, evidently, this little sum every week to spend on sweets.

There was silence from below; had they gone? No; in a moment she heard a low tuneless humming, the chink of some tool on stone. Joseph was weeding the bed as he'd been ordered, secure in the knowledge that afterward he could go into the village for his peppermint creams.

Joseph was going into the village.

Joseph—she'd discounted him from the first. But any chance must be seized for what it was worth.

Pat's mind began to work very cool and fast. Joseph—like all his kind—was childishly unable to concentrate very long or hard; like a child, his interest might be caught momentarily by the bright-colored, the unusual. He couldn't be trusted to take a message in the real sense—but he might carry one in the literal sense. If—if—if!

It wasn't a chance at all—it was just a crazy idea.

She ran out to the bedroom, to her handbag on the desk, and tumbled its contents out hastily. . . . Last night she'd been in the brief grip of the dark despair that had seized her again just now; she had known with awful finality that her silly little postcard with its secret message would never be understood or acted upon, that she was lost unless she could help herself or get out a real S.O.S. Wild schemes had gone through her mind, impossible: at one point she had conceived the notion of bribing Anna secretly to send out a plea for help, tucking it unobtrusively in her apron pocket with some signed traveler's checks. (Anna probably didn't know what traveler's checks were.) Well, she had not been thinking clearly: she had had some of the brandy, maybe too much on her unaccustomed low diet. That was mad, as mad as Mrs. Trefoile. The postcard still lying there on the desk proved it—she must have been half-drunk, or going crazy herself. If Anna could be bribed to take out a message, it need go no farther than the village constable; if Anna would betray herself so far, there was no need for a message. But in the first flush of that maudlin idea, Pat had actually addressed the other card—absurd, absurd—again to Glentower. . . . The first card still in her mind, her hope that he understood it; he was still her highest hope.

That didn't matter now, that the space on the back of the card for the address was filled in with his: or that she'd even got out her stamp book and put on a twopenny stamp, ready. She'd got that far before impulse and enthusiasm died. The card was important now only because its face bore a very highly-colored photograph of the Lake of Berwyn at sunset, which might—just possibly might—catch Joseph's simple eye.

And he might pick it up, and he might put it in his pocket, and he might not show it or say anything about it to anyone here *but* he might show it to someone in the village—a someone with more brains who could read a message——

Too many ifs altogether. But she had to take every chance.

She uncapped her fountain pen hurriedly and bent to the card, meaning to write something like *To the Abervy Police* to begin with.

The pen was dry.

She shook it frantically, knowing it was no good. She disliked ballpoints and never used them; this was her pet old-fashioned side-filling fountain pen, reliable—but the best of pens needed refueling. It must have have been nearly empty when she wrote the first card; now it had dried up completely.

The only bottle of ink in the desk had also dried up, years ago.

Pat heard herself sob once in frustration more angry than self-pitying. Suddenly it seemed very important to try this terrifically long chance for freedom and safety. She *had* to try—but it would be no good if it did come off and someone in the village saw the card, if it was just a postcard with nothing on it——

And any minute Joseph might finish that bed and go away.

She looked around desperately. Something sharp——

She snatched out the little two-pronged pin-curler from her pocket. Its prongs weren't very sharp; but she felt very much as she imagined the wild animal might who gnaws off a leg to escape from the trap. She jabbed it cruelly, again and again, into her third left fingertip, perhaps (she thought later) with some vague memory of blood samples taken for testing. Hardly feeling the pain, she gave a little gasp of relief when she saw a tiny drop of blood well up, and dug the crude tool in again, twisting it. More blood came; she squeezed the finger hard, collected blood on the little prong held upright, and began to mark the card.

But it took so *much.* Scarcely half of one letter formed, and the prong was dry. . . . She jabbed and squeezed, and traced the one word—

painfully, crookedly, running downhill across the white space on the card.

She wrapped her handkerchief round her left hand. Money. Joseph liked peppermint creams. They hadn't touched her traveler's checks or cash purse; oh, no, she thought almost hysterically, they were quite honest! She opened the purse and scooped out all the change. The blood on the card wasn't dry, but she couldn't wait.

Such a long chance.

She went back to the bathroom. God bless the backward English for not having screens to their windows! Was he still there? She listened, and heard the tuneless humming. She stood on tiptoe, and dropped out the card first, unable to see it fall: waited a second, and dropped the handful of copper and silver. She heard that fall, some of it at least, on paving.

And it was no use worrying that Hector was somewhere to see that, or that there was another window underneath—perhaps the kitchen—and Anna had seen. Or that Joseph would talk about it to them.

It was a chance, another chance, and she had taken it.

FOURTEEN

*Garry had begged a package of sandwiches from his mother that morn*ing; he was often out all day in holiday time, and she gave in readily. He ate them under a tree at the back of Llandaffy house. He'd lost Joseph in the thick growth of trees in front, about an hour before, and fearful of being caught and run off by Hector, he'd reconnoitered with extreme care. Finally, about noon, he'd worked his way round to the back and saw Joseph on his knees by a bed up against the house wall, a hundred feet away. Garry couldn't see what he was doing, but he wasn't moving much. Like he was just kneeling there looking down at something.

When Anna called from the kitchen door and Joseph got up and went in, Garry ate his sandwiches, thinking. This was Thursday, and every Thursday—the whole village knew—Joseph got some money, not much, and he always came to Garry's mum-and-dad's store to buy chocolate peppermint creams. Likely after he'd had his noon meal Joseph would be off to the village.

Garry buried his sandwich paper under fallen leaves and worked his way back to the stand of trees in front of the house. He chose a spot where he had a good view of the drive and settled down to wait.

About half an hour later he was rewarded with the sight of Joseph coming down the drive. But before he passed Garry, Joseph turned off among the trees. After a moment's debate Garry got up and started after him. He wasn't afraid of Joseph, for all he was so big; Joseph was just like a little kid, he never hurt nobody—didn't know how, and wouldn't think to do such. And Garry had a strong suspicion that Joseph had a secret hiding place for the little things he picked up. Maybe that was where he was going now.

It wasn't easy to be quiet in the undergrowth and dried leaves, but he was quiet as he could be. Up ahead he heard Joseph stop, and stopped himself. Pushing aside branches carefully, he saw Joseph there by an old tree, and he was reaching his arm inside a hollow in it——

Garry felt an upsurge of righteous indignation at the thought of his good solid brass compass maybe inside an old hollow tree, and he ran out at Joseph openly. "What you got there? Show me!"

Joseph started around, his almost colorless eyes wild. "N-nothin'! Nothin'! You—scared me. Ain't doin' nothin'." He was three times Garry's size, but he backed away a few steps nervously; he looked like a startled wild thing shying from the scent of man.

"Come *on,* show me!" said Garry, conscious of superiority. In two ways; this was a stroke of luck. It'd be no good if he tackled Joseph about the compass, bullied him into showing what was in his pockets and it wasn't there; but this looked like being where Joseph hid his things, and if he hadn't it on him, it'd be in the hollow.

"I—I—I *won't!* You can't make——'Tain't *fair!"* The big simpleton was almost blubbering to have his secret place found out.

"Oh, don't take on!" said Garry, impatient. "I ain't orf t' take anything belongs to you, Joseph—I just got to see if there's somethin' o' *mine.* It's O.K., nobody's goin' to hurt you, I know you don't mean t' go thievin', but I just want t' see. Show me what you got—what's that in your pocket?" For Joseph's hand had gone to his shirt pocket protectively. "Come on, Joseph, I'm not orf t' take it if it ain't mine—just let me see."

"You—you won't keep nothin'? Jus' look?"

"That's right."

Slowly Joseph emptied his pocket, and his pants pocket too. There was something wrapped up in a piece of cloth, and Garry pounced on that eagerly and then dropped it in disgust. Only an old ring, from Woolworth's likely, the stone wasn't shiny a bit. A postcard. A grimy handkerchief with a few spots of red on it. A lot of money in coin. He whistled. "You been savin' up, Joseph?" There were a lot of pennies, but silver too. But he wasn't interested in that; the compass wasn't there. "Orl right, lessee what's in that hollow."

"No—no——"

"I ain't goin' take nothin'," he repeated, fishing. His arm wasn't as long as Joseph's and he had to scrabble up the trunk a way to get it all out. He looked at the stuff in contemptuous disappointment while Joseph stuttered and cried and protested. Lot of dirty old stuff nobody'd want. And no compass.

He said all the bad words he knew. So Joseph hadn't got the compass after all. If only he knew where he'd lost it—none of the kids, not even Billy Luff or Dave Barke, 'd dare to keep it, they couldn't show it or use it. Could they? Oh, damn.

"Orl right," he said disgustedly, "you can shove it back—I just wanted t' see. I'm sorry, Joseph, didn't go to scare you."

"You won't take nothin'——"

"Not me, o' that lot." But he hung around a minute, moodily amused —outside his new speculations about where the compass could've got to —at Joseph's collection of treasures. The simpleton was muttering tenderly over them, wrapping them up again carefully; and last of all he picked up the picture postcard to add to the bundle. "Hi," said Garry idly, "you don't want t' put that there, I reckon some'n give you that to post. There's a stamp on it, see."

Joseph looked at him uncomprehendingly. And what silly idiot ever trusted Joseph to post anything—just like Garry'd always thought, they was all loonies at this place.

"Pretty pitcher," said Joseph. "Nice."

"Sure, but it's for the post, all stamped. You give it here, I'll do it. You can't *have* it, Joseph, it's s'posed to be *posted.* Give it me, silly fool."

Joseph let it go with unexpected willingness after a stubborn moment, and Garry stuck it in his own pocket.

"You—won't tell no'un? Won't——"

"About what? Oh, yer hidey-hole. No, o' course not—it's O.K., Joseph." But it wasn't O.K. about the compass. Garry tramped off moodily, wondering if that little devil Billy Luff'd really dare. . . . Somebody must've found it by now. He couldn't quite remember every place he'd been that day, but he didn't think he'd been much off the main road or the village street, places it'd be spotted.

Damn.

He decided to find Billy and bully the truth out of him. You could always make Billy back down if you acted tough.

He didn't remember the postcard until he passed the box at this end of the village, and then he stopped and took it out. Someone had mucked up the writing-space with red ink, not making letters that he could tell, just like the pen had splashed. Well, there you were: loonies, like he said. But it was addressed and stamped. In Garry's world nobody wasted tuppence on something to be thrown away, even a stamp.

But the postcard just flitted across his field of vision without setting up any train of thought. He dropped it in the box and went on his way. In any case, it was last year he'd been enthralled by *Boy Detective* and all that and made up fantasies about messages in blood and sinister Russians and atomic secrets. This year most of his waking thoughts were devoted to sports cars and the official races for same.

Except for his new solid brass compass.

The last postal collection from that box was at six o'clock, and by then the postcard found itself in the middle of a slim bunch of other cards and letters. Mrs. Laughlin the postmistress had had a busy day, and been up with a sick baby most of the night before; she was still anxious about the baby, and concerned only to finish up her day's work and get home. There never was much to go out, but it had to be sorted and got ready for the mail truck due at six-thirty. The truck took it on to the county town, where it'd be put in with the appropriate bigger bundles for south, central, midwest, north, London and so on.

She worked mechanically, wielding her little rubber stamp, glancing at the addresses only. She was very tired. By six-thirty she had it all made up in three slim packets; when Tad Paget clattered up in the truck she had shut the post office and was waiting outside. She handed the bag over to him and started home.

The British Post Office system carried the postcard some twenty miles out of its way, roundabout to the county town, before it was sorted again and sent in another sack rattling southeast in another mail truck. Eventually, at eight-fifteen the next morning, it fell into the hands of Thomas Reynolds of the Newcastle Emlyn Post Office, along with the rest of his morning's scheduled deliveries, and in the course of sorting out his bag by streets, Reynolds noticed it. But many queer things pass under the eyes of postmen, and he registered it only as an unspecified joke of some sort; the address was clear enough, and he duly delivered it to the Black Lion at about eleven o'clock.

Glentower was usually a moderate drinker, and in consequence wakened with a nasty hangover. He took three aspirins with a great deal of tap water, told the maid in a faint voice to ask Burley for the standard remedy—never mind, he'd know what was meant—and went back to bed. At least, mercifully, the hangover and aspirin dulled his renewed bitterness somewhat.

It was noon when he came downstairs. Burley, who had never known Mr. Glentower to overdrink but once or twice—and he'd known him, on and off, most of twenty years—was cautiously and curiously sympathetic.

"Hope you're feeling better, sir. There'll be a nice sole for luncheon——"

"I don't want anything, thanks. Send me a drink in to the lounge, will you, sherry—no, not sherry—oh, a gin and Italian." They'd had sherry together that evening.

"Yes, sir. Oh, there's summat in the rack for you."

"All right." Glentower was not very curious about what further communication, from whom, the post had brought him; but he went on down the hall, past the lounge door, and looked under his room number on the rack, and took down the postcard.

He stared at it for a full minute before it registered. He went on staring at it.

He heard himself say something, but he never knew what he'd said.

"You're gin-and-it, sir."

"What?" He stared blankly down at a waiter with something on a tray. "What—oh. Yes. Thanks." He picked up the glass and drained it at one swallow. And then he said, "My God—the other card!" and made for the stair at a run, nearly knocking the man over.

The gray jacket—he'd had on the gray tweed yesterday, hadn't he? He didn't take time to shut the room door, but plunged across to the chair where he'd draped the jacket, groped in the breast pocket. The card, the other card——

There must be something, there must be. It wasn't *right.* Dimly that had penetrated his mind, but the surface sense of it had so——so demoralized him, the subtler thing had been overshadowed. Now he read it with desperate concentration, still clutching in his left hand this thing just come to him, this incredible other thing. He read it over and over, searching for some inner message it held—that it must hold.

This other thing that said she was in trouble, in danger. How or why he couldn't stop to question. The address in ink, but on the other side—that was blood, dried blood, smeared the way blood would smear, not ink, and at first glance it looked just a confused splatter, but if you looked close you could see what looked like an H and an L and another longer downstroke——Somebody had tried to write *Help* on that card, and in blood, and it was wild, fantastic, incredible, anything you liked, but the address in ink was in the same pointed thin script as that on this other card signed *Pat,* and she was in some danger——

Steady, Think, Use your mind on it. God, this damn hangover slowed and dulled his mind——She'd been watched when she wrote this first card, she wasn't allowed to say anything directly—was that what the second card told him besides? So she'd have tried to write a secret message, and that was why the surface meaning was wrong—odd; yes, for the terms they had been on. The *tone* of it was wrong, as addressed to a man she had known for six hours. A man she didn't know loved her.

Use your mind on it.

He read the words over again, and started violently as someone behind him asked timidly, "Is—anything wrong, sir? Shouldn't I do up the room now?"

He had not noticed the maid, half through making up the bed. He carried the card across to the window for better light. There was something—maybe just a slip of the pen——

The girl jumped as he swung around on her. "A Bible!—I want a Bible! Is there such a thing in the house? For God's sake hurry, go ask Burley—any Bible——"

"Yes, sir, I will." She fled.

Was that it, was it? He paced the room impatiently, stopping to reread the card.

In thin pointed script it said, in the little space reserved for a message:

Darling, I've left my charming hostess and wandered on. *So* desolated I can't meet you Thursday! You know I'd be singing Psalms if I could, and you promised to show me those 3′ fascinating Teifi Pools too and all sorts of things. But I'm unavoidably prevented as the saying goes! Maybe see you in Town later, darling. Love, Pat

The Teifi Pools. There were more than three—and the figure was used, not the word, and there was a mark right after it, a downstroke just a bit longer than an apostrophe. To the first glance, it might be just a place the pen had slipped, touched inadvertently: look at it again, and it made that 3 into 31. And there weren't thirty-one Teifi Pools either.

He went to the door. Burley himself was coming up the stair. "Now what in the world might you be wanting with a Bible, Mr. Glentower? Getting religion in your old age? I've had to fetch you my own, or that is my old mother's, not to say I'm not respectable C. of E., but I don't get to church all so often——"

"Yes, thanks very much," said Glentower, and took the Bible and shut the door on him.

Psalms, Psalms—he leafed through it impatiently, before it occurred to him that there might be a table of contents; there was; he found the page, hunted on from there for Psalm 31, and found it.

In thee, O Lord, do I put my trust; let me never be ashamed: deliver me in thy righteousness.

Bow down thine ear to me; deliver me speedily: be thou my strong rock, for an house of defence to save me.

For thou art my rock and my fortress; therefore for thy name's sake lead me, and guide me.

Pull me out of the net that they have laid privily for me: for thou art my strength.

Into thine hand I commit my spirit: thou hast redeemed me, O Lord God of truth.

I have hated them that regard lying vanities: but I trust in the Lord.

I will be glad and rejoice in thy mercy: for thou hast considered my trouble; thou hast known my soul in adversities;

And hast not shut me up into the hand of the enemy: thou hast set my feet in a large room.

Have mercy upon me, O Lord, for I am in trouble: mine eye is consumed with grief, yea, my soul and my belly.

For my life is spent with grief——

He stopped there, skimming over the rest. *The net that they have laid. Deliver me. I am in trouble.*

But, God, God, how and where? What could——

The postmark was plain as print on that card. Welshpool. The other —the stamp had slipped, or there'd been too much ink on it—it was only a blurred black mark, indecipherable.

Welshpool.

He thrust both cards into his breast pocket, began feverishly throwing his clothes in any order into his bag; interrupted himself to shout for Burley out the door. By the time the man came in he was ready to leave.

"What do I owe you? I'm leaving. Oh, hell, don't bother to reckon it —here, this should cover it——" He found a couple of bills and ran past for the stair, hardly conscious of the weight of his bag.

The car park where he'd left the Humber was only round the corner. He thrust another bill at the attendant, tossed his bag into the boot and switched on almost in one motion. He had just enough common sense left to look at the gauge and see he'd better fill the tank before he got on the road.

"Now what d'you suppose is up with Mr. Glentower?" wondered Burley, rubbing his jaw in perplexity. "Ordinarily he's a nice quiet gentleman. Especially the last few years since he's settled down like. I do remember when he was what they call an undergraduate up at Cambridge, he used bring his young pals down, a few times, and there'd be —um—pranks as you'd say. Harmless, o' course. An' then again, blood will out. The Glentowers is nice steady-as-you-please folk most o' the time, but you don't want to get across 'em, any road."

"He fair startled the wits out o' me," said the girl. "Rushing in like a crazy man, an' all after nought but a liddle postcard. An' shoutin' out like that for a Bible——"

"Very queer," said Burley, "about the Bible. The Glentowers never was much in the way o' religious. Honest enough folk, an' gentlefolk, o' course. But in their own way. There's some as do say the family goes back to old Owen Glentower and his kin as was kings about here 'way back so I understand, and that might be. It's a fact—his dad was the same—mild as milk mostly, but you get across him some way, well! And stubborn—couldn't turn him for love nor coin."

"Startled the wits out o' me, he did. Hardly know if I'm on my head or heels yet, Mr. Burley, I give you my word."

"Ah, well," said Mr. Burley, "he's a writer, you know, Gracie. Besides bein' a Glentower. Writers, you just never know what they'll be up to, poor things."

FIFTEEN

The inspector of police sighed and refolded his plump hands the opposite way round. "I'm bound to say, sir, I don't think there's anything in it, and I've been in the force thirty years and ought to know. If you want my opinion, there's a perfectly natural explanation of everything you've told me."

"But this card—are you going to tell me it isn't blood? It——"

"No, sir, I don't think it is."

"Have it analyzed, damn it——"

"Oh, I don't think we need go so far as that," said the inspector. "I see this has got you disturbed, sir, and you think something's wrong, but you haven't really much to go on, have you? These postcards—well," he cocked his sandy bullet head at them, "you've reached quite a ways to make out your secret message on this one, and I've told you my opinion of the other."

"A natural——Or a joke, you said! Who in God's name would——"

"Oh, people do these things. I grant you it's a—um—primitive sense of humor, but——"

"She's not like——"

"Now just think about it, sir," said the inspector patiently. "You say this little red mess here is blood, and you make out that somebody's tried to write *Help* in it—though I'm blessed if *I* can see it. But whoever sent this card had a pen and ink to write the address plain enough. If they wanted to write *Help* or anything else, why not use the pen? It doesn't make sense, sir."

"Maybe the pen went dry," said Glentower, and it sounded foolish even to himself.

"And maybe whoever it was—all right, it's the young lady's writing, you say—maybe she decided not to send it, and some kids found it where she threw it away, or it got posted by mistake. Maybe she upset her nail varnish on it——"

"She doesn't wear red nail polish."

"Excuse me, sir, how well did you say you knew Miss Carroll?"

Glentower sighed and raised his head. He'd had time to think on the way here to Welshpool, and the inspector hadn't said anything he hadn't expected. "I know," he said. "I know exactly what you're thinking, and going to say. I met her by chance about five o'clock in the afternoon a week ago yesterday, and I spent the evening with her and had breakfast with her next morning. That's all. You're going to tell me she had—second thoughts—about meeting me in Newcastle, and sent that card to get out of it. So I ask you if that's the message a—a respectable girl would write to a man she'd known just a few hours, and you say to me——"

"Well, yes, sir, she's American, you said." The inspector coughed. "They're apt to be a bit free and easy in manner, you know."

"And you think I'm woolgathering to find any reference to the Thirty-first Psalm——"

"Well, I do, sir. You've reached for that one. Excuse me, sir, but just what do you think might have happened to Miss Carroll?"

"I don't know, damn it—how should I know? I——"

"Exactly," said the inspector. "Now, if she *was* in some trouble and could get this mesage out to you—and mind you, I'd think it far more likely that she'd be trying to get in touch with the local police or the American Ambassador!—she'd surely have had sense enough to try to tell you where she was and what trouble she was in? This just says nothing at all," and he flicked the cards on his desk.

"Suppose she was prevented from writing anything specific—that that card was read by—by some people holding her——"

"One of these sinister gangs like Mr. Edgar Wallace used to write about, perhaps?" The inspector was amused and gallantly tried not to show it. "For why, Mr. Glentower? For ransom, or because she's the long-lost heiress to a fortune, or knows some secret about the chief villain? This is real life, sir. These things don't happen. The young lady was a free agent when you met her, not worried or upset about anything, not running away from anything, just a young lady having a good time on a long holiday—yes? She had plenty of money and a new car. Just so. She's sent you this postcard postponing your meeting, and the writing looks quite normal, though I don't, of course, know what her usual writing looks like. Do you?"

Glentower shook his head. "That's the first time I've seen it."

"Well, there you are. It's all perfectly straightforward. Now we know the young lady wasn't staying anywhere in Welshpool when that card was posted, because you persuaded me to have that checked before I—um—heard the details of this business. So she was passing through, in whatever direction, and just happened to post the card here. As for the second card, sir, well, we can't make anything out of the postmark, but I'll give you my considered opinion for what it's worth. I think she started to write out the same message to you, more or less, on that card, and then it got spoiled—as we see—either her nail varnish or red ink got spilled on it. And so she left it, say, on a post-office counter or in the wastebasket of some room where she was staying. And some well-meaning idiot, or a dumb maid, spotted it and posted it. Quite a few methodical people address and stamp a postcard or envelope before writing the message, you know—I do myself," said the inspector comfortably.

"Yes, I see. In other words, you think I'm an overimaginative fool," said Glentower.

"I didn't say that, sir. I see you believe there's something really wrong—but if you'll think about it for a minute, I'm sure you're bound to admit——"

"No," said Glentower. He got up, picked the cards off the desk and put them back in his pocket. "I know your explanation could be right. I know it's—the logical view. The thing most *likely* to have happened. But I don't believe it. And I can't give you any nice solid evidence to make you believe *me*. It's all—nuances. She doesn't color her nails," he said vaguely. "Is there red ink on post-office counters? I've never seen any. She wasn't planning to come up into Montgomeryshire at all. She's American, yes, but she wouldn't naturally have used those phrases to me. And, God damn it, that *is* blood!"

"Excuse me for asking, sir—you see any service?"

Glentower put a hand to his head, which was still aching. "Occupation duty—after the war. Germany. Not action, if that's what you mean. But it doesn't need a battle-scarred veteran to identify blood! If you'd——"

"Now I'm sure you take my point, sir. We're here to help the public and I don't want to give you the idea that public complaint and information doesn't get acted on. But there's no evidence here of anything remotely wrong. Foreigners—*and* our own citizens—can get into trouble driving around strange territory, certainly. But the time's gone by, Mr. Glentower—if there ever was such a time—they get into the kind of trouble that involves being abducted and—er—tortured, or any such wild nonsense. If you'll forgive me, sir——"

"Don't bother to say it again," said Glentower bitterly. "The young lady wasn't as much impressed with me, and has brushed me off, and I'm making up fantastic stories to get out of admitting it to myself. You said that before. You should have been a psychiatrist, inspector. All right, I'll go away quietly and stop bothering you. Thanks at least for checking all the hostels."

He came out of the police station seething, but not as hotly as he had an hour before. It was ninety miles from Newcastle up to Welshpool; he'd made it in something under an hour and a half, but that had been time to do a lot of thinking. Everything the inspector had said he'd thought out for himself before. Nightmarishly, he had doubted: was he building this all out of nothing? Just to bolster up his vanity, that she *had* meant to meet him? He smiled twistedly. To say nothing but force would keep a girl away!

—And clung, every time the doubt came, to the little nuances that told him the first estimate was the right one. Had to be.

How many ordinary brief messages, scrawled down hastily, would yield a reference to a part of the Bible? Just at random? It was like that old one about setting a bunch of chimpanzees at typewriters to reproduce Shakespeare. . . . No statistics available.

Just what, asked the inspector, did he think had happened to the young lady? Well, what? In this peaceful rural countryside, in this well-protected civilized day and age?

He ought to have some theory to work on. Well, consider the possibles, keeping what he thought was evidence in mind. She'd been allowed to write that card, to put him off—or—the appalling possibility suddenly occurred to him—forced to write it, as an excuse for not meeting him. They had known about that, and—feared he'd come hunting her? He couldn't know where. Without the card, he might have inquired about road accidents, but he'd have been helpless to follow her up further. . . . Never mind. She was being confined somewhere, and that message was read by whoever held her, that was why it could not be more specific.

Confined. Held. It was all very thin. Pure Edgar Wallace, just as the inspector had said . . . damn him.

Glentower looked at his watch; it was after four o'clock. He was not sure what to do or where to go, but he thought he'd better have a meal. He walked up to the center of town from the police station and found a café, went in and ordered at random. It was too early for dinner, but the girl doubtfully promised eggs.

All right. Think. There *were* criminals all about; and damn Edgar Wallace, even some gangs. That gang the papers had been voluble about lately, a ring of car thieves. Say some crowd like that had made an attempt on her car, and she'd inadvertently learned something about——

Well, all right. How wild could you get? He didn't write detective stories; he didn't know if the run-of-the-mill mystery plot was far-fetched or not, where it concerned real-life crime statistics. Never mind *what* had happened. What was he going to do about it?

And—wasn't this almost of first importance—where had it happened and when?

He ate eggs and toast absently, not knowing what he was eating, and drank very strong overboiled black tea.

It came to him that he'd have to backtrack her, that was the only chance. Go where he knew she'd been, and follow on from there. People would have noticed that new bright-red Jaguar, and a pretty American girl in it, wherever she stopped.

She had been going to Llandaffy up north in Cardigan, to stay with this old woman, the mother of the man she'd been engaged to. She hadn't meant to stay long: a couple of days. Say to last Monday. But they'd know there where she'd meant to go next. So, go and ask.

And hurry. A sense of urgency filled him; this would be a tedious and probably long job, starting on her trail of four or five days back. The second card had been posted yesterday, *but when had she addressed it?* Had it been Pat who tried to write that one word in blood, or someone else? Was she—able to do that now?

Never mind what fantastic conclusions all this suggested, what incredible shades from every blood-and-thunder thriller ever written it conjured up. Follow it up and find out for sure.

He paid for his meal. He felt better, with definite purpose directing him. He went back to his car, rummaged in the pocket for maps, found the right one. He was northeast of the Cardigan border here, it was barely a forty-mile run as the crow flies but he'd have to go roundabout a bit to keep on even a secondary road. Call it fifty-five miles.

He got the tank filled and started off.

"Righteous and virtuous acceptance of the laws of God," said the old woman in a rapid gabble. It seemed to Pat that she had repeated that, almost meaninglessly, several times.

She turned her head on the pillow and looked at Mrs. Trefoile. The other woman was looking down at her: slowly Pat realized how she had changed in seven days. Not the fussy little aged Queen Victoria any longer. Her gray hair had partly escaped from its bun to straggle in wild wisps about her white face; she wore the same black gown, but it was stained with food droppings where her hand shook and she did not notice, or care. There was a convulsive involuntary tic at one corner of her crumpled little mouth.

Once yesterday she had done this, thought Pat with no particular feeling. Suddenly lost the meaning of what she was saying, and gone on mouthing one phrase over and over. The pale eyes fixed and staring, and the little tic distorting her words.

"Righteous-and-virtuous-acceptance-of-the-laws-of-God," said Mrs. Trefoile loudly and rapidly, and raised a shaking hand to wipe her mouth. "You have—we must—let the blood flow, let the blood flow. You must have pain, that is an excellent way." Pat did not stir as the hand came out to pull open her dress.

She knew that her temperature must be above normal, if only a degree or so; she was uncomfortably warm and felt frighteningly weak. Her leg throbbed with pain. When they went away, she must get up and bathe it again in the brandy or it would get infected. Like the wound in her shoulder, it would get infected.

She moved her head again, trying to shut her ears to the voice, to see whether they had taken the clothes away. . . . Yes, gone. Taken—where? Like the slashed and torn relics of all her own clothes—burned, or what had been done with them? Because there must always be one more hope, faint curiosity and speculation stirred in her mind. Was there some system of rubbish collection in a rural village like this? Would they unthinkingly put those things in with household refuse, if so? And someone—someone perhaps noticing——

"—Evil. Always so active and ever-present and cunning. I have fought it, I will never cease to——The eternal enemy to be fought——"

She is not talking *to* me any more, thought Pat; she is talking about me. It's only a pretense. In seven days she's gone right over the line; before that she was mad, but it was covered up, she could—hold the pose—of just eccentricity. I've driven her really mad. Just by being here.

She knew the other woman, Anna, was there but did not look at her. She was saving all her strength for when she should be alone.

And it came; they had gone. In a moment Pat got stiffly off the bed. She limped across to the desk, got out the newly opened second bottle of brandy. There was fresh, cool air coming in now from the shattered window. Since last night—last night: last night when she had almost done it, almost got away. . . .

It was the clothes she had suddenly thought of, last night, in the middle of listening to the Book of Esther. All Julian Trefoile's clothes there in the chest: trousers and jackets. If they could be knotted securely together, sleeves to trouser legs——? Impatient to try, her heart beating with excited hope, she thought she'd never be left alone. And she knew better now than to leave the light on. She had got them all out of the chest and separated trousers from jackets, ready, where she knew where they were by feel, and switched off the light, and set to work. It felt like good stout material, strong; she worked patiently, difficult as it was to make such thick awkward knots, pulling them as tight as her strength let her. She had no way of gauging what length she achieved; she just went on until she'd used every piece. It alarmed her to find how much strength she'd lost even in a week; she had to rest before she could begin making fast one end of her clumsy makeshift escape rope to the leg of the desk. She tested it and it held firm. Whether it would hold under her full weight—well, that was something she'd find out.

She stood up, feeling her heart thud. She *would* get away this time, she would make it! But wait now, before she started, to get her breath back and all the strength she had—for once down, she'd have to run, and run a long way: all down that long curving drive to the gates, and please God they'd be open or pursuit wouldn't be so close that she couldn't open them in time—and on to the village.

Now.

She groped for the smallest chair in the dark room. The windows were two pale rectangles of lesser dimness; she thought the moon was rising. She drove the chair savagely through the right-hand one, again and again, knocking out as much of the pane as possible. Bent and picked up her awkward rope, tossed it out. She'd always been nervous about heights, but she scarcely thought of the drop below, enough to break bones if not to kill. And she'd never been athletically inclined, and if she'd stopped to think she'd not have had the least idea of how to climb backward out of a window and slide down a rope. But now, after that hideous racket the breaking glass had made, she had to hurry—

hurry! She never knew afterward how she'd done it, but somehow she was half out of the window, her back to the drop. Clutching desperately at the rope—rough stout cloth under her hands——

And just as her weight came on it, she saw—too late—below, the little rectangle of light shining out from an uncurtained window under this one.

Too late. Hurry. She hung swaying, her stomach hollow like going up in an elevator, and slid bumpily downward. She never knew how far, before the rope gave—the jagged edges of glass above cutting it, or a knot pulling loose—and she fell. She fell hard, on one knee and shoulder, sidewise so that she slid along the crazy paving a little way of her own momentum. But she was out—away—now get up and run! She tried to get to her feet, feeling sharp exquisite pain in her knee—heard a door open and slam quite near—but she was up; and then the man had her.

She fought him desperately, but she had not much strength left to call on. She tried to scream—at night, everything quiet, *could* she be heard in the village?—or someone coming home late along the road——His big hand over her mouth, smelling of tobacco and grass—and he was lifting her, carrying her back in——

Pat never remembered fainting in her life, but she must have then. When her mind came back to her, she was alone, back in the room again; the makeshift rope still hung out the window, but when—a long time later—she examined it, she saw that it had pulled apart only a foot or two below the outside sill. The night air coming in through the broken pane was cold.

She could walk, so she hadn't broken anything. Taking inventory in the bathroom, she found a deep, bloody, painful gash and pavement burn where she had slid, on her right knee and down to the calf; the knee felt wrenched and sore. Another deep bloody scrape along her right arm down from the shoulder. Various bruises; her whole body felt bruised; and a number of cuts, not felt at the time, from the edge of the window as she went through.

Maybe lucky? she had thought numbly. If I'd broken an ankle or an arm—they'd never get a doctor in, of course—just let it go. . . .

Today she had wakened stiff and sore all over. And the wound in her shoulder had got infected after all, as she'd feared; it looked larger, and had an ominous dirty yellow center, with the skin an angry red all round it. When the ragged nails had dug into it this morning, yellow pus had flowed out with the blood.

This morning, this morning . . . The old woman right over the edge now, often not even coherent; little pretense of her former preaching and pleading at a confirmed sinner—no—as if she'd forgotten how and why she acquired this victim, clearly realized only that there *was* a victim, for her twisted pleasure. . . .

The sun was going down now. On Friday. I must remember and keep track of the days, she thought. Friday. Just a week ago today I came here—a week and a few hours ago. Impossible, only a week. A week—quite a short period of time, and the time I have been here——

She took the bottle of brandy into the bathroom. It was fire and agony on her shoulder, on her leg, on her arm, and the alcohol hadn't been enough to halt infection in the shoulder, but it was automatic reaction to use it now. The opened and reopened wound was oozing pus and blood, slow and ugly. If only she had something to bandage it, keep it covered—even a clean handkerchief——

Sitting on the stool, she drank out of the bottle. And laughed weakly to herself. Once she'd thought it—things get too bad, I can always get drunk—but she couldn't even do that. She didn't dare. They'd know—she might be noisy, she didn't know how she *would* act, she'd never been drunk—and they'd find it, and take it away. It was really very funny, that she couldn't even get drunk on poor Mr. Trefoile's pathetic cache of liquor.

Once she started she couldn't stop laughing. Hysterics—nonsense, stop it at once—disgraceful, weak——She put her hands over her mouth, staggered up to reach the bowl and splash her face with cold water.

It was only a brief loss of control, but it frightened her. She took another swallow of brandy and went back to the desk to hide the bottle away. The chill dusk air from the window cleared her head further.

From these windows on the second floor she could just catch a glimpse through the trees of an occasional light in the village of Abervy—what?—a half-mile, more, away. A half-mile direct, perhaps, but longer by the drive and the road. There was a spurious kind of companionship about the little points of light, and at the same time they were maddening. Burning away there, lighting a family supper or a woman's knitting or a man's newspaper. People, snug in their homes, going about their ordinary daily affairs, and never suspecting—never dreaming——

SIXTEEN

Glentower dropped downhill into the village of Llandaffy at just on a quarter to six; you could make good time on these lonely North Wales roads where there was seldom much traffic. He thought Llandaffy was the most godforsaken hole he'd ever come across, but that couldn't matter less. She'd been here, and someone here knew—must know—where she'd been going when she left.

It was awkward that he didn't know the woman's name; she hadn't mentioned it. But he knew enough of the circumstances, surely, to identify her.

He parked the Humber a door down from the inn and went in, to a subdued mutter of talk and a smell of ale and feeble electric light. The man behind the bar was a little bantam of a fellow with bright-red hair. There were only three other men in the one public room. Every eye went to him as he came in; strangers would be a rarity here.

Two men at one table were talking Welsh; the barman and his third customer had been using the same tongue, and the former broke off to ask Glentower in English what he might serve him.

"Whisky, please, straight. And perhaps you can give me some information. I'm looking for a lady who lives here, or near here, and I don't know her name, but she's a widow, and she had one son in the R.A.F. who was killed in America last year." Sufficiently unusual circumstances that any resident should be able to tell him the name at once.

Instead there was silence. "Indeed?" said the barman. "I can't call to mind any like that in Llandaffy. Would you be sure you've the right place, sir?"

"Yes, I'm sure. There must be."

The barman poured his whisky. "Well, now. A widow lady. And you don't know her name. That's very strange indeed." He looked at Glentower obliquely.

"There's nothing strange about it. I—have an appointment with someone who came here to stay with this woman—I don't know her myself." Glentower shoved over a ten-shilling note.

"A widow lady," said the barman dreamily, taking it, "with a son in the R.A.F. There'll be a-many of those even just roundabout North Wales." He opened a cash drawer leisurely and produced a shilling and sixpence change.

Glentower was annoyed; and for the first time in his life he needn't worry about money, but that got to be a habit, especially with a Welshman. "What is this, gold bond twenty-year-old imported back from Canada? It doesn't taste it. I bought a bottle of Scotch last night for thirty shillings."

"Likely cut stuff," said the barman. "I will show you the bottle, sir."

"Never mind. Someone must know this woman, I gather she's lived here some time. If you'd——"

One of the men behind him said in Welsh, "Ask me, I'd say the man's had as much as is good for him already. Looking for a widow he is and not knowing her name."

"Better a widow than a wife," said his companion reasonably.

These little secret far-flung villages, still suspicious of the outlander and the Englishman. He should have remembered that and made a more leisurely approach. Glentower swung round and tossed off the rest of the whisky. He said in Welsh, "Don't miscall me, my son." He hadn't used the language in a long time; it came awkward to his tongue at first. "The first drink today, barring an English gin in Newcastle."

Nobody was at all abashed. "Then you've had a dry day," said the barman.

"And a bad one otherwise. It isn't any choice of mine to come up into Cardigan where they rook a Carmarthen man as soon as look at him—but I'll lay you'd not have tried to rook me so far unless you thought I was English."

"Fourpence in the shilling only," said the barman imperturbably, and opened the drawer and handed him another shilling and sixpence.

"Take shame, Garryd," said another man. "And the regular landlord away too. The gentleman is of our own. Sit down, sir. Now how could we help you?"

Glentower said, "The same all round then, on me, and have one yourself," and sat down at the table. "This woman, I'd think it wasn't a cottage, but a fairly big house. She must be known here, my—friend was coming to visit her. Her son—his name was Stephen——" He'd just remembered that. It was a very damned odd thing, but not once up to now had he thought about Stephen. What kind of man he'd been, what he'd looked like—that man she had presumably loved, been going to marry—who had kissed her, held her. A dead man. He wasn't jealous of a dead man. She had said, "I've—you know—got over it." "He was killed on some sort of experimental flight from an American base, a year ago."

They both shook their heads at him. The third customer came up and thanked him politely for the drink. "There's no one like that in Llandaffy. You'll have the wrong place, sir, very likely. It's maybe Llandaff you want."

"Damn it, I know it's Llandaffy. She was coming here, my—this friend of mine, I mean. She said so."

They went on saying no. Glentower felt blank dismay; and all the while that sense of urgency kept pushing at him. It hadn't occurred to him that there'd be any difficulty about finding this woman; just ask, to learn the name. Damn it, she *had* said Llandaffy. He remembered distinctly, because they'd talked about the language at one point and he'd laughed at her surprise that the *Ll* wasn't pronounced that way at all but like *Sht,* and how different names sounded pronounced in the Welsh —*he'd* said Llandaffy, and other names. He hadn't got it confused? He was sure he hadn't.

"It'll be Llandaff or Llandyllid you want, sir. There's a widow or so here, and a couple of sons in the R.A.F. too, but all alive and well, saving poor Dave Jones and *that* were in the Battle o' Britain as they call it. Nobody just like her you're looking for in Llandaffy."

Hell, had he got it confused? He wasn't sure now; they had made him unsure. Llandaff, Llandyllid? Hell.

He had driven a hundred and forty miles and had an unpleasant, annoying session with that police inspector in the last six hours; he realized that he was tired and hungry—the meal in Welshpool had been meager. He asked if the landlord could give him a scratch dinner. "Anything'll do."

"I reckon, sir. A bit later, or now? If you're figuring to go on tonight ——It's a fair eighty miles to Llandaff, we could put you up the night. The regular landlord's away, up to Merioneth with they sheep, but——"

"No. Yes. No——I'll go on, I'm in a hurry. I must go on tonight."

"I'll see what I can do, sir."

The talk turned to desultory village matters; innately courteous like all countrymen, they would not ask about his business that brought him among them. Glentower's cigarettes were shared out and he was thanked. He sat smoking nervously; presently the barman brought him a plate of cold beef, half a fresh loaf of home-baked bread, and the inevitable watery boiled potatoes. "There's a pudding made yesterday, if you should want it after."

"This is all right, thanks." He ate and listened to slow speculation as to how Daffyd would do with they sheep—the flock could be better this year. . . . It did begin to look that Elsie Morgan'd catch young Ivor Jones at last, by what Andy was telling. . . . A great pity it was about the Reverend, poor chap, flat on his back with what they called this virus. Aye, but Mary Tresswell was a good nurse, she'd have him fighting-fit in no time. You couldn't keep the Reverend down, fat as he was—the gallant old cock (this with affection). Indeed Llandaffy was lucky in him, a reasonable sort of minister not forever preaching at folk, and him appreciating a drink or a pretty girl as much as any man.

A general chuckle. "Isn't that so, now. I mind how gallant the old chap behaved to that pretty American lass last week. You was here, Garryd, you'll——"

"What's that?" exclaimed Glentower excitedly. "An American girl? When? Where did she go from here, d'you know? That's—it's an American girl I'm—she's the one I'm looking for, really, who was going to stay with this woman. What——"

"Oh, indeed? Well, it was Daffyd and the Reverend talked with her mostly—the Reverend took her off to his house for lunch before she started on. A lovely new red Jaguar motor she had."

"Yes, that's—go on, what——?"

The barman was summoned to tell what he could. "The young lady, she was looking for a Mrs. Something as she thought lived here—now I think, much the same as you, sir—only she didn't say 'twas a widow and so on. I misremember the name. It was Daffyd thought to ask Morgan the Post about any misdirected letters he might've sent back, see you, and in the end they got it straightened out where it was likely the young lady'd find the right house. . . . I couldn't say, I don't remember the name at all."

"The minister will, or——"

"I doubt whether you could see Mr. Fallow, poor chap—I hear from Mrs. Tresswell he's been delirious—a bad case of this virus thing. And

Daffyd being away—but Morgan the Post might remember, so he might."

"Where does he live?" Glentower abandoned the meal and sprang up. "I must see him, find out——"

"It'll be an important matter, I see," said the barman.

"Yes, I think—very important. I must see him at once."

"Take it easy and finish your dinner, man," said one of the others, friendly. "I'll slip up the road and fetch him, he'll be here in five minutes and we'll see does he recall the name of the place. I've no doubt he will, for he's not the brainiest fellow in Cardigan, but once he hears a thing he never forgets it. He'll be able to tell you where your young lady went."

"There now," said Mrs. Evans, "I said you'd get it back safe, an' you going round with a face long as a preacher's list o' sins sayin' some'un thieved it. Say thank you to Mr. Andrews for fetchin' it to you, now."

Garry did so enthusiastically, clutching his compass and examining it surreptitiously for damage.

The choirmaster smoothed back his long hair. He was a London import of the rector's, he disliked this dreary rural place intensely and was only beginning to suspect that the vague airy promises of a respectable wage would not materialize. "Oh, er, quite all right. I wouldn't have kept it so long, I believe it was Monday I found it—but I had no idea who it might belong to—it was only when I happened to mention it just now——"

"That's O.K., sir, thanks a lot!"

"Anna."

She looked up; it wasn't often he called her in her right name like that, and he sounded fretted about something. "Well?"

"The girl hurt any by that business last night?"

"I dunno, didn't ask." She looked back to her mending.

"Didn't *ask!*" he said. "That's a Christian way to go on. She didn't look so good to me, look I had at her just bringin' her in. She didn't get that knock on the head fallin' last night, it was a day or so old by the color. Anna, girl—what's the old woman up to with her?"

"I—dunno, really, Harry. Jus' preachin', like I said, I guess."

"Don't try t' put me off on that. Preachin' don't knock no 'un on the head. You're there ever' time *she* goes in, you said that. Tell me straight, now—she's tormentin' the girl some?"

"She—well—some," she nodded reluctantly, driven to admitting it.

"I don't like that," he said in a troubled voice. "Not right, you can't get round it."

"Oh, trust *you* all right—sorry for a pretty girl—what's the odds, anyway? Nothin' to us, she ain't——"

"You can bark at me, 'n' twist around 'n' try make excuses all you want, you know 'tisn't right either. Don't be a fool, my girl. The old bitch is gettin' crazier by the day, think I can't see it plain as you? An' doin' the girl mischief out o' her craziness. Sometimes—it don't take much mischief to—to do a thing for good 'n' all. If you know what I mean."

"Oh, don't take *on* about it!" she said crossly. "What can *we* do, any road? I say anything, do anything, she's on us like a knife—an' you back in t' Moor——"

"That's maybe better nor you in Holloway!" he said brutally, bluntly. "I never did like the whole crazy notion, but it's gone from bad to worse with this. Ain't you got sense t' see it? It's like I said, some'un's bound t' find out soon or late—she'll get away like she near did last night, or—what I'd be afeared of—the old woman'll go—a mite far. Too far. An' there we are with a body. God, do *I* know how easy it is—find y'rself with a body! Bodies you can't hide up. An' ever'thing comin' out, you'd be right up in the dock alongside her, when you've gone 'n' stood by 'n' jus' watched her tormentin'——"

"Oh, shut *up* about it!" Anna put her hands to her face. It just made the picture a little clearer, what he said. She'd gone to his trial, heard it all. Everybody acting so awful polite, and bowing and scraping, and never using a little word where a big one 'd do, but the end of it——Of course she knew—all that. There'd been times, just for a flash like, she'd felt terrible ashamed of the things she'd done to the girl. But every time, quick and loud, her mind rushed in to say, You *had* to, she was fighting you—she was going to get away, and that'd mean everybody'd know, and Harry'd get taken again—you had to! But all the time she knew she'd—halfway, more than halfway—liked doing it, because—because——

"Liddle tart, all her fine clothes 'n' scent 'n'——Never worked a day in her life, likely—lookin' down her nose at folk like us——" The defiance was automatic.

"What's that got t' do with it? The law's the law. I don't know, Anna—I don't know. We got to figure some way, try to make a break. . . . She's crazier by the minute, nearly. You seen it too. It could be—it jus' could be—she'd be too crazy to tell anything, now—make any listen to her. If we jus' took that car 'n' made a run for it, like I said——"

"No," whispered Anna. "She would. She's not all so crazy—not yet, Harry. She talked real sharp and straight to me about the greens not bein' fresh tonight."

For a while there was silence in the big kitchen. She sat looking listlessly down at the sewing in her lap; he got up to fill his pipe from the tobacco jar on the mantel. Presently he said, "Funny—them old clothes still bein' there."

"You know all the stories. I heard about that right when—when it happened. 'Twas the year I left home 'n' went to Lunnon, turned seventeen I was. Nobody talked about nothin' else for months. Ellen Parr as married Ted Paget, she was housemaid there then, an' she told—how nothin' was took out o' the room but the big mirror, *she* wouldn't abide such under the roof even in a room locked up—an' t' door locked an' sealed up fast."

"I've heard. Poor bastard."

"You would say such, him bein' another man."

"Reckon he had excuse for aught he done," said the man mildly. "What'd you do with 'em?"

"They're wrapped up in paper in t' pantry—I thought you could put 'em down in y'r compost heap, like I did——Or maybe nex' time you burn leaves 'n' such——"

He grunted, and then looked at her. "Like you did what?"

"I dunno what you mean. Nothin'. Anyways, get rid of 'em."

"Some're still good, looked like. 'Bout my size, I reckon. It seem like a waste."

"You'd never dare," she said dully.

"By God, I'd dare most anything, get us safe out o' this mess!" he said violently. "An' not only that—it's you, my girl—you've changed, some way. You're not like y'r old self——"

"Well, who *would* be? Stop talkin' about it, Harry! There's nought we can do, so why waste breath?" She took up her sewing again with sudden determined vigor and he fell silent, watching her uneasily.

It was only a thirty-mile run down to the village of Abervy, Morgan the Post told Glentower; he should make it inside an hour. He would have, and been there by eight o'clock, but first he had a puncture and then he got off the road. He was tired—starting out with the hangover this morning, his various frustrations and anxieties coupled with the long drive had resulted in another blinding headache. He had the puncture about ten miles out of Llandaffy, and he was not much good at that kind of thing; he made a slow, awkward job of getting the spare on. A fine steady drizzle had started to come down; he was wet and very tired when he got back into the car, and it was nearly eight o'clock.

Which was probably how he got off on the local track; the main road twisting, his eyes tired straining ahead, and the gray drizzle—he found the tires bumping over earth, and said to himself, A detour, they're resurfacing, and went on. Then the headlamps began to show him deep-grooved cart tracks, and finally the track narrowed down to a footpath and he braked and swore. He had no idea how far off the road he'd come; and he knew how easy it was to get hopelessly lost in these great lonely bare sweeps of country.

With difficulty he turned the car and went back; wherever the track curved he slowed, peering to each side for the road. In this gently undulating, moor-bare country the County Council didn't trouble for white posts to mark the roadside. He made several false casts, once found himself bumping over open moor.

When he got back on the road at last, it turned out not to be the one he'd been on; the next signpost made no mention of Abervy, and though it seemed a waste of time he did the sensible thing and went on to the next village to ask directions. He was almost twenty miles out of his way by then, and the rain falling harder.

It was twenty minutes to ten when he drove into a village he thought was Abervy. There was a lighted inn halfway up the high street: The Dog and Gun. He parked and went in.

SEVENTEEN

"Good evening, sir. Just time for a quick one before closing time, eh? Whisky, yes, sir . . . This is Abervy, indeed."

Glentower repeated his description of the widow. The landlord was a florid, not unhandsome man with a head of wavy silver hair; he eyed Glentower with curiosity and speculation and said at once, "That'll be Mrs. Trefoile, sir, at the house called Llandaffy."

"Ah." Morgan the Post hadn't remembered the woman's name, only that it was Tre-something. "Thanks very much." But it was too late, damn it, to go and see her tonight. He couldn't go on tonight anyway, even when he knew which direction to go; no point in it. "Can you put me up tonight?"

"Well, we don't often have visitors, sir, but daresay we can take care of you o'ernight. You'll be wanting to see Mrs. Trefoile, then?"

Of course they'd be curious, a stranger coming out of the blue: but Glentower also registered the fact that visitors to Mrs. Trefoile were an unusual circumstance. Undoubtedly—would she be one of the landholders here, in gentry society, in the old phrase?—the village would have taken note of another visitor. "Yes," he said, sketching a plausible tale rapidly, "I must see her in the morning, but perhaps you could help me too. I'm a lawyer, and I'm trying to locate a young American lady who was staying with Mrs. Trefoile last week. She's on holiday, you see, just driving about, and I don't know where to get in touch with her—I thought Mrs. Trefoile might be able to tell me where she was making for when she left here."

Everyone in earshot looked at him with lively interest. Next him at the bar was a little wiry dark man with a clever ugly face; he said, "Oh, right enough, sir, that young lady was at Mrs. Trefoile's, last Friday-

Sa'd'y it'd be. T' one as was engaged to young Mr. Trefoile an' he killed in a naroplane over in t' States year ago July. We was all a bit curious like to see her, if you understand me, sir—for this 'n' that reason——"

"Indeed," rumbled the landlord. "But none did, her only bein' o'ernight or justabout—exceptin' Tom here's woman——"

"As we've the general shop, see, sir, an' t' young lady stopped nex' morning—the Sa'd'y that'd be—an' bought two postcards. A very nice-lookin' young lady, Gwen said, an' friendly." Some memory put a brief laugh in his little dark eyes.

"Saturday?" said Glentower blankly. "I'd thought—she was planning to stay a few days." Hell, a week ago tomorrow—she could be at the other end of England. No; remember the first card was posted at Welshpool on Wednesday.

"Ar? Well, seems she didn't. She said that to Gwen, time Sa'd'y she was in t' shop. Leavin' that day, she said."

Found it too awkward and difficult, he deduced, and made some excuse to get away. "I see. Well, as I say, Mrs. Trefoile may know where she planned to go from here. She didn't say anything about that to your wife?"

The little man shook his head and retired into his beer. The landlord said in his surprisingly smooth bass rumble, "Beg pardon, sir, I'm John Davies and this here's Tom Evans." Glentower introduced himself. "I seen the young lady myself that very morning. Came by on the way t' church with Mrs. Trefoile, an' that was something out of usual too, I can tell you—Mrs. Trefoile not settin' foot in church a good five year, along o' the quarrel with rector she put up—but that's by the way, you won't be interested in that. Nor I don't reckon as she's been in the village in six-eight months or longer, either—she keeps to herself, shut up in her own house, if you take me——"

Glentower said, "Miss Carroll told me she—Mrs. Trefoile—is rather ——?" He raised an eyebrow.

Both men relaxed and grinned. "Say it twice, sir," said Davies solemnly. "Straighter-laced nor old Queen Victoria as my granddad used talked about. You know the sort. Girl slaps on a little lipstick, she's bound straight for perdition—and all such-like ideas. No odds what she wants t' believe, but folk take it amiss when she tries to make 'em toe the line according, an' that's another idea she's got too, her gentry an' us ignorant peasantry like they say an' we did ought bow an' scrape to her."

A big burly man next to Evans said thoughtfully, "I had words wi' her over Eiluned. Had t' gall she did t' tell me Eiluned was no better 'n she should be, all along o' Mis' Trefoile seein' Jim kiss her behind a hedge—las' time old woman came into the village that were. Now Eiluned 'n' Jim are engaged, 'n' the banns up soon as he's done his service. Tell *me* my girl's no better 'n a tart! I said to her, I says, Mis' Trefoile, you mind your own affairs, I said. I heard this 'n' that, I says, tells me maybe you ain't so pure-perfect your own self."

This was evidently not the first time he'd told the story; there was a concerted murmur of amusement and confirmation, and someone said, "An' then *she* said——"

"*She* said, 'You mind your manners, my man!' But she went white as a sheet all t' same," said the first man in satisfaction.

Glentower wasn't interested in Mrs. Trefoile. "Did any of you see Miss Carroll drive away that morning—which way she went?"

"No, sir, don't reckon. My boy Garry, our last at home an' a handful he is too, he seen her come—about teatime on t' Friday. Ravin' over her fine new car he was. But I reckon when she went on, 'twas t'other way, not through t' village. Way she come, see?"

Davies rapped on the bar after a glance at the clock. "Time! Time, boys! Drink up and go. . . . I'll see a room's fixed up for you, Mr. Glentower. You stayin' in the house, you can buy another drink if you please."

Glentower went out to the car for his bag, and was taken upstairs to a tiny bedroom where a girl was just making up the bed. . . . *Saturday.* Damn, another two days to trace her. He was a fool to have come here; all this time wasted! He should have tried to trace her from Welshpool, casting every road asking if she'd been seen, stopped for petrol . . . Hadn't been thinking straight, to start this far back. He knew she'd been in Welshpool on Wednesday.

Did he? In the middle of unpacking to get at his pajamas, he stopped. Did he? That was only if she had been a free agent. That card had been intended as a blind; this whole fantastic notion hung on that. She'd been compelled to write it, an excuse to him, to put him off. They—whoever they were—would not post it from the place they actually held her?

It all sounded thinner and thinner . . . real life: these things just don't happen . . . pure Edgar Wallace.

Damn it, there *was* something—not right.

Late on the trail, he thought. Six days, seven days. But do what was possible. Tomorrow morning, see the eccentric and difficult Mrs.

Trefoile and ask her—if she knew—where Pat had intended to go from here.

She woke slowly, aware as soon as half-consciousness returned of the lassitude, the reluctance to face another day. The insufficient food, the physical treatment she'd suffered, combined to keep her draggingly low in spirits now. Each time she flogged herself to new hope, trying to make some new plan, it was a little harder.

After a while she forced herself out of bed. It was not as cold this morning, perhaps the summer was coming in at last; but it was still cool this early, and she shivered as the air struck her bare flesh. She took up the wreck of her dress, the cardigan, slipped into her shoes. She got the brandy from the desk, went into the bathroom: largely a futile gesture, applying brandy to the wound in her shoulder—it looked much worse, puffy and red—but perhaps it was helping the deep scrapes on her arm and leg. She washed in cold water, put on her dress and cardigan and had a drink of brandy.

Very bad, drinking first thing she got up, she thought vaguely. But there was quite a calorie count in most liquor, wasn't there? She couldn't remember whether it was carbohydrate or what. Something, anyway.

More of this second bottle of brandy had gone (vainly, perhaps) for external treatment than she'd drunk, but there was only about a teacupful left. Have to open another one today. Wonderful of Mr. Trefoile to leave it there for her; a little spurious comfort, at least. She wondered, not for the first time, what he'd died of, poor man.

But it wouldn't do, sitting here not thinking. Today she'd think of something—today something would happen, and she'd get out——

They took her by surprise; she hadn't expected them for another half-hour—but there was the rattle of the bolt. Pat's heart jumped—the brandy bottle——She tilted it up and swallowed all that was left in three hasty gulps, almost gagging at too much of the fiery stuff at once, and slid the empty bottle under the old-fashioned bathtub as she got up from the stool. She stood in the doorway looking at them, two ugly women she was afraid of, and tried to keep any fear from her eyes.

In a moment she felt the brandy hitting her; in sudden queasy alarm she thought, Too much—on an empty stomach, equivalent of four or five drinks—I'll do something, say something silly. Be careful. But I'm not afraid of them any longer. That's good.

There was something different. Mrs. Trefoile did not carry her little

Bible. No reading today? And the other woman carried no tray. Another fast-day? The hell with them, said the brandy; they'll never hear me begging!

"You know something, Anna?" she said. "This is all going to come to an end sometime, you know—maybe very soon, today or tomorrow—and whatever Hector's wanted for, they'll find him and take him. And they'll take you too—and you'll need a lawyer for your trial, because I don't suppose even you are so crazy as to think Mrs. Trefoile'd pay for *that.* So *I* think you'd be very smart to take my offer of a thousand pounds, don't you? Seeing that I'll get out anyway—or someone come to fetch me out—sooner or later. One way, you've got nothing and are arrested as soon as I get out—the other way, I get out today and you've got a thousand pounds."

Anna stood silent, head down, sullen. "I have prayed," said Mrs. Trefoile suddenly, loudly.

"I'm not surprised," said Pat. She wished she'd had another drink of brandy. "You're good at that." She walked across to the old woman, careful to walk straight. "You're good at everything except taking a little of your own medicine, aren't you?" She struck her a resounding sudden slap, hard as she could. One part of her mind said in civilized horror, An old woman; most of her tingled with joy at giving even a little back.

Mrs. Trefoile's head snapped back under the force of the blow; and then her eyes went quite wild and she lashed out with the hand that held the pistol. Pat thought she heard the crack as it struck her, and knew she was falling; she heard Anna say something in a frightened voice, and then everything went away from her.

When she recovered consciousness, she was lying there on the dusty carpet where she'd fallen. Her head was throbbing savagely; putting a wavering hand to her temple she felt a little crust of caked blood. As her mind began to clear and she remembered, she thought numbly that she'd been lucky . . . the old woman had done nothing else to her, at least—yet. That one moment her eyes had held murder. But she had gone away. Or had Anna, frightened at last, taken her away?

Pat sat up. Such a fool—it was the brandy. Oughtn't to have drunk all that brandy—just to hide it. They never went into the bathroom anyway. Fool.

She got up to her feet unsteadily, staggered into the bathroom, and clumsily bathed her temple until the dried blood was gone and she could feel only the tender bruise.

Fool. What would the woman do now, after this?

She was so hungry that her whole body felt sore, aside from her bruises. Evidently they didn't intend to feed her today. For an unspecified time she sat there huddled on the stool, lax, feeling sorry for herself; the tears kept flowing hot and wet down her face, she kept smearing them away, uncaring how she looked or how stupid and dangerous it was to let herself get so far—demoralized.

At last she made a great effort to force herself up from this black pit of despair. It simply could not happen that in this day and age, wherever or however, anyone could hold an unwilling prisoner in a private house very long. *Something* would happen. A week, a week today. Almost exactly a week ago today she had been walking to the church in the village with Mrs. Trefoile—and thinking, in an hour or two I can escape—buying postcards from gossipy Mrs. Evans at the shop. A week wasn't really very long. Something would——

Postcards. They hadn't been any good at all, either of them. She had known they wouldn't be; all her silly contriving. Alan Glentower had read the first one and been momentarily disappointed and tossed it away. And Joseph must have picked up the second one or it would have been found by Anna or Hector and something said, but he hadn't shown it to anyone—maybe he'd thrown it away by now.

She *must* not let herself feel hopeless. Make another plan, however wild; make herself *believe* something would happen; she'd make something happen, and——

She got up and went out to the bedroom on uncertain feet. Sat down at the desk, because her legs were unsteady, and wrestled with the little bent prongs of the pin-curler to open another bottle. It was false strength and courage, but any kind of strength and courage was her lifeblood here and now. She drank out of the bottle. For a moment her stomach rebelled, and then decided to keep it. She sat, head bent, waiting for the brandy to reach her.

The false warmth and a little new confidence began to flow back into her before the bolt was drawn back and they came in.

Pat got up from the chair and leaned on the desk behind her. She looked first at Anna, and the small spurious new hope leaped higher, for Anna looked frightened.

"I have prayed," said the other woman in a loud rapt voice. And Pat looked at her and saw that she held in her right hand not the little pistol but a long knife. "I have prayed for guidance—God has spoken to me——"

Oh, dear God, thought Pat. She did not move; there was nowhere to run to. And then, in the second of time before the old woman spoke again, a door banged somewhere below and there came the pound of heavy footsteps up the stair, and a man's voice calling, a fist pounding at this door.

"Car comin' up the drive—som'un coming—take care——"

Someone from Outside! Pat whirled, stumbling, for the broken window and got out one scream before Anna was on her. Heard the room door open——She fought clear with the surging strength of desperation, and ran for the door blindly, and came up against the solid rock of the man. In one astonishingly clear glimpse she saw Mrs. Trefoile just standing there motionless, rapt-eyed, knife in hand. It was the other two so instantly understood the need for action.

"We can't let—hold her, don't let——"

Hand over her mouth. She bit, she twisted and squirmed in that hard grasp. Felt herself lifted to the bed. Fought free one second and screamed again, and was caught and held firm——"Got to gag her, no choice," he was panting; queer, queer, all this time and this the first she'd heard Hector speak so close, seen him—taking part—in this. "Anna—quick—your apron, girl, I'll do it, you hold her for God's sake, I'll——"

A brief nightmare glimpse of Anna's face distorted with panic, as she whipped off her apron—folds of ill-smelling cloth in her mouth, about her mouth, and their hard labored breathing over her, holding her jointly as she struggled frantically. Then she was flung over on her side, her wrists caught, and something rigid drawn round and round them together while the woman's hands held her——

And the hands withdrawn. A confusion of sounds and voices. The knocker on the house door below. "Madam——" *"I have heard God's voice——"* "Madam, don't you hear? 'Tis the knocker—some'un—you got t' go down an' act ordinary—madam——" "God, girl, she's—I *tol'* you——My God, what's she up to wi' that knife?" "I don't know, Harry—I said—but we can't let any'un suspicion——"

Suddenly they were all gone. The door slammed, the bolt shot.

A visitor. Someone from Outside. Oh, God, was it—could it be—Alan Glentower, alerted by her secret S.O.S.? She lay here helpless, the apron stuffed into her throat and bound round her jaws, her wrists bound behind her with—was it a man's belt? It felt like it. She struggled against it, desperate, determined—listening in despair, frenzy, agony, to the knocker falling on the house door.

Glentower looked about the room, waiting for its mistress. The drab middle-aged maid who'd admitted him—looking breathless and flurried, probably left something boiling in the kitchen—had been very much what he'd expected; so was the room. Perfect period piece. What they'd said of the woman last night, he couldn't wonder that Pat had stayed only a day.

He'd heard a little more oblique gossip from Davies over breakfast an hour ago. One of these fanatics, religious and otherwise. Money, Davies said; quite a lot of money—"her fambly, you understand, I've heard it said the grandfather was a mine owner and rich as Midas——" but she was mean. Well, one way to hang on to money, and there never seemed to be a happy mean achieved in that, he thought vaguely, between penuriousness and extravagance. . . . And where was she?

He'd settled on nine-thirty as the earliest possible time, but Davies had laughed. "You'll find her up long afore that, sir. Not that the two she's got with her now, that Anna and Hector, go talkin' much, o' course—outlander he is, from Lunnon—Anna was born here but she's a Rhys an' they allus was glum-silent folk—but word gets round. Anna says this 'n' that to her niece, and when Gloria dies they'll need to kill her tongue separate. The old lady's up at crack o' dawn, readin' her Bible an' such."

It was barely nine o'clock now.

He wasn't much interested in Mrs. Trefoile—it was a type, and a dull one; but that was a false premise in a way, for no human person is ever wholly a type, and his interest quickened a little when she came in. Absently, aside from his interest in what she might be able to tell him.

Queen Victoria gone to seed, he thought, eyeing the stained black gown thirty years out of date, the untidy gray hair. She stood just inside the door, and he thought her sight must be poor by the way her eyes stared past him, just in his general direction; she did not ask him to sit down.

"Mrs. Trefoile?"

"Yes—yes. What was it—you wished?" Her voice was thin and breathy.

He told her his plausible story. After his interview with the inspector, he knew how most people would receive the truth. (The truth? Damn it, he had to find out for sure!) Very urgent to get in touch with Miss Carroll; known she was to be staying here; did Mrs. Trefoile know where she had intended to go when she left?

"Miss Carroll," said the woman. "Miss Carroll. You are asking—where she has gone. Miss *Carroll.*"

Rather more than eccentric. A bit off. "Yes, that's right. I understand she left here a week ago today."

"She has left," said Mrs. Trefoile. "Yes. She is gone. She had a motor car—she was alone. So foolish and dangerous—a young woman—traveling alone. I said that at the time, did I not?"

"Did she say anything to you about where she meant to go? Which way did she drive off, north or south?"

"I do not know where she has gone. I do not know where she has gone," said the woman. Yes, rather more than a type; he thought it might not be long before Abervy lost its eccentric widow to the local asylum or a home for seniles and incompetents. He saw her make an effort for surface conventionality, as if dimly aware that she was talking strangely; she made a vague gesture and said, "We are quite out of the world here, of course—I live very quietly, as you see. Only a modest establishment—everything is so very dear these days."

"Perhaps one of your servants would know which direction Miss Carroll took?" But if she'd driven through the village, going south, someone would have seen her, surely.

"Direction? I do not think so. Miss *Carroll,*" she said; and for the first time her eyes met his directly and he felt a little shock for their pale coldness. "You are asking about—I would have her in my house no longer! A very wicked loose young woman, deep in the ways of sin. I have struggled with evil all my life—I know it well! I would not abide her presence—and so I informed her—and she has gone."

"I see," said Glentower. He was rather surprised that Pat had stayed overnight. She had said she wasn't looking forward to this, and her fears had evidently been justified. "There's no more to be said then, thanks very much," and he came toward her for the door.

She did not move aside. "Who are you—asking for—I had not thought——"

"I introduced myself a moment ago—my name's Glentower," he said icily.

"Glentower!" she exclaimed. "The man who—go, get out of my house! Anna! Anna! I will not tolerate——"

"With pleasure," said Glentower grimly, and marched out. The drab maid was coming up in a hurry, from the back premises; she looked frightened. My God, what a woman. And nothing helpful to be got here at all. Why the hell had he taken the trouble to come this far back on

Pat's trail? Had to have a starting point somewhere. . . . There was a man just outside the front door, a gardener—big stocky fellow on his knees over a flower bed. Glentower stopped. "The young lady who was here last week—she left on the Saturday morning——"

"Aye, sir—that's right," muttered the man.

"Did you happen to notice which way she turned from the gates?" He had a ten-shilling note in his hand, suggestively.

The man straightened and looked at him. Not a bad-looking fellow in a broad, oddly Slavic way; maybe a man who'd come down in the world to his present job. "I couldn't say, sir," he said expressionlessly.

Glentower shrugged, pocketed the note, and got into the Humber. As he backed and turned the car, he was conscious of the man's eyes on him.

EIGHTEEN

He went back to the inn, collected his bag and paid his bill, and found the one petrol station. No one there had seen the young American lady or her new red Jaguar. He started south from the village, arguing to himself—even if no one had seen her pass, it might have been the noon hour and most people indoors—she wouldn't have headed north again, where she'd come from the day before. There weren't many petrol stations or secondary roads along here, or villages; but he tried them all, and there were enough to make it slow work. He veered off on every side road and went on until he found somewhere to ask—a house, a filling station, a village. And drew blank, and came back to the main road, and went on again.

It was maddeningly tedious work. By one o'clock he had worked his way down nearly to the Carmarthen border, and got nothing—nothing. Here the road forked and became two main roads, one running east-west—the county town of Cardigan west; Brecknock, Hereford and all England east—and one continuing on south for Carmarthen and the Bristol Channel ports. He had investigated eleven side roads, asked questions of thirty-odd people. He was only twenty miles from Abervy in direct line.

Nobody had seen her.

He stopped at this latest village and had lunch. It was surely odd that *someone* hadn't seen her. In this lonely rural countryside, a new bright-red sports Jaguar would be noticed, a sufficiently rare sight. And wherever she stopped, for food or petrol, she'd be marked as American, and remembered—American tourists didn't often get this far into Wales. Another thing, it was school-holiday time and hordes of small boys would be loose, and if there was one thing boys noticed it was automobiles. He remembered—there was a game about it——"I got a *Rolls Royce* today, that's worth three Wolseleys and four Rileys and *eight* Fords——" collecting the cars you saw pass. Did boys still do that? Maybe not in the real country, where there wouldn't be the chances; but they'd notice cars.

He should have found boys to question, not grownups.

He didn't want the meal; he felt discouraged and—oddly, absurdly—panicky. His mind cried at him like a frightened child, *Where is she?* He felt he was wasting time, fumbling about at the problem ineptly; he could not think, just for the moment, what to do next. Cast back, and find those bright, noticing boys to repeat his questions to, or go on from here?

He got out the postcards to look at again, for the fiftieth time tried to decipher the anonymous black-ink blur of postmark on the second one. It was just a blur. All it said to him was that she had bought it—both cards—somewhere in Cardigan. The Lake of Berwyn. The Teifi Pools. He was a fool; he knew where she'd got the cards, Tom Evans had told him, the general shop in Abervy, last Saturday. And it didn't matter where she'd bought them, of course.

Deliver me speedily . . . an house of defence to save me . . . the net that they have laid privily for me . . . I am in trouble. . . .

He called abruptly for his bill, and went out to the car. Use his mind on it. He got out an ordnance map and studied it. By what Davies and Evans said, she must have got away from Abervy—after going to church with the old woman, God knew why—about eleven o'clock. All right. Call it forty miles or at a push fifty before she stopped for lunch. If she'd gone due south, that would put her somewhere around Kidwelly, even as far as Llanelly, Laugharne, Ammanford. She'd have had to come south from Abervy to the first east-west road, if she meant to turn either way: twenty or thirty miles on, east or west of this point, would put her at Carmarthen town, or over the Pembroke border somewhere, west—and east, over into Brecknock, or southeast, into the Black Mountains, say at Cray.

She'd come from Brecknock. She expected to be in Newcastle—expected to let him guide her around Carmarthen—later on, so she wouldn't have headed there, was that a fair deduction? Expecting to come back to Newcastle Emlyn within a few days, where might she have intended to go? Around the Pembroke coast, perhaps—down from Newport past Fishguard, to Milford Haven—plenty to see. Or southeast through the mountains into Monmouth the other way.

He couldn't sit here wasting time; he must decide which way to go on. Toss a coin or something.

Irrationally, suddenly, he decided on the west. People for some reason were always drawn westward—all the myths put the pagan Blessed Isles west—mysterious human impulse or superstition, he thought he would make a cast that way. Back toward Newcastle and over the Pembroke border, toward the sea.

For the first time, as he switched on, he noticed the sort of day it was. Thunder weather. The air was muggy and there was the indefinable tension—air pressure, wasn't it?—always present before a storm. The sky was dull pewter, dark at the horizon. Something was building up: rain and thunder by tonight.

That probably accounted for the peculiar breathless sense of renewed urgency driving him on.

He turned the Humber in the village street and took the right fork on the main road west.

"God's voice," said Mrs. Trefoile. "I do not know. I do not know. That man—asking. I must be certain—of God's voice speaking to me."

Pat held herself upright in the chair with immense effort. She seemed to be all pain, not bright sharp pain that in some perverted way could be stimulating, but one great dull throb—her head, her knee, her shoulder. The pain, and the hunger, made her a little lightheaded; she clung obstinately to the quite irrational determination not to let the woman see her weakness.

She did not speak; it would be no use at all; Mrs. Trefoile was not hearing what anyone said to her now.

"I am an old woman, it said. He will call me to His throne before He takes you. I cannot keep you safe—it said—for Stephen. I must remember it is all for Stephen—his virgin bride—remain holily pure, as God's laws dictate. Yes. It said—cannot keep you forever—of myself——"

Pat looked at the other woman. Anna, standing rigid there, quite expressionless, but a kind of wild uncertainty in her eyes. "Anna," said Pat softly. "Anna. Do you believe me now? Will you do it now? You can't—you can't——"

"It said—the only way—the right way. She must be kept pure. She must be—taught the truth. With the knife, it said—to make her ugly, so no man forever will look at her, desire her—as—a—woman. I do not know—now. I must be sure. I thought—but *I* must not be made to suffer—God's instrument. I must pray—I must pray. I must be certain."

"Anna!" said Pat.

The other woman looked past her and said nothing; but her eyes moved whitely.

Nothing, nothing, nothing.

Glentower came out of the inn in Newport and stood beside the Humber, lax, uncertain. The inn was starred in all the best-known travel brochures; if she'd got to Newport at teatime, dinnertime, ten to one she'd have stopped there. She hadn't. All along the way, nobody had seen her.

He tried to reckon sums in his head. Say she was getting, what, twenty-five miles to the gallon—less, on a new car?—say the tank had been full at Abervy. She could have got much farther than Newport—Llanelly, Cray, Presteigne, Neyland—any damn place within a hundred miles, before filling up. But she'd have stopped for meals.

Somebody should have seen her, if she'd come this way. God, if it had been an open car!—all the more likely—his lovely Pat, sun shining on her dark-chestnut hair——But what more noticeable could you ask for than a brand-new bright-red sports Jaguar? Somebody——

And nobody had. All right, so she hadn't come west. She'd gone east or southeast, down through Brecknock into Glamorgan, thinking to drive up round the south coast by Barry and Port Talbot and Swansea, leisurely, and over into Pembroke, to come up into Carmarthen from St. David's or somewhere.

He'd have to cast back, that was all.

It was five o'clock. He'd wasted the whole damn day. No. He knew she hadn't come this way, that he knew at least. He'd covered one possibility.

What was happening to her, while he drove about North Wales asking stupid questions?

His head was still aching slightly. He laid a hand on the door of the Humber, but tentatively; he wasn't sure what he meant to do, where he meant to go.

The atmosphere had grown closer, unbearably humid, and the dark line on the horizon had widened. There was breathless expectant tension over the whole world. In an hour, two, three, the rain would break through, and the electrical charges built up would discharge themselves in riotous thunder and lightning. It was nonsense to call man civilized:

in his modern stone cities he felt the forces of nature as deep as the fox and badger burrowed under earth. The tension in the atmosphere (gravitational pressure?) built up tensions in humans. . . .

He could not stand here forever, or until the storm broke, with his hand on the car door.

Glentower got into the car; and in that instant he knew what he wanted to do. He wanted to go back to Abervy.

There was no reason in it. She had left that place. All the evidence he had said so. She had run into danger and trouble, but there was no danger there—except that of boredom and insult in that old woman's house. Why did he want to go back there, why did he feel it was—necessary?

Glentower was a Welshman. An intelligent, educated man—and brought up in a fair-sized town—exposed to no rank random superstition in his formative years, and an avowed agnostic. But a Welshman; and despite himself, all his rational mind, he could not be rid of the Celtic remnant in him. The primitive, instinctive conviction of This or That to help or harm.

Whichever it was, whatever it meant, it whispered to him now, Go back to Abervy.

And always that terrible sense of urgency pushing at him.

He swore aloud, violently. He was frightened to hear his voice frightened. In that moment he'd have been heart-wholly relieved to have it proved to him that the Welshpool police inspector was right, she'd just decided not to meet him, and scrawled a hasty excuse and gone on—somewhere. Just so she was safe. Driving off lightheartedly—somewhere——And safe. And safe.

He switched on the engine. He turned the car and drove out of Newport north, and at the fork where the signpost said *Cardigan,* northeast, and *Pembroke,* south, he turned northeast. It would not be dark for four hours normally, but the storm was making up fast. Unless he was lucky he'd do the last half of the journey in blinding rain. The hell with it.

He didn't know why he was heading back.

She'd *left* Abervy. Last Saturday.

Because he was a rational, intelligent man, he had to find some excuse for himself. He found it, slim and meaningless as it was, after thought.

Mrs. Trefoile, that almost-mad and certainly queer old woman, had recognized his name. She had said, *The man who*——The man who, what? And then, "Get out of my house!"

So Pat had mentioned his name; what did that say? The man whom the wicked and sinful Miss Carroll had mentioned? But why the disapproval? Was it sinful in Mrs. Trefoile's creed to pay for a young lady's dinner?

Nothing in it. She had left Abervy. Everyone said so. . . . True, no one had seen her pass. But—but——

And he did not know why he kept his foot hard on the accelerator, cursing at the bends slowing his pace. . . . He'd driven many miles today, but hadn't got far from Abervy. Call it thirty-five, forty miles; he'd be back there in time for dinner.

Why was he going back there?

The storm would never break. The darkness kept building up as he drove northeast; the humidity increased minute by minute. When he passed the occasional stand of trees, he saw the leaves all turning their undersides, paler green; and the atmosphere was like a great taut drumhead awaiting the first stroke of the stick.

He pulled up before The Dog and Gun again at six-thirty. He got his bag out of the boot and locked the Humber and took the dozen steps to the door of the inn.

As he laid his hand on the door, the storm broke. There was a blinding, long, brilliant stroke of lightning, and almost as it died the thunder sounded, a great ominous rumble. A moment of breathless silence, and the rain began.

Glentower thought, Now the air will be better, cooler.

He pushed open the door and went in.

"I never seen you act that way afore," he said. "Didn't know as you could. Hitting her like that—no call, hit her. We had t' stop her yellin', or gettin' away—but no call hurt her more'n need be."

"Oh, stop goin' *on* about it!" said Anna. "Come to that, you wasn't so gentle yourself!—hadda stop her, like you say——"

"So we did. But no call go slappin' and maulin' her about—just for fun, like. Like you did. I seen how you looked when you did, girl—I know—you *liked* hitting her that way."

"Damn liddle tart—come 'n' make all this trouble," she burst out with something like a sob. "She——"

"That's no way t' think," he said. He was still staring at her. "Just a girl, like as it might be—be Gloria, say. Just walkin' into this thing innocent——"

"Don't you say she's like Gloria! Painted-up liddle American trollop, lookin' down her nose——"

"Damn it, you sound 's bad as the old woman! That's not straight thinkin' no ways, girl——" He laid a hand on her shoulder. "What's to do, Anna? What's put you like this? Never saw you lay a rough hand on any afore—you're not yourself, girl—Anna? Anna, what—what's she got in her mind about that knife?"

"I don't know 'n' I don't care! Leave me be, Harry! What's it to us, anyways?"

"You know. You got t' know, there all the time—listenin' to her. You've changed somehow . . . Anna? Anna, you mind what I said t'other night—you got to think straight about it. Look at me, girl. You know, 'twasn't for you, I'd 'a' made a break long afore now—put the old woman out 'n' run for it—only way—but I couldn't bring you in, nothin' like that. I—you got to *see* it—bad business all round, an' I can't see any way through it but we're done, however it come out—but we don't want t' make it worse nor it's got to be! Anna——"

"I don't want to talk about it. Leave me be."

He said slowly, "It was like—you *wanted* to hit her—hurt her any old way, like the old woman. No call. Anna——"

"I said stop talkin' about it! Leave me be or I'll never get t' dinner done."

"That was allus the talk," agreed Davies to something Tom Evans had just said. "Ten year afore I come here, I wouldn't know ins an' outs, but that's what I allus heard."

"He were some distaff relation o' the Ffolliotts, 'n orphan, 'n' raised here—him 'n' old John Ffolliott together. But he didn't have no money —poor relation. Off to Shrewsbury he were awhile, tryin' t' sell motor cars I heard it, after he were out o' t' army—but it weren't no good."

"Ah, so I heard," said Davies.

Though it was Saturday night, not so many had ventured out in the storm to gather at The Dog and Gun. Glentower had been received back with civility, secret curiosity, but no questions; he had not made up any tale to explain his return. He sat now over the remains of his dinner in the public bar; at the next table three men sat talking, and Davies had joined them companionably. The only other customers were what looked to be a couple of shepherds in a far corner, silent over their beer.

Glentower was aware of glances stolen at him; they were interested and curious. Now the landlord rose and took the few steps to his table, to ask politely, "Is there aught else you'd be wanting, sir?"

"Bring me a Scotch and water, will you?" Abruptly Glentower half-turned his chair to face the other men. "None of you happened to see Miss Carroll—the young American lady—when she was here? Or——" But no, there'd be nothing to get; he knew that. Waste of time asking. Why the hell had he come back?

The storm was in full fury outside, loud on the roof; at brief intervals the windows were lit by a stroke of lightning, and the thunder was almost continuous. A deluge—like the night they'd met, but worse. Presently it would slacken off, its force spent, but the rain might go on all night.

Tomorrow, start out again, cast in a different direction.

"Young lady weren't here long, sir, like you know." It was a big broad young fellow spoke, one he'd not seen before; boyish-looking, freckled, but his blue eyes were shrewd and steady. Evans was there too, and the third man was a cut above—white collar and tie, prim manner; he was drinking gin, the others beer.

"An' no wonder at all," said Evans. "By what Gwen said, t' young lady'd had her fill o' Mis' Trefoile o'ernight." An amused murmur.

"No, I'm not surprised. I saw the woman this morning. I shouldn't wonder if you saw her carted off to the asylum one day," said Glentower. There was nothing he could do tonight; relax, he'd accomplish nothing by sitting here worrying. "She struck me as mad as a hatter."

"That wouldn't surprise me," said Davies, setting the bottle of Scotch on the table before him with two glasses, one of water. "Bound to say she do seem to tend that way, an' I reckon it gets worse as she gets older. Beg pardon, sir, but she couldn't help you about the young lady at all, then?"

"No. Damn it, she had the gall to say she was a—a 'loose young woman' and she—Mrs. Trefoile, I mean—had ordered her out of the house."

"You don't say! There's something now," said the big young man indignantly.

The prim white-collared man said, "Religious mania. They do get like that. I'll have another, Mr. Davies, please. We shall all get wet going home tonight, a regular Niagara it sounds like."

"All the more reason for summat inside to keep out the cold," said Davies genially. With Glentower's little confidence they had all relaxed to companionship with him. "This is our chemist, sir, Mr. Ormsby, an' you can see *he* knows what t' do to keep nasty summer colds off. An' this here's the local representative o' law and order, Davy Griffiths the pollis, who didn't ought t' be drinkin' on licensed premises."

"I just come in out o' the rain," said the constable with a grin. "You ain't located the young lady as you're lookin' for, sir? I daresay you know, if it's summat important, like a legal matter or such, you can get 'em to broadcast for her. They do it at the end o' the news."

"Yes, I know," said Glentower; it had occurred to him this afternoon. But would it be of any use? If it didn't bring her forward, that was no evidence that she wasn't a free agent; the police would just say she didn't choose to answer. And would the B.B.C. broadcast for her, when he couldn't supply any reason except one the police had refused to act on? "I may—have to do that. . . . What did your wife say?" he asked Evans.

Evans chuckled and drank beer. "Why, they come into t' shop that morning, see, on way t' church. T' young lady come in first, an' bought two postcards, an' talked a bit to Gwen—said who she was 'n' so on. Gwen said you could tell she was t' kind o' smart young lady as 'd be wearin' powder 'n' lipstick usual, an' jewelry too, all got up nice—not tarty, just like all t' girls do nowadays—but she hadn't a bit on *then.* An' when she paid for t' cards, she said she was leavin' that day, she'd got a urgent appointment—solemn as a judge, she says that, an' she dropped a wink at Gwen, t' old lady bein' behind her. Gwen says 'twas all she could do not to wink back. She knew well enough what t' young lady meant. Likely Mis' Trefoile'd made her come out without her powder 'n' lipstick 'n' so on, an' been nasty other ways along o' her funny notions, see, an' t' young lady was gettin' out of it fast as she could."

Glentower joined in the laugh with an effort. "Yes, I see. I don't wonder. They went to the church together, on Saturday morning? That seems funny—if she'd ordered Miss Carroll away beforehand."

"Maybe 'twas after. I wouldn't want to say what Mrs. Trefoile might take into her head," said Griffiths thoughtfully. "I reckon you're not far off the mark, sir, say she'll maybe end up in asylum. Let me have another pint, John."

"I must say," said Mr. Ormsby to his gin, "I always felt sorry for the boy."

"Stephen Trefoile," said Glentower. He poured himself more Scotch;

random curiosity stirred in him. Odd that he felt so little about the dead man, the man she had—presumably—loved. "What was he like?"

The atmosphere relaxed more, indefinably. A wet night, a cozy fire within, plenty to drink at hand, and pleasurable gossip. It was a lie to call women the gossips: a human impulse. "He was what she made him," said Ormsby. "A very good-looking young man—he looked like his father—but weak, if you know what I mean. We were all surprised he ever got out from under her thumb."

"So we was," said Evans.

Glentower asked idly, "What was the father like?"

There was an unexpected moment of silence. Then Griffiths said, "If I'd been constable then, summat more 'd have come of it. Gentry or no gentry—or money or no money."

"There wasn't," said Ormsby, "any evidence that *was* evidence."

"The talk was," said Davies to Glentower, "she killed him, you see. Yes, sir, her husband."

"She'd never've got a husband, 'twasn't for t' money," said Evans. *"I* were here an' seen it an' heard it all, which t' rest o' you never—leastways, Dave, you were here but only a snotty-nosed youngster wi' no sense at the time, an' 'twas afore John or Mr. Ormsby came to the village. I can tell you."

"And have, many's the time," said Davies with a grin.

"No odds. I don't say the man was no saint, but I do say he had excuse in plenty. We was just talkin' about him awhile ago, sir, maybe you heard—Cap'n Trefoile as he liked to be called. Brought up at Rhydenn by t' Ffolliotts he were, some sort o' poor relation. He'd be about my age. Allus a real friendly, fair-spoken chap, as was liked well. Only trouble wi' Cap'n Trefoile, he liked his pleasures an' he hadn't no money. He were in t' army awhile, that's where he got the cap'n, but reckon he couldn't keep up wi' other orfcers at standin' drinks 'n' so on. It was a bad day he met *that* one."

" 'Twas his own choice marry her," said Griffiths.

"She had the money," said Glentower. "Was that it?"

"Indeed she did, sir—an' has. He met her somewhere up north—we heard, her just come into all her fambly's money. A good ten year older 'n him, an' plain as mud in the bargain. But he weren't t' only chap as ever swallered his pride to wed money, were he? You bein' a lawyer, you'll back me up there, sir."

"Oh—certainly," agreed Glentower. "It happens all the time."

"As you say. An' the Cap'n, I'd say he meant t' be as good a husband as he could be to her, honest an' aboveboard. Only it didn't come out that way, on account o' her bein' how she is. I reckon—if you follow me —she wanted the—the look o' bein married, because it's the thing for females t' do—an' that's for why she took him. But anything else—well, you see what I mean—old maid married, for certain." Evans laughed and shrugged his thin shoulders. "An' I'm all for morals like Reverend preach, but I reckon all on us here got some common sense about folk, 'n' all I say is, t' Cap'n, he weren't a man as liked a cold bed, an' who t' hell were he doin' harm to, wi' Kitty Ford or Nance Luff? Certain not his lawful wife, as—by what t' housemaids say as were there then—couldn't abide him noways, forever callin' him a wicked sinner 'n' so on. So he liked his drink 'n' he liked his women—'twasn't no harm—girls he went with hadn't no reputations or maidenheads t' lose."

"It were harm when he got to Cerridwen Lewis," said Griffiths. "So I've heard."

"All *right!*" said Evans. "So it were. I allus thought myself as t' Cap'n was romantic in love wi' t' lass, like she certainly were wi' him. Only he was—weak, like. He wanted to do t' right thing by her, maybe, only he couldn't bring himself give up his lawful wife's money. Not that he saw much of it, or so I'd guess. She's allus been mean about partin' wi' coin. But a good living he had, 'n' enough for his drink an' t' hack horse he kept 'n' his fine clothes—nor he wasn't a chap as 'd earn a living very easy. Right clever-good he was at puttin' up a show as a gennelman—fine easy manners he had, like a lord, an' he knew about horses 'n' dogs 'n' guns 'n' all such-like—but as for earnin' wages, well! A gennelman he were. He meant well enough, but he was weak."

It was a familiar story. "He got this girl in trouble?" asked Glentower. "And his wife found out?"

"Along o' Jack Lewis, her dad. I don't blame him—any on us 'd do t' same, daughter in t' fambly way by a married man. I allus heard as Cap'n promised get rid o' his wife legal 'n' wed Cerridwen—but 'twasn't to be. Any road, Mis' Trefoile got to know. She was allus awful religious, an' I reckon——"

"No need t' be trottin' to church seven times a week to figure that immoral," said the constable. "Not that I say she'd any right to do murder. Though it wouldn't 've been murder, I don't reckon, but manslaughter or some such. If there'd been aught done. If *I'd* been constable then——"

"You mean she really killed him? What happened?"

Ormsby said, "I believe I'll have one more, Mr. Davies. There was no evidence at all, by what I understand, but perhaps that was more—er—luck than good management as they say. There was a quarrel——"

"That Ellen Parr heard—she was housemaid there at the time, see, sir—but she couldn't swear to seein' nothin'. She——"

"I've seen the statements," said Griffiths. "In the files they still are at the station. The maid said as she come down the upstair passage, one bedroom to t' other, makin' up the beds that morning. Cap'n Trefoile had his own room—best in the house, private bath and all—and a bolt on the inside o' the door, so he could do a bit o' private drinkin' without her walkin' in to lecture him. Any road, there the maid was, and she said they was going at it hammer and tongs, Mrs. Trefoile at the top o' the stair and him a step or two below her—like she's stopped him just as he were goin' out, see. The maid went into Mrs. Trefoile's bedroom, but she could still hear 'em. Her callin' him a fornicator and so on, and him tryin' to calm her down. And then the maid hears a hell of a noise, and she comes running out and there's Captain Trefoile fallen backwards down the stairs and broke his neck."

"She pushed him," said Ormsby softly. "Of course she did. She caught him off balance—a big, heavy man he was, wasn't he, Tom?—he'd no chance to save himself at all, you see."

"Yes," said Glentower, "I can see that happening. A nasty little story. What happened to the girl—suicide?"

Evans smiled and finished his beer. "That's only in storybooks, ain't it, sir? Most folk don't give up so awful easy. No, Cerridwen went off to Lunnon—we never heard did she have t' babby or get rid of it, see—any road, she was only nineteen about, an' she took some sort o' trainin', secretary or such, 'n' got a good job. Jack Lewis is dead ten year, but she sends five pound a month reg'lar as clockwork to her ma, I knows that."

"One hopes," said Ormsby primly, "that she has found happiness after such a tragedy. I do believe the rain is letting up—I must be getting along home. Good night, sir—Mr. Davies—good night, all."

"Ar, Gwen'll be thinkin' I'm drunk or drownded. Reckon 'tis time we was gettin' along." Evans got up reluctantly.

NINETEEN

A rather usual little story, thought Glentower, taking himself to bed. A tragedy if you liked—or just more evidence of human nature. The kind of thing that had happened before and would happen again.

He didn't think much about it. He thought about what he'd do tomorrow. Another cast—southeast. It was odd, if she *had* left Abervy before the noon hour, that no one had seen her pass; *had* she gone back north? Why? No; it was just happenstance that no one had seen her go. Try southeast, into Brecknock; she might have intended to head for Monmouth or Glamorgan.

Before he fell asleep the rain was slackening, the thunder long silent.

He woke to a golden summer morning—still damp, the gutters dripping, but the sun out full and early. Thank God, he needn't lose time driving through rain, questioning people surly for the weather. . . . Get on with it: the time he'd wasted!

Well, yes, he'd had to spend the night somewhere, but there were only two roads she could have taken from here—north or south; he'd covered the ten miles on from here to where she'd have another choice. He'd have done better to stop at Lampeter on the border, carried on from there.

He shaved and dressed hastily; he meant to get an early start. The fact that it was Sunday made the hunt just a little more difficult; some places shut, and people not as available.

Davies asked as he served him breakfast if he'd be wanting the room tonight. "No, thanks, I won't be back." He didn't know why he'd come back at all.

"I hope you'll find the young lady, sir," said Davies politely. "A pity she didn't leave word where she'd be, but some folk do like to go jauntering about without any plans that way. But if 'tis an important legal business, like Griffiths was saying, you could get them to broadcast."

"Yes. . . . How much do I owe you?"

And Glentower the rational man did not believe in mysterious supernormal powers—in the existence of This or That to help or harm—or he hadn't, up to that Sunday morning. After that he'd never feel quite sure. Call it coincidence that he had forgotten his cigarette case; it was a likely enough thing for him to do; he often wondered why he carried it, for he seldom took the trouble to fill it. Bob had given it to him the Christmas before he died in Korea, and perhaps it was just sentimentality.

At any rate, he had left it upstairs on the bureau, and as he opened the car door he remembered it, and went back. The maid had already found it, and was just coming down the stair to hand it to Davies. Glentower thanked her, rewarded her suitably and came out to the car again, putting it away in his pocket.

Just in time to collide with the girl passing the inn.

"I beg your pardon!" He caught her arm to steady her; in a hurry, he'd knocked her off balance.

" 'S O.K.," she said, flashing him an automatic smile. "No harm done, s' long as I haven't started a run in my nylons. . . . No, all's well. Never do t' go t' church with a run, daresay Reverend'd have me turned out!" She tucked her bag firmer under her arm with another grin and went on.

He took three steps toward the car and stopped. Something—something—was saying urgently to him, *Pat.* Sudden, nostalgic, vivid memory surged up in him—unprecedentedly real and warm, a physical sense—the sensation of her as she had been, sitting opposite him that night, close, over the hearth fire at the Tregarth Arms—the sight and sound and scent——

Scent. Her perfume—something unusual, spicy and strange——That girl was wearing the same scent, one he'd never known before, something very different——

He turned and ran after her. Calling like a—a damned department-store floorwalker. "Miss! Oh, miss!"

She stopped. He came up to her, feeling suddenly foolish. She was about twenty, a pertly pretty girl with a lot of ash-blond hair, a little too much in the way of make-up. "I—I beg your pardon," he said. Belatedly he thought, Scent—anybody can buy it. A hundred different brands, available to anyone with the money to pay for it—rural village as well as London, with mail-order business these days.

"Yes?" she said, a little puzzled, a little curious.

"I——" He summoned a smile, reading her as to type: the good-natured careless sort, a talker, friendly. "Don't laugh," he said, "but I couldn't help noticing your perfume—it's nice—I like it. I'd like to get some for my sister, I think she'd like it too. Would you mind telling me what it is, what it's called?"

The girl relaxed, gave him an automatic provocative smile. "Your sister, indeed! There's a story! *'Tis* nice, isn't it? And good—I mean it stays on a long while. It's called Ginger Carnation, it's from America—some company I never heard of before, in New York. I 'xpect it's awful expensive here."

"You expect?" he said teasingly. "Was it a present from the boy friend, then?" She was the sort of girl who'd respond mechanically to flirtation, meaning nothing by it.

She giggled. "Aren't you smart? Sure it was, a present I mean—my auntie give it me for my birthday on Tuesday, if you want to know. . . . You're the lawyer gentleman here looking for the American girl as come to see Mrs. Trefoile." Her glance was frankly curious.

Villages. Everything known five minutes after it happened. "That's right," said Glentower. "I just happened to notice it—couldn't help it, could I, you practically falling into my arms? My sister's got a birthday coming up, and I know she'd like it—where could I get it, d'you know? Could I order it somewhere? Where'd your aunt get it?"

She giggled again. "Sister! Ask me, you want it for your girl friend, chaps don't buy scent for sisters, they get chocolates or some such——"

"She's on a diet," said Glentower.

"Indeed! I dunno, I 'xpect some big department store in Lunnon could get it for you. I couldn't say where Auntie got it—maybe she saw an advert and ordered it. She sure didn't get it around here, I know—must've ordered it from Lunnon."

"Oh, she lives here?"

"That's right. Auntie's with this funny old Mrs. Trefoile as you went t' see yesterday. Didn't you? I reckon as she saw an advert in some magazine and ordered it. 'Tis nice, I'm crazy about it. I s'pose, like I say, a Lunnon store could get it for you."

"I see, thanks. Thanks very much. I'll ask, anyway—when I get back to town. I—know my sister 'd like it."

She patted her pompadour of ash-blond hair and gave him an impudent grin. "Sister! You're welcome, I'm sure. And I'll be late for early service." She teetered off down the street on her stilt heels.

Ginger Carnation. An American company. That funny old Mrs. Trefoile.

Auntie. The drab middle-aged maid who'd admitted him?

Glentower stood there beside the car, not so much thinking as feeling.

He felt he didn't want to drive away from this place. Just as he'd felt he wanted to come back last night. Why?

The scent. Pat's scent. He didn't know much about such things, but he had a vague idea that import duties and so on would make it unprofitable to import any but the very famous and exclusive name brands. Was this one of those? No—the girl had said she'd never heard the name before, and that sort of girl would be well up on things like that.

Auntie. At Llandaffy house.

He thought, So, an explanation. A reasonable explanation, for a girl in very rural Wales wearing Pat's American scent. Pat had left Mrs. Trefoile and Llandaffy house in a hurry—hadn't she—after the insults implied by that odd and malevolent old woman; and so she forgot a bottle of scent. Auntie—the drab maid—found it, and passed it on to her niece as a birthday gift.

An unopened bottle? How could she have forgotten that?—it wouldn't have been taken out of her bag, would it? Because surely otherwise, if it was an opened bottle, even almost full, Auntie wouldn't have made it a formal birthday gift? It would have been: "The American girl left it, an' I don't use such fol-de-rols, you take it"—and the girl, knowing who he was, that he was interested in the young American lady, would have mentioned it—"She left it behind, and Auntie passed it on to me." Wouldn't she?

He didn't know where he was about this.

It wasn't anything—it wasn't important.

Was it?

Deliver me speedily. . . . I am in trouble. . . .

He didn't *know.*

He stood there with his hand on the car door and for one awful moment his mind was quite blank; all rationality slipped away from him. What—where—how—and why?

He had to find her. What trouble she was in, what danger.

The whole thing was eminently nonrational, blood-and-thunder fantasy. A postcard with a secret message. A postcard stained with blood.

Scent. An American company. Expensive. She wasn't rich; she had worked for her living, until she got this little legacy. She would be accustomed to budgeting her money, taking care of what she bought.

Glentower shut the door of the Humber carefully. He told himself he was wasting time, not getting on with the business of trying to trace the road she'd taken, asking questions. But for no very logical reason he wanted to know the story of that bottle of scent, American scent which had gone from Llandaffy house, from Auntie, to an ash-blond, flirtatious, nameless niece.

Llandaffy house, north along the road from the village.

He lit a cigarette and strolled up the high street, past the Evanses' store and the outlying cottages. A hundred yards, two hundred, round the sharp bend in the road, there were the iron gates with *Llandaffy* painted on them.

Anything to that story Evans had told last night? Probably she *had* pushed him.

The gates were partly open. He went in, started up the curving drive. He would ring the bell—the maid, Auntie, would answer—and ask her about the scent.

Why? It was self-evident what had happened. Pat had forgotten it, and Auntie committed a very small felony in taking it.

The bolt—Julian Trefoile's inside bolt—Pat struggled with it frantically, sobbing. It would never move—but it moved at last, reluctantly, and shot home. She staggered backward to collapse on the bed.

They could not come in any more, any more. It had come to an end —one end.

The knife in the old woman's hand. God's voice, she said. The only way. Use the knife—to make it so that no man would look on her but with loathing.

It would be better, if it came to a choice, to go out the window. She thought that bleakly. Risk the broken bones, the broken neck.

Hour by hour she had been learning the deeper lessons of fear, this week. They began, *This cannot happen.* They went on to end, *I will die before——*

How much use to know the woman was mad! When, if, it was found out, it would be too late for Pat Carroll.

Get away, you must get away, screamed her mind.

Anna. Could she count at all on Anna? No.

An hour ago, ten minutes ago—time had ceased to mean anything—

the old woman mouthing incoherences, about God's voice, the divine instruction she had received, and the knife in her hand—"To mutilate, to destroy, the only way—" Pat would never know where she found the strength, the courage. But Anna was frightened—if not for that, she'd never have been able to do it, fighting them both. The old woman stronger than one might expect, but still an old woman—and Anna very frightened. Somehow, an ugly nightmare of physical struggle, she had beaten them off, toward the door, and they were *out*——But she had known she could never get past them out there in the narrow hall, they'd been taken by surprise but they'd stop her there——And then she remembered the bolt, and slammed the door as the old woman turned on her in the doorway.

They could not get in again. She could not get in, pistol or long knife.

I would rather go out the window, she thought.

They had only gone to church, she and Aunt, at Easter and Christmas, odd times like that. *O God our help in ages past. A mighty fortress——*

God, please, she found her mind saying. Only that. God, please.

She was finished; it was done, all she could do. She was safe from the madwoman—but for how long? Bolts could be forced——

"Hello," said Glentower, and stopped. The man had dodged out into the drive from the trees at the side, oddly furtive. Another gardener? It didn't seem likely that a reputedly mean woman would keep many servants.

The man stopped dead still, looking at him. He was very big, but with a closer look Glentower saw what he was: what they used to call a natural. "Hello," he said again. "Do you work here?"

The natural looked at him nervously, warily, head down and barely raising his eyes. "Work—that ol' Hector a-catchin' me, I does. Don't like t' pull weeds, I don't."

"I don't blame you," said Glentower. "Do you remember the pretty girl who was here awhile ago? What's your name?"

That was a mistake, two questions at once. It was only the last one got answered. "Joseph."

"Do you remember the pretty girl, Joseph?"

The almost colorless eyes were blank on him. And it was a waste of time and effort, this one wouldn't have noticed or remembered anything, but—try him. "She came in a motor car, a bright-red motor car, and she stayed overnight."

"I like red," said Joseph, smiling. "I had a nice red shirt once."

"Yes, it's a pretty color. Did you see the red motor car?"

"T' owd badger don't like it noways, though. He were right scared. I see him scuttle back t' burrow quick. No call folk got, scare owd badger."

"The car scared him?"

"Car——" said Joseph vaguely. " 'Twas a motor car, sure-ly. Dark 'twas goin', for t' mist, 'n' owd badger think it's real night, 'n' come out. He run back quick, he done so."

Absently Glentower fished out a couple of coins and handed them over. The badger was frightened—dusk falling, so that would have been when she arrived, "about teatime," someone had said. "Joseph, did you see the motor car again, when it went away—*down* the drive?"

Joseph looked at him blankly. "The red motor car," said Glentower. "The one that scared the badger. Did you see it again?"

Joseph shook his head. "You give me two sixpences. I know pennies 'n' florins 'n' sixpences. You're a nice gennelman. I—I—I show you somethin' purty I got." He fumbled at his shirt pocket.

"Never mind that, Joseph. The *motor car*—did you see it again?" But the simpleton only stuttered, shaking his head, still fumbling at his pocket; nothing more to be got. Glentower went on up the drive.

When he came in sight of the house he saw the big gardener he'd spoken to yesterday, and the maid. The man was at the foot of the house steps, the woman above him and the door open behind her, as if she'd just come out for a moment to speak to him. At the little sound of Glentower's steps on the turf, they both turned, and the woman put a hand to her mouth in a frightened, startled gesture.

"Good morning," said Glentower. Some household crisis? he thought. The man looked worried, the woman distraught—not too strong a word. Perhaps the old woman had gone all the way off her head and was dancing naked in the sitting room, or something.

Neither of them spoke immediately, and then with an effort the man said, "G' morning—sir. What was it you wanted?"

"You c-can't t' see madam," said the maid. "Madam's—poorly an' can't see no'un."

"I don't want to see Mrs. Trefoile, I want to ask you a couple of questions," said Glentower pleasantly. "I didn't see you when I left yesterday. You saw Miss Carroll when she left that morning, didn't you?" She nodded once, sullen. "Did she say anything to you about

where she was going? Did you see which way she turned from the gates?"

"You can't see the gates from here, sir," said the man.

"No, I didn't see nor I didn't take no interest, I got my work t' do." She kept looking around nervously; her voice was low.

"She was in a hurry, wasn't she, to forget that expensive bottle of scent?"

"What—what d'you mean?" She looked terrified suddenly.

"The one you gave your niece for her birthday. Miss Carroll's special American perfume."

"I—I——"

"D'you take summat o' the girl's, Anna?" It was jolted out of the man by surprise. "You shouldn't ought to've——"

"How'd you know—'bout that? An' I never, anyways! I didn't say nothin' to Gloria, how'd you——"

"But it was Miss Carroll's, wasn't it?"

"I—not that it's any o' your business, but she *give* it me. I—said as how 'twas nice, I'd like get some for Gloria—an'—she gave me an extra bottle she had—on account I wouldn't have time—get it sent up from Lunnon."

It was as palpable a lie as he'd ever heard. And what did that mean? That she'd deliberately stolen it from Pat's bag, probably. And Pat hadn't missed it before she left.

The big simpleton slouched up behind him. "He's a nice gennelman, he give me *two* sixpences."

"You needn't go tryin' t' get any sense out o' Joseph," she said sharply. "He don't know nothin' about—no more 'n any o' the rest of us, see? Young lady come an' went, that's all any can say—'n' why for'd we take any notice which way? We all got *work* to do!"

There was a muffled thud from somewhere in the house, as if something heavy fell. It came again after an interval, and again. Both the man and woman moved, looked toward the open door. The old woman breaking up the furniture, thought Glentower only half humorously.

"I—I got work t' do," repeated the maid called Anna almost desperately, "can't stand here listenin' to silly questions——" As she turned to the door, old Mrs. Trefoile's voice called her name imperiously, and she ran in and banged the door behind her.

Glentower felt deflated. What the hell did it matter that the woman had stolen anything from Pat? What the hell was he doing here, anyway? Wasting time—this wasn't tracing her, finding out. The sense of time passing while he dawdled about blindly oppressed him suddenly like a physical weight—he must get on to some useful action—what he'd decided, cast southeast for traces of her. Hanging about here like a damned fool, asking irrelevant questions——

He turned abruptly without farewell to the gardener; when he was six steps away the man said in a queerly tentative tone, "Sir——"

"Well, yes?"

"I—nothin'. Nothin'. Just thought t' say, if that Joseph tell you aught—you don't want t' be too sure he knows what he's sayin'. But you can see he's got no sense—sir."

Glentower said yes impatiently and went on, anxious to get back to the car and carry on with the job. Why the *hell* he had wasted this time——

The simpleton had slid off somewhere while he talked to the other two, and now reappeared, again from the trees bordering the drive. "Goin' t' *town,*" he confided. "Goin' t' get *chocolates.*"

"That's fine," said Glentower absently, lengthening his stride.

"Ne'er had *two* sixpences afore. You're a nice gennelman. I—I—I show you somethin' purty, maybe you give me 'nother sixpence?" An eager pawing hand on his arm.

"I haven't got time, Joseph."

"It's luck-full, it is. Things green allus holds luck. I—I let you see it—for 'nother sixpence." The Josephs could be tenacious when an idea occurred to them.

"Oh, hell," said Glentower, fumbling in his pocket without stopping, "all right, here's your sixpence."

"But you didn't see it yet, I show you——" He was keeping up with Glentower; they were nearly to the gates now. Glentower tried to shake off the big dirty hand; and then the other hand was held out insistently six inches under his nose, and he stopped dead in his tracks.

"Purty," said Joseph, pleased at attracting his attention.

That was Pat's ring. The big silver ring with the oval green turquoise, that she'd been wearing that night.

TWENTY

Pat heaved and pulled at the highboy frantically, and just when she thought she'd never do it, it began to move: a foot, two feet—almost there now——She fell against it, shoving with all her weight, until it was squarely in front of the door.

The heavy regular blows on the door sounded like the steps of doom in that symphony, which one was it?—she didn't know what the woman was using, an ax or something duller, but she could see the door shake at every blow. They were——

They? Anna too? She thought Anna was thoroughly frightened at last. Ten minutes ago she'd heard the old woman calling her, ordering her—"You will do this better than I, I must save my strength"—and Anna, "No—madam, you got to see, I—it ain't——" and the other voice rising to a thin shriek with anger. But if Anna was frightened of the consequences, she was more frightened of Mrs. Trefoile—what help would she be?

Damned bleating sheep of a woman, thought Pat, tugging at the chest. If she had any sense she'd call the man, they could handle the old woman between them—or run to the village for help. No. Caught between two evils, the ones like Anna would always hesitate, wringing their hands, until it was too late.

Oddly enough she felt quite cool herself. This was the very worst, and perhaps the very last—that door wouldn't hold forever, and they said mad people showed surprising strength. But she hadn't the least impulse to have hysterics or scream foolishly out the window.

She got the chest over in front of the highboy, and tried to shift the desk. All the furniture might gain her another ten minutes after the door was down. Never get the desk all the way across the room——

If she gets in, Pat thought, very rational and emotionless, I'll jump out the window.

"Anna—Anna!" A breathing space when the blows on the door stopped.

"Madam—please, madam, don't——"

Never shift the desk unless she took the drawers out. Pat began to do that. Impersonally she felt rather surprised at herself—she wouldn't have said she'd show up so well in such a crisis; pity there wasn't someone there to admire her and tell about it afterward. Let it never be said she didn't die game, she thought. Or stopped fighting back up to the last minute.

When she took out the middle left drawer she picked up the bottle of brandy and took another drink. And then another. Never knew, it might be her last. In a little while she might even be meeting Julian Trefoile, and she mustn't forget to tell him how much she'd appreciated his legacy of liquor. It had helped her through some bad moments.

Of course she wasn't going to die. Even now, at the last and worst, something would——

That door wouldn't last much longer.

Pat gave the desk a final shove and leaned on it, panting. That should stop her a while even after the door gave. She straightened and went back to the window, as far as possible from the door. She had done everything she could, and now there was no more for her to do but—wait—The fear came up like a great black tide in her.

She looked out the window and knew she'd never have the courage to jump. She groped for the bottle and drank. Disgraceful, to die drunk—if she had to die, she could die like a lady. Aunt wouldn't approve if she died drunk. She heard herself laugh hysterically.

Pat's ring. She valued it—it had been her father's, she said. She must have been very sorry to lose it. Or have it stolen.

"Where'd you get this?"

Joseph eyed him uncertainly, and then closed his hand over the ring and backed away. "I—I——"

Glentower made a grab for him. "Give it to me, Joseph. That's not yours—did you steal it? It's wrong to steal, you know. Where'd you get it?" He took the ring, prying open Joseph's hand.

Joseph was frightened; he began to cry. "Give me back—give me back—I *found* 'un—'s mine! Didn't neither thieve—'tain't *fair*——"

"It belongs to the young lady, Joseph—the one who came in the red motor car, remember? Where did you find it?"

"In t' clover I *found* 'un—give me back! 'S mine! Wasn't no'un there——"

"You can't have it back, but—but I'll pay you for it," said Glentower, "because you took good care of it for her, see, Joseph?" He gave Joseph a pound note, and saw that Joseph had no idea what it was, so he took it back and gave him all the silver and copper in his pocket. Joseph looked slightly mollified and backed away farther.

"The young lady in the red motor car, Joseph. The one that scared the old badger. Did you see her go away?"

"You 'on't—give it back? I—I—I——"

"Listen, Joseph. The car that came and scared the badger, did you——"

"You want t' see *that?"* asked Joseph. Another idea had occurred to him now; he looked at Glentower slyly and grinned. "That ol' Hector. I show you my purty thing 'n' you thieve it—'d you thieve *that* from ol' Hector, do I show you? I like see that!"

"What? Show me what?"

"That there motor car, see. In t' shed," said Joseph triumphantly. "Ol' Hector, he got t' door lock' up, but you c'n see through cracks. I show you, 'n' you—you thieve it away?"

Incredibly she was thinking how hungry she was. A cigarette would taste good, too. She should really be thinking of something more serious if these were—equally incredible—her last minutes on earth.

She had another drink of brandy. If she was going to have to jump out the window, she felt she'd like to be good and drunk when she did. Which was a very unedifying and unsuitable thought. Aunt Tilda wouldn't approve at *all.*

She was rather surprised the door had held this long. Now the blows stopped again, and Pat turned quickly to listen for voices—turned too quickly, what with all the brandy she'd had, and fell headlong over one of the desk drawers. And her handbag, put on top of it when she moved the desk. She knocked the bag over, and its contents spilled out on the floor beside her.

Bracing herself on hands and knees to rise, she stared down disbelievingly at the thing near her left hand. The little thing they must have missed in ransacking the bag—in the inner zippered compartment, or caught up among papers—the little thing that all this time had been there, if she'd only known——

A packet of matches.

Fire brigade. Must be one in the village, if only a small volunteer force. But fire brigade or no, that would fetch people up—people from Outside. People always flocked to see a fire.

She staggered up, clutching the packet. It was nearly full. She grabbed up handfuls of the stationery from the top desk drawer, crumpled it up in a pile beneath the floor-length sleazy curtains over the broken window, knelt and struck a match. Her hands shook; the match flared and went out, and she struck another. That time the paper caught, smoldered and began to turn black; then suddenly it flamed up wildly toward the curtain. Pat sprang back. The curtain caught; the flames shot up higher, faster than she'd expected. In a moment there'd be smoke streaming out the window, but it might be quite a little time before the smoke was seen in the village—if the household was roused, in their sudden panic they'd send for help before realizing——

She snatched up the little chair and turned to the other window, intending to knock out the pane and shout—and she saw something quite incredible.

She saw Alan Glentower come running around this side of the house, with Joseph after him.

What's this? thought Glentower. He looked at Joseph blankly. "The red motor car?"

Joseph nodded eagerly.

Quite suddenly a very queer feeling moved up Glentower's spine. He thought, *No one saw her leave.* "Show me!" he said sharply. "Where, Joseph?"

Joseph started back up the drive. "Hurry!" said Glentower.

"I—I—show you, 'n' you thieve it from ol' Hector——"

Almost to the house the drive forked, the right-hand track leading around the house toward stables or a garage; Joseph trotted up that way. Stables, converted. The double doors shut, but they were warped loose and gaped a couple of inches open in the center, even with the padlock securing them.

"You *look,"* said Joseph proudly.

Glentower looked, and through the little gap he saw the dim outline of Pat's brand-new bright-red sports Jaguar inside.

"My *God!"* he said. And then, without wasting time thinking about this incredible thing, he turned and ran for the house the quickest way.

He burst out through a rough tangle of hedge into the open garden about the side of the house. The front door was round to the left; he turned that way. He heard a crash of breaking glass from above, and he looked up and saw Pat.

If he hadn't loved her he mightn't have recognized her. Her hair was limp and tangled about her pale pinched-looking face, her dress was torn apart to gape widely above her waist, and her eyes were wild, unfocused on him. She staggered against the window frame and tried to call something to him, but her voice was only a thick croak.

He heard dull regular heavy blows being struck against something in the house.

Glentower turned and ran. The big gardener was standing there on the steps as if he hadn't moved since Glentower had last seen him; he seemed to be listening to those thuds from inside. He started to speak, but Glentower shoved him aside roughly and flung himself at the door. It was locked. He tore off his jacket, wrapped it around his arm and drove his fist through the nearest window, three times, and climbed in over the jagged edges to a dim stale-smelling dining room. He heard the other man shout after him. He ran out to the hall and took the stairs three treads at a time—and brought up against the newel post on the landing, staring for one incredulous second at the scene before him.

The old woman, her face a distorted mask of fury and madness, attacking a door with upraised ax, and the other woman huddled against the wall, watching with helpless frightened eyes.

In that instant the door gave, a panel smashed in and he saw that there was furniture shoved into the doorway inside.

He took two strides and caught Mrs. Trefoile by the shoulders, and she turned on him viciously, blindly, and swung the ax at him. He got her wrist—she was astonishingly strong—and they struggled pantingly before he twisted the ax away.

"Pat! Pat—clear the stuff from the door—it's all right, I've——"

The woman was on him again like a tiger, from behind—clawing at him, mouthing obscenities. He hit her without compunction, as he'd have hit a man, and she fell sprawling. He dropped the ax and put his shoulder to the door, calling Pat's name—heard a stir behind him, and whirled.

The other woman standing up at last, uncertain, staring. Mrs.

Trefoile up again and on him—"For God's sake," he panted, "help me hold her!" Where the hell was the man? Couldn't he hear this row?

The woman came up and took Mrs. Trefoile's shoulder. "I—I help hold her—" The old woman turned on her in a flash; it was done before he could move or shout. She bent and came up with the ax, and swung it like an executioner. The blade struck the younger woman across the breast, and she reeled back to the top of the stairs and over, falling backward, a great crimson splash already spreading on her body.

Glentower dodged the ax as it fell, grappling with her. No time even for incredulity, one frail-looking little old woman——He got the wrist, he wrenched it until it gave and he could seize the ax, he sent it flying over the bannister down the stairwell, out of reach. He hit her again and again, and she fell against the wall and lay still.

"Pat! Help me—get that stuff out of the way——" He attacked the door, and heard sounds inside; and then the whole center panel fell in, and she was there, struggling clumsily to shove past the piled furniture into the doorway. He saw her eyes, and reached to catch her as she fell toward him.

He never glanced at the old woman, but carried Pat past her down the stairs. At the foot the other woman's body sprawled head downward, broken and still, and the big gardener stood looking at it. He turned a gray empty face to Glentower.

"Telephone! Is there one? For God's sake——"

"Telephone," said the man. "Yes, sir. It don't matter now, do it? It don't matter at all. I don't mind it. There's a telephone at back o' the hall, sir."

"My darling, my darling—don't try to move now, you'll be all right, don't be frightened any more—what have they done to you, my darling——"

Pat listened dreamily to his incoherent phrases, thinking, How funny—evidently I told Mrs. Trefoile the truth—he's saying he *is* in love with me. How very odd, all at once. Don't know if I ever could be with him—maybe—maybe *ought* to be as a sort of reward for rescuing me.

"They'll be here soon, darling—police and doctor and—don't try to move, dearest, you're too weak——"

" 'M not so much weak as drunk," said Pat with dignity. "Too much of Mr. Trefoile's brandy. 'D you send for—fire brigade too, because—think—house might be burnin' down, you know——"

"Yes, darling——"

"Much too much brandy," said Pat. "But it *was* nice of him—leave it there for me, wasn't it?"

"It was damn nice of him," said Glentower with something between a laugh and a sob.

"Must look—awful. Did you really—all of a sudden like that—? Don't know *why."*

"There aren't any rules about it."

"Guess not," agreed Pat sleepily. "Funny. Think about it later."

"Yes, darling," he said, and heard a car coming up the drive, and got up from where he bent over her on the sitting-room couch. "Here they are, thank God. They'll want your story, but it'll wait until a doctor's— —Pat? Pat!"

She didn't answer. She was sound asleep, and smiling.